By Rona Jaffe

Rona Jaffe THE

Simon and Schuster
New York

LAST CHANCE

DESIGNED BY IRVING PERKINS
MANUFACTURED IN THE UNITED STATES OF AMERICA

1   2   3   4   5   6   7   8   9   10

LIBRARY OF CONGRESS CATALOGING IN PUBLICATION DATA

JAFFE, RONA.
THE LAST CHANCE.

I. TITLE.
PZ4.J2Las [PS3519.A453]   813'.5'4   76-7564
ISBN 0-671-22274-0

For Phyllis

PROLOGUE:
DECEMBER
1975

Prologue: December 1975

SOMETHING WAS WRONG about this funeral. Not that it wasn't impeccable; the mourners, the flowers, the music, the service, the choice of Frank E. Campbell's on Madison Avenue, the arrival of all those long black limousines so clean and shiny . . . she might even have liked it. Her family and friends hoped she would, for they could think of nothing else to do for her. The people who had loved her were there, and the people who had disliked her, and even the people who had hardly known her at all. *She* should not have been there, they were thinking, it was all wrong.

Outside, in the streets of New York, it was the Christmas season, with stores decorated and shoppers struggling through the crowds loaded down with packages. False-bearded Santas rang their bells on street corners, and the chestnut and soft-pretzel venders sent their clouds of aromatic smoke sailing up to the cold white sky. There were not so many lights as in former years because of the energy shortage, and the giant tree in Rockefeller Center was not as pretty as in years gone by, but better than last year's most people agreed. The loss of the lighted trees along Park Avenue was sad, but still it was Christmas, you knew it, and a funeral would have seemed incongruous even if it had been that of a very old, sick person.

But this was the funeral of a young woman who had died before her time of an unnatural death. It should never have happened, and yet when you looked back on it, in a way it had a kind of inevitability.

The three women sat together. Their glances met briefly and each knew the others were thinking the same thing. They had been four close friends, and now they were three. The fourth was up there in that coffin. They were the survivors, not in the sense of "survived by," as it says in obituary columns, but in the real sense. It could have been any one of them.

Each of them had wanted control of her own destiny, and had moved toward it, unaware that her destiny was really stalking her. That had to be the only explanation. And yet none of them could really believe it, even now. They had all made choices. That had to have some meaning. They could not believe choices were meaningless. Three of them were still alive. . . . Even she, at the very end, had made a choice.

But they knew they were telling themselves all this so they would not be so afraid.

THE
YEAR
BEFORE:
JANUARY

January 1975

At five a.m. in New York at the beginning of January it is black and silent. The new carbon arc lights that are supposed to make the streets safe from muggers illuminate the fact that not even a mugger wants to be out in that lonely cold. Every ten minutes, perhaps, a lone taxi might cruise by, doors locked, bulletproof shield between the driver and his passengers firmly closed, smeared with the fingerprints of the night's innocent travelers, who hated shouting their destinations through the money slot. The large alarm clock next to Margot King's bed went off with a shriek that seemed to shatter her brain. The pain of it made her heart pound, but she didn't shut it off until she was sitting up on the side of the bed, otherwise she knew she would go back to sleep.

It's my job and they need me. I promised. She had never been a morning person, and five a.m. was unspeakable. She had to bear it for two weeks, because she was doing the morning news while the regular newscaster was away. She wondered if he was sleeping now in the Bahamas where he had taken his vacation. Margot did the evening news every night on local television, and sometimes the late night news as well if a substitute was needed. She thought of it as the swing shift. Ten years as a television reporter, going to be forty years old at the end of the summer, thankful for the myopic camera that missed all the tiny lines she had begun to notice, and no steady slot of her own. People knew her, but she wasn't really a name. It was her own fault. She had never fought for anything and had even turned down promotions when it seemed they would take up too much of her time. She remembered when she had been fresh out of college, so long ago, turning down a job as a researcher at Time-Life because the personnel director told her she would have irregular hours and never be able to make a date in advance. "I don't want my job to interfere with my life," Margot had said. And now she realized that her job was her only life.

She brushed her teeth, squinting against the harsh bathroom light. Two drops of eyedrops in each eye ("for forty-year-old eyes," the commercial said—next year she would have them). She washed her face in the shower because it took less time, although she knew soap and water were lethal for delicate skin. But then she slathered on moisturizer, quickly so as not to dwell on the wrinkles, and watched them smooth away under the yellow liquid. Television makeup wasn't helping her skin any. Maybe she would have a facial this week. She stepped on the scale, not surprised and yet always relieved that the needle never wavered from the point where it had been the day before.

There would be coffee at the studio, but it would be even worse than her own instant, so while she waited for her coffee to cool she made the bed. It seemed futile and depressing because no one would see it, but you never knew. She might invite a man home for a drink. She thought that every morning, but she hadn't had a lover for nearly a year, and while part of her felt old because of it, another part didn't care. Sometimes she felt frustrated, but she couldn't seem to turn the feeling toward any of the men she met every day who would have been delighted to help her out. The more she didn't have sex, the more distant it seemed, the more difficult, as if she were a virgin again.

The last man who had lived with her had drifted away, not walking out cleanly but nicking at little bits of her until she felt as if she were covered with tiny wounds. Finally she took his key away and told him not to call. It had taken a long time to recover. Maybe it was true that when you got older everything took longer to heal.

She walked to work. The streets were deserted, and she walked out toward the middle of the sidewalk in case anyone was hiding in a doorway, and kept the handle of her bag firmly knotted around her wrist. Her steps were swift and aggressive out of habit, and her glance darted all along both sides of the street, but she was not afraid. It was only six blocks. She had deliberately moved to West Fifty-seventh Street so she would not be at the mercy of transportation. She liked to be independent. She had more anger than fear in this city because she had always loved New York and now it had been ruined. It was filthy, noisy, filled with junkies, rapists, muggers, murderers, and the paranoid hostility of the average citizen who felt he had been taken. We've all been taken, Margot thought, but nobody made us come here. We all wanted to come here. This was dream city. There *is* no place else.

In her office she started typing the news items she wanted from the Teletype machine. That machine had always fascinated her, sputtering out the endless roll of paper with items of mayhem from places so far away they seemed not to exist. And in between a garden party. She chose just the right combination of world and local news, knowing her viewers were as interested in a tenement fire in the Bronx in which one child had died as they were in a catastrophe in Asia in which a hundred had.

"Little Denise could have been saved if it had not been for the rash of false alarms that left her neighborhood without any fire engines. It took twenty minutes for fire fighters to come from . . ."

"Henry Kissinger said today . . ."

17

"Convicted Watergate conspirator . . ."

"In the nursing home scandal . . ."

There had been a time when everything had affected her, and now she no longer cared. She could watch a man sob and shove a mike into his face, her only feeling the fleeting hope that he wouldn't push it away. Some reporters never stopped caring, and they were the best ones. Margot had become numb, but it had seemed the only way she could save herself from caring too much. She worked better this way. She could write sharply, she could be funny or make people cry, but inside she remained untouched. Outside was unreal; her inner life was all that mattered. She wondered if that was good, and what would become of her.

On her desk there was a note someone had left for her about a phone call that had come last night after she'd gone home. She realized she'd forgotten to call her service again. Gone to bed with a drink and a sleeping pill, turned off the phone, thinking only of getting up at five. It was a frantic message from Ellen. All Ellen's messages were frantic if they concerned Ellen. She had been Margot's roommate at college, had gotten married soon after graduation, had two teen-aged daughters, and spent her entire existence relentlessly trying not to become a housewife. This desire, however, did not extend to having a steady job. *Call Ellen Rennie. Urgent.* Ellen called only when she wanted something.

Margot looked at her watch, clipped the message to the top of the folder containing things to do after the show, and tried to decide if she should scratch the Watergate item in favor of giving more time to the new story that had just come in about a man who had died as a result of last evening's trapped subway. Hell, everyone was sick and tired of Watergate, but they had to take the subway every day. If the world she presented to her viewers kept getting smaller, perhaps that was good. Maybe it would give them something they felt they could do something about. The worst feeling in the world was to feel helpless.

She went into the makeup room when she saw that both chairs were unoccupied. Everyone on the show knew that you were not allowed to speak to Margot in the morning. She had let them

18

know she was a grouch, but the truth was she couldn't stand to be near smoker's breath that early. Ever since she had given up smoking two years ago she had become a fanatic. The only one she spoke to before the show was the makeup man.

"Save me, Ralph, I'm in your hands," she sighed, and sank into the chair.

ELLEN RENNIE WOKE UP at five thirty that morning, wide awake with anticipation. She had hardly slept at all, formulating her plans for getting a job, making lists in her mind of whom she could call, what she should tell them. Naturally she would see Margot first. Margot knew everybody. Ellen was more jealous of Margot than she liked to admit, always had been, even though she was fond of saying to her friends, "Poor Margot, we *must* find her a man."

Poor Margot, pretty and slim and ethereal and brilliant, always being deserted by men because she chose the wrong ones, while she, Ellen, trapped in a marriage, was always attracting the right man, the perfect, considerate lover, and was never able to stay permanently with any of them because she was stuck with this clod.

She looked at Hank, sleeping peacefully on his side of their king-sized bed. What kind of man hadn't touched his wife for six years, even though they slept in the same bed, just because she had told him not to? What kind of man would stay with his wife for seventeen years even though he knew she had lovers? How could you respect a man like that? It would be different if she thought he had someone, anyone, even his ugly secretary, but she knew Hank was faithful, and somehow that annoyed her even more. If he would just do one thing that wasn't predictable. The thing that was most predictable was his failure.

His large, clean white feet with the tufts of blond hair on the toes were sticking out from the covers. Six feet four of white bread, Margot had called him. Oh, Margot could kill with her tongue when she wanted to. Ellen stifled a giggle. She remem-

19

bered what fun they'd had at college, all the men phoning them and camping on their doorstep, the two most popular girls in the dorm. In those days when someone wanted to get Ellen a blind date she never asked, "Is he cute?"—she asked, "Is he tall?" She'd thought tall was sexy. Perhaps because she was tall, and in the fifties that wasn't considered sexy in a woman, it was liability. She liked big hands holding her breasts in a parked car, huge arms holding her on the dance floor.

All those long, lazy hours of foreplay in parked cars before curfew, without ever arriving at the moment of truth. A girl had to stay a virgin, she couldn't risk getting pregnant. Although it was rumored half the girls in the dorm weren't virgins, Ellen was, and Margot was until her senior year. Ellen was afraid. She didn't want to risk not getting the best husband in the world because he might disapprove of her past. She had totally bought the myth of marriage and children and happily ever after. She would have liked to be somebody, to have an interesting job, but she was afraid to be alone. All the wonderful touching in the cars—she had orgasms from just necking, and she knew that some of the girls who had gone all the way didn't even know what an orgasm was. She was afraid of what she would do if she was lonely and single. She would be a wonderful wife.

She and Margot shared an apartment in New York after they graduated, subsidized by their parents. Living together was supposed to keep them pure. Margot began to have an affair with her married boss. Wrong from the start, but nothing Ellen told her could change her mind. "I'm too young to get married right now anyway," Margot had said cheerfully. Having Margot sleeping home every night was no protection at all, Ellen discovered. All her dates had their own apartments. They could jump on you before dinner when you were sitting there totally unsuspecting, listening to their records, having a drink.

Hank Rennie respected her. So tall and blond and well dressed, already at twenty-five the owner of his own business because his father had died and left it to him. He sold big, expensive cars. But instead of necking with Ellen in one of them, he used cars for transportation, driving her to romantic restaurants in Westchester where they could watch ducks on a lake and play with each other's fingers over a dimly lit table. They were grown-ups now. Grown-ups didn't just fool around. When Hank proposed, Ellen accepted immediately. The happiest day of her life was when she quit that damn typing pool where the other girls hadn't even gone to college, and she had been Phi Beta Kappa, magna cum laude, and all they cared about was how many words a minute.

Ellen and her mother and Hank spent the entire spring preparing for the wedding. The china, the silver, the linens, the trousseau, the apartment they rented "until the children come and we move to the country." It was a June church wedding, with the reception at the Plaza Hotel. Upstairs they had rented a suite for Ellen and Hank to spend their wedding night. The next morning they would fly to Bermuda.

Margot and three of Ellen's other friends were bridesmaids. Margot had been annoyed because the bridesmaids had to pay for their own dresses but Ellen had picked them, and they were Margot's worst color. Ellen had done it deliberately, not wanting to be upstaged. Even then . . .

Before the wedding, waiting for her grand entrance, Ellen had cried. She didn't know why. She felt trapped. She didn't love Hank.

"Why are you crying?" Margot asked, her arms around Ellen, letting her smear mascara on the dress Margot hated anyway.

"Why did he get a haircut?" Ellen sobbed. "I hate his hair so short."

"Bride's nerves," Ellen's mother said cheerfully, rushing with a towel to clean Margot's dress and a whole makeup kit for Ellen's ruined face.

It was barbaric to have to change into her traveling suit and jump into a taxi, drive around the block, and go into a side entrance and upstairs to their wedding suite to be officially deflowered. Everybody who mattered knew what they were going to do. Her mother, his mother, her father . . . oh, God, how humiliating. Ellen wondered if her father was blocking it all out of his mind the way he did everything that bothered him. She was tired and embarrassed and hot and Hank was too. She wished they could run away, or put on jeans and go to P. J. Clarke's and get drunk, or just go to sleep. But not have to go into that huge white marble bathroom and change to her white satin nightgown with the matching peignoir and go out to the living room to face this stranger she was welded to now, who was in his bathrobe too and even had the mandatory bottle of champagne waiting in a cooler, just like in a bad movie.

She couldn't tell him how she felt. Girls didn't tell men how they felt about things. She had to let him undress her like in that same bad movie and try to pretend she didn't notice how scared he was. This time they wouldn't be necking and touching and doing all those wonderful sensual things that drove her crazy. They were Married now and they had to Do It. He even had a condom ready on the night table. She had never felt less like Doing It in her life.

She knew he didn't feel like it either. She had never been close to Hank without his getting an erection, but this time it just lay there, and she pretended not to look. She had never seen him fully naked before. Not even in a bathing suit, because they had met in the winter. She had never seen any man naked.

He took her hand and put it on his penis. He couldn't even speak to her, ask her, tell her what to do, and his embarrassment compounded hers until she felt nauseated. She began to stroke it with the hand that had the wedding ring on it. She was so used to the boys doing everything to her, trying to go as far as they could, that she had never done anything to them. But it didn't bother her. She had been curious to know what a bare penis felt like. It just lay there in her hand.

Then she felt his hand on the back of her neck, pushing her head down. She knew what he wanted her to do but she wasn't going to do it. How dare he? Why didn't he *ask* her instead of shoving her? If he'd only said something, if he'd been a person instead of this frantic frightened animal, she would have done it for him. She didn't know what to do, but she let him put it into her mouth and she felt it finally grow big, no, enormous, and she wanted to gag. I hate you, Ellen thought. I hate you, you make me sick, and I will hate you for the rest of my life.

She lay passively while he consummated their marriage, and she wondered if her mother knew what a hoax it all was and why she had never told her.

The next morning they went to Bermuda and the weather was perfect. They swam, sunned until they were mahogany color, snorkeled, rented bicycles, ate lobster, drank champagne, and took "a nap" every afternoon. Hank never had any more trouble and Ellen never had to do that thing again, but she was determined never to do it even if he begged her. He became aware after a while that she remained totally unmoved, and finally he even asked her timidly what she would like, and she told him, but nothing he did made her feel anything but cold and dead. Anger burned inside of her for having been cheated. She felt as if they were mirror skaters, doing everything perfectly in synchronization but never touching.

When they came back from their honeymoon she met his brother, who had been in the Army overseas and had just been released. Tony was short and lively, not much like Hank at all, and Ellen fell madly in love with him. They had a brief, passionate affair, heightened by the knowledge that they were doing a terrible thing to Hank and there was no way they could keep on doing it. The day they finally decided was the last time they would ever sleep together and that Tony would go to live in Europe until he got over her, Ellen did to him the thing Hank had made her do to him on their wedding night. It was her idea. She didn't mind doing it at all, in fact she enjoyed it. It made her feel happy.

Ellen discovered that a wedding ring was an aphrodisiac to men at parties. She had thought that marriage would put her out of the game, but instead she found that men were after her more than ever. It did not occur to her until many years and many affairs later that it was not the gold band that drew them to her but her own aura of secret sexuality. She was tall and rangy, the

23

sort of woman other women were not afraid of, but men sensed the rest of her. She liked to hold forth on her intellectual opinions, she read widely and retained well, she wasn't afraid to argue, but underneath this façade which lulled the wives there was that burning which awoke the husbands, made them try to be alone with her, made them phone her at home in the mornings from their offices when they knew Hank would be in his. She had her pick, and she was careful. She became involved with a man only when she fell madly in love. Each of her affairs lasted for over a year, and when Ellen broke it off to save her marriage, the man always remained her devoted friend.

Jill, their oldest daughter, nearly sixteen now, was born in New York, and then Ellen and Hank moved to the suburbs. Stacey was born two years later. They had decided to have only two children even if the second was a girl. Hank wanted to be able to give them the best. Ellen always liked Jill better than Stacey because Jill was so beautiful. Jill was slender and graceful and lovely, while Stacey looked like a little fireplug. Stacey looked like Hank's mother. But she was cheerful and sweet and had dimples. When Jill was ready for high school Ellen decided she couldn't stand to live in the suburbs another minute, it was a trap, they were going to go back to New York where there were things to do. She was tired of being a chauffeur, she wanted to go to museums and the theater. They sold their house, found a beautiful apartment, and put the girls into private school. Hank's business was doing well enough. He should have been doing better but he didn't have a head for business. His brother, who had no head for business at all, was living in Paris married to a French girl. There was only Hank supporting all of them, including his mother.

It was around that time that Ellen realized Hank knew she had been cheating on him but had never said anything. She wondered if he was afraid a confrontation would make her leave him. She didn't want to leave him because of the kids. The girls adored Hank, and in all fairness, he was a wonderful father, patient, attentive. It was just that he was so weak! What would he do without her? What would she do without him? He let her alone to do

24

what she wanted and he was someone to take her out at night. She could always depend on him. In his doglike way he had come to depend on her completely. They never fought. She just blocked him out when he annoyed her, the way her father had blocked out things he disliked so many years ago. Everything was really all right until the gasoline shortage and the recession.

One of the businesses hardest hit was big cars. The sales figures were so low they were frightening. There were Hank's monoliths sitting there, rapidly becoming extinct, a product that was dated and unsalable. Every month the interest on the bank loan came due, every week there was a payroll to be met, but how? The millions of dollars that had moved so easily on paper were now a real debt, a real threat. The calls came from people in Hank's office; at night, frightened voices. Sometimes there were calls during the day, usually on Friday, from Al or Bernie. Tell your husband he has to face his business problems. Even Al and Bernie didn't respect him. Is there trouble at home? Al asked. *Is there trouble at home?*

Hank was stubborn. He was sure the economy would turn around. But he was also frightened, Ellen could see that. The worst thing of all was that years ago, when they were first married, Hank had been offered a wonderful chance to switch from big cars to the then-new Volkswagen, and he had refused. His friends had advised him to consider it, and Ellen had agreed with his friends. "People are used to quality," Hank had said stubbornly. "They don't want it any other way. I'm known for quality."

Now he would be known for bankruptcy. How like Hank to have missed his chance, and to keep pretending even now that he had some kind of foresight. He said that over the holidays people didn't buy cars. He said wait until spring. They were just words.

They were living on their savings. Ellen wondered if there would be enough for the girls' private school next year and she worried. She didn't want them going to public school, she'd heard too many horror stories about how the kids carried knives. And drugs—thank God the girls weren't into that. They had always been open with her. She figured out how much money they had left in the bank and how much it would cost them to live this year if they were frugal, and she realized it wasn't going to work. She would have to get a job. She couldn't imagine what she could do that would bring in enough money to support them all, but at least her salary would be better than nothing.

That was why she had called Margot. Margot knew everything about working in interesting fields. Margot would help her. Margot didn't like Hank, because she considered him spineless and dull, so she would be sympathetic to Ellen's plight. It was going to be all right, it had to be. There was just no other alternative than all right.

IN WILTON, CONNECTICUT, Nikki Gellhorn woke up at six o'clock. The first thing she always did was look out the window to make sure it hadn't snowed during the night. She hated snow, it seemed a personal affront just to make commuting more miserable. She didn't mind getting up at six, but she hated all the rest of it—the fear that the car wouldn't start in the cold, the rush to the train and the hope it wouldn't get stuck or be late—which it usually was anyway—the hike from Grand Central Station to her office lugging all those heavy manuscripts because there never were enough taxis when you needed them, and then the same rotten thing all over again to get home, except that by then she was exhausted and had different manuscripts to lug. She was a senior editor at Heller & Strauss, she loved her job, she adored her husband and her children and was delighted with her life except for the total inconvenience of their illogical living arrangement.

Robert, her husband, was a lawyer in Stamford, which was nearer to Wilton than to New York, and therefore, since they'd lived in this reconverted farmhouse ever since the twins were born nineteen years ago and it was their *home*, he drove easily to work in Stamford and she had to commute a total of four hours every day to get to and from her job in New York. It was always the

26

woman who had to make the sacrifices. It annoyed the hell out of her.

She went into the kitchen and plugged in the electric coffee maker, which she'd prepared the night before. Robert could sleep until seven. At least that gave her solo bathroom privileges, although now that the twins, Dorothy and Lynn, were away at college there were two free bathrooms she could use. There was no reason any more to live here except that she and Robert loved it on weekends in the summer—and that was not much of a compensation for the rest of it. They could use it for weekends and have a place in New York, but then *he* would have to make the long haul, and his job was more important.

Who says his job is more important? Nikki thought again as she was beginning to think every morning. His job is more important to him, but mine is just as important to me.

She did love him. He was sexy and bright and cuddly, but she felt she was beginning to need more; not another man, but a part of her own life where she could be completely selfish. She was forty-two, with fresh, bright coloring and bouncy hair, a firm, curvy body—she looked no more than thirty. Even in the middle of summer she always looked as if she'd just come from a bath in a wonderful air-conditioned room. Her clothes were never wrinkled, her nail polish (she was the only woman she knew who even bothered to wear any) was never chipped. She was always carrying tote bags the size of small suitcases in order to look that way, but it was all part of her struggle to have something just for herself.

She had met Robert when she was in college and he was at law school; he was three years older. She was twenty when she graduated, and they were married the day after her graduation. They had both grown up in the suburbs and it seemed natural to them to buy the farmhouse as soon as they could afford the first down payment. When the twins were old enough to walk to the school bus by themselves she started working part time in New York because she was bored. First she was a fill-in secretary, then

27

a reader, and then an editor. She was working full time when the girls were in high school, and it never seemed to bother them any. They always enjoyed their time together more, and she was pleased to be able to say that Dorothy and Lynn were nice people, that she would have liked them even if they weren't her daughters.

She was dressed and having her second cup of coffee when Robert came into the kitchen. She kissed the back of his neck and his hand lingered on her rear end. "Nice ass," he said. He said that every morning.

"Thank you. It's comforting to be appreciated at my age." She grinned when she said it because she really did think she was thirty; it was always a shock to see the numbers when she had to write her date of birth on a document.

"You're just a baby," he said.

"I'm going to be late tonight, sweetheart. I have to have business drinks. Do you feel like driving into New York and taking me to dinner, or should I leave something here, or what?"

"Or what," he said.

"No, come on, tell me."

"How late will you be?"

"Nine thirty if I have to come back, seven thirty if we meet in New York."

"I'll wait and take you out to dinner here. Take the express to Stamford and I'll meet you at the station. Then you won't have to cook. I have some work to do anyway."

"Then I'll leave my car here and you can drive me to the station now." She saw his raised eyebrow. "I mean, *will* you drive me to the station?"

"Sure. When I'm dressed."

She looked at her watch. "Shit, it's not going to work."

"Why not?"

"I have a meeting at nine. It's important. If I wait for you to drive me, I'll miss my train."

"Well, then, why don't you just come home and we'll eat something here?"

"Okay." She took two steaks out of the freezer and put them on a shelf in the refrigerator. "They'll be thawed by tonight."

"Goodbye," he said, taking his cup of coffee into the bathroom.

"Bye, darling."

That was really a scintillating conversation, Nikki thought with unaccustomed anger as she drove her car out of the garage. I wouldn't have missed that conversation for the world. It was worth traveling two hours this morning and getting up at six A.M. just to have that conversation. What do a brilliant lawyer and a successful editor talk about at home, folks? Now you know.

The train was only five minutes late, and Nikki settled into a window seat with the manuscript she was going to read on the trip. She was a fast reader and could usually finish a whole manuscript each way. She hadn't bothered to tell Robert that her business drink wasn't exactly a business drink, even though she could put it on her expense account because Margot King was a television personality who might want to write a book some day. But Margot was mainly her friend, and keeping her girl friends was an important part of Nikki's personal life. Because she had commuted for so long she didn't have much of a relationship with the married women they knew in the country. She and Robert saw them and their husbands on weekends, as couples. Her lunch dates were all business ones, no time for just a lunch with a girl friend. She had business cocktail dates too, more than she would have preferred. There was never enough time for anything. She felt rushed and pushed and frustrated, knowing there were so many things she couldn't fit into her life. This evening she would just sit in the bar at the Plaza for an hour with Margot, maybe get a little smashed, and they would talk about all the things that bored husbands and boyfriends. It would make her feel whole again for a while anyway.

RACHEL FOWLER, ORNAMENT, wife of Lawrence Fowler, international banker, woke up in the king-sized bed of the master bedroom in their Fifth Avenue duplex apartment at just ten minutes past noon. She always slept late, even when she didn't feel like it. It made the day shorter. She had Porthault sheets and a Porthault breakfast set to match. She buzzed for the maid, and by the time she had emerged from the bathroom her breakfast was waiting for her on a white wicker tray table on the bed, the sheets having thoughtfully been smoothed as if she were an invalid.

The breakfast tray contained half a grapefruit, a pot of tea, some artificial sweetener, a rose in a bud vase, and *The New York Times*. She read the headlines, skimmed the front page, and turned to the crossword puzzle. She liked to do it in ink; it was one of the few things she did well. Once she had been a model, and she had done that well. Now she was thirty-five, still very beautiful, tall and slender, terrified of losing her looks, and she did being a wife very well.

Being Lawrence's wife was not an ordinary job. He gave dinner parties every night if he was home. Large ones on certain weekends, medium-sized ones for thirty on certain week nights, six for cocktails if it was a private little thing before an opening. Rachel kept a leather-bound book with the names of the guests on each date, the food and wine served, which table linen had been used, what kind of flowers, and what she had worn, so that nothing would be duplicated. She had a round leather disc into which she could slip place cards as if it were their dinner table and move them until she found the perfect seating arrangement. She drew the circle with the names in her book too.

There were things she did not write but which she remembered: who had his or her eye on whom, who had clicked, and whose mate had found out. It was as important to keep certain people apart as to keep others together.

None of this being a hostess was really very difficult. There were phone calls to be made to the florist and the liquor store. To the butcher and grocer if the cook was preparing the food, otherwise to the caterer if it was a large party. She had standing appointments at the hairdresser's, the gym, and the salon where she had her facials. A masseuse had come to the apartment three times a week until Rachel read that massage could give you

30

broken capillaries, then she had stopped. Last year, at thirty-four, she'd had an eye lift. It was better to have these things done when only you noticed they were needed, before other people noticed.

The new important novels and nonfiction books were piled on the bedroom desk. Rachel read two every week in order to have something to talk about. If they invited anyone who had written a book, of course she would read it before the author came, but she never said more than one thing about the book to the author unless it was obvious that more was called for. She wanted to seem informed but not pushy. The one thing she said about the book was always a carefully chosen compliment even if she thought the book was garbage.

Lawrence never took a vacation. Sometimes he went to Europe on business and took her with him. Rachel had learned to speak several languages rather well in order to make the other people feel at ease when they went out socially in foreign countries. Lawrence spoke only English no matter which country he was in. He said that when you were doing business you couldn't afford to make mistakes. He always used a translator, although he could speak and understand most languages better than Rachel did.

He was older than she was; they had been married for ten years, and they were hardly ever alone together. When they weren't entertaining people at home or being invited out he was out with businessmen. He seemed to like that best of all. He went to different bars or sometimes drank in offices where executives had their own bars, talking business or just having a good time with the men, and he never came home before eight. If she felt lonely she couldn't call him, because she never knew where he was. When he did come home, if they were alone they ate in front of the television set. He was a very fast eater. She ate almost nothing. It took them fifteen minutes to have their entire dinner, including coffee, and then Lawrence liked to go into his den to work. At eleven he emerged and watched the evening news on television, then he went to sleep. He was up and gone to the office long before Rachel ever woke up in the mornings. Once in a while, when he remembered, they had sex together. He was very

31

observant, he knew exactly what she liked in bed, just as he knew what sort of presents she liked to be surprised with on the birthdays and anniversaries he never forgot. She had a safe deposit box at the bank full of Fabergé *objets*. She used to keep them out on the tables in the living room, but then one of them disappeared. It was expensive and irreplaceable. Rachel knew the maid hadn't taken it, because it wasn't the sort of thing a maid would steal, and besides she trusted the help. She was sure it had been one of their guests. That made her feel creepy, because you tried to invite the best people into your home, you made yourself vulnerable to them, and then one of them turned out to be a kleptomaniac or, worse, a common thief.

Lawrence hadn't been upset when she told him. He bought her another *objet* like it. Rachel, however, couldn't forget about it for a long time. She kept half expecting to see her Fabergé egg sitting on somebody's coffee table when they went to a party, but of course she never did.

ELLEN HAD LUNCH with Margot that day. Margot had made a reservation at the Russian Tea Room, and Ellen was a little nervous because the tables were so small and close together and the place was so crowded that she was afraid people would hear her discussing personal business. But it was also very noisy, and there was a certain anonymity in that. Besides, she didn't know them. The hell with them. Her survival came first.

"I hope this is all right," Margot said. "If you hate Russian food you're out of luck."

"If you think I care what I eat . . . Hank's on the verge of going bankrupt, Margot."

"Oh, no!"

"I don't know what I'm going to do. It's so typical of him. Only Hank could inherit a perfectly good business from his father and then let it fail. He had his chance to switch to small cars years ago. But Hank is incapable of an original thought. What was good enough for Daddy was good enough for him. And now nobody wants big cars. We're broke and in debt and I'm hysterical."

"I'm so sorry, Ellen," Margot said. "That's just terrible." Ellen could see she really meant it. "You know what I think of Hank, but I can't help thinking how rotten it must be for him too, losing his father's business—the Oedipal thing."

"Margot, when you're about to go on Welfare you don't have Oedipal problems, you have real problems. I need a job."

"I'll be glad to help," Margot said. "I'll look."

"Isn't there something at your station I could do?"

"They're not hiring anybody right now. Wait . . . wait, let me think. Nikki! I'm going to make a call."

Margot went to the phone booth and called Nikki Gellhorn at Heller & Strauss. She knew Nikki would be out to lunch but always left word where she'd be, and Margot then called her at the restaurant.

"What's up?" Nikki asked. "Are you calling off our drink date?"

"No. I wanted to know if that opening in your publicity department has been filled yet."

"Not yet, but they're seeing some people tomorrow."

"I have someone for them to see today. It's a big personal favor for me," Margot said. "I can send her over this afternoon. You've met her, it's Ellen Rennie, my friend since college."

"But it's a kid's job," Nikki said. "It's boring, and the most it would pay is two hundred a week."

"She really needs the money," Margot said. "And besides, Ellen's so aggressive she's perfect for publicity."

Nikki giggled. "I always like to do a favor for a friend. Especially a pushy one. Tell her to come by at three thirty. I'll pave the way before."

"Thanks a million, Nikki. I'll tell you the whole story later. You'll understand how much she appreciates it."

"You can pay for the drinks," Nikki said.

Margot came back to the table beaming. "I've got you a job, I think. You have an interview at three thirty. You remember my friend Nikki Gellhorn. She's a senior editor at Heller & Strauss."

33

"The commuter," Ellen said. "What's the job?"

"It's in the publicity department. They need someone to book tours for authors: get plane tickets, coordinate schedules, reserve cars and hotel rooms in various cities, make sure that when an author shows up at seven forty-five in the morning to do a television show, they know he's coming and he knows where to go."

"I can do that," Ellen said. "I'm very efficient."

"It only pays two hundred a week, but you haven't got a résumé and . . ."

"Are you kidding? That's a thousand dollars a month! Do you realize the terrible weight you'd be lifting from my heart with a thousand dollars a month?"

"It's independence," Margot said.

"It's beautiful. Tell me everything about the company so they'll think I'm smart."

"Well, let's see. Heller & Strauss is one of the biggest and richest publishing companies. They have a very good list. Both Heller and Strauss, who founded it, are long since retired—or dead, for all I know—and nobody really knew much about Heller except that he was very rich and very ugly, and he had a horrendous wife who insisted on looking over every secretary and reader in the entire company to make sure she wasn't pretty. If she was pretty, she got fired. Mrs. Heller was sure that every woman in the world was after her husband, even when he was eighty."

"How did Nikki get the job, then?"

"She came from elsewhere after Heller had retired. Strauss, on the other hand, became quite well known because he was the darling of the talk shows. Now that I think of it, he *is* dead. He gave the company a kind of panache and a lot of good publicity. Now the company is run by a publisher, a president, the editor in chief, the executive editor, and some senior editors, one of whom is Nikki, and under them some ordinary editors and readers. Then there's the copy department, the art department, the sales department, and of course the publicity department, where you will be."

"It sounds like they have a lot of authors," Ellen said.

34

"They do. But they don't all tour. Just the ones who can get on talk shows and be interviewed by newspapers."

"I don't actually book them for that?"

"No, you'll be sort of the in-house travel agent. Move them around and make sure nothing gets screwed up."

"I can hardly wait!" Ellen said. "You're a real friend, Margot."

RACHEL AND LAWRENCE FOWLER were giving a large party to help one hundred of their closest friends recover from the after-holiday doldrums. Margot and Nikki were both invited, Margot as "Celebrity—TV" and Nikki as "Intellectual—Publishing." Neither was aware of the categories in which they were listed in Rachel's party book, but they suspected. Actually, they both liked Rachel, for they had decided that there was more to her as a person than the role that life, her husband, and she herself had put her into. Ellen and Hank were invited too, having been on Lawrence Fowler's "Large Party" list ever since Hank had sold him his first limousine at a discount. Lawrence had switched to a Mercedes several years ago, but he didn't like to drop people, and the Rennies seemed personable enough.

The party was held on a Friday night, starting at eight. Rachel had decided that people should dress up. There was a buffet dinner, a lot to drink of course—mostly white wine, because people wanted that lately—and she had hired a pianist. Handsome young men sent from the caterer were running all over the place. Rachel preferred them to maids. It made the wives feel sexier, even though the waiters were homosexual.

Dressed, Lawrence presented himself to her for her approval. It was nice of him to do that, she thought, it made her feel important to him, and it was one of the few times she felt that he, not just his environment, needed her. She in turn presented herself to him for his approval. They shared a glass of champagne together in the library before the guests came. It would probably

35

be the last time they would see each other until the party was over.

The Christmas decorations were long gone, and Rachel had managed to have spring flowers flown in. The large apartment looked fresh, blooming and cheerful. She supposed everything would go right, it always did. It was too bad she couldn't get drunk and enjoy herself, but champagne was fattening. She would just be charming and bored.

Ellen was thrilled. She had wanted to be the first to arrive so she would have time to chat with the Fowlers, but then she decided Hank was a detriment and it would be better to arrive later so she could lose him in the crowd. When they got there Nikki and Robert were already there.

"I love your wife," Nikki said to Hank. "I think she's enchanting. She's going to be so good at her new job. Everyone loves her."

Hank looked pleased but uncomfortable. "Don't be jealous, dear," Ellen said to him.

"Oh, why would he be jealous?" Nikki said cheerfully. She was bubbling and bouncing all over the place like a blond cheerleader. In a minute there were three other men around her, all admiring her. Robert hovered over her for a while and then went to the bar.

Ellen lost Hank as soon as possible. In a few minutes she had her own group of men around her. One of them brought her a drink. They were a banker, an advertising executive, a doctor, and an actor. They were all married, except for the actor, who had a possessive date at least twenty years younger than he who kept clutching onto him. No wonder poor Margot never finds anybody, Ellen thought. All the men are divine but they're all taken.

Margot, in the library where it was quieter, kept looking at her watch. She had to be back at the studio soon to prepare the news. There was a very attractive boy standing by the fireplace, maybe twenty, watching everything with that cool, self-possessed air young kids put on when they're uncomfortable. She was immediately attracted to him in a way she hadn't felt for a long time, and she thought how funny it would be if at last he turned out to

36

be the one who could move her. He looked at her, right into her eyes, and smiled. "Hello," he said without moving toward her.

She moved toward him.

"You keep looking at the time," he said. He had a soft, sweet voice, sexy. But just a kid. Nothing for her—she'd have to be crazy.

"I have to go to work soon," Margot said. "I do live news on TV."

"I've seen you," he said. "Margot King. Murder and mayhem at eleven." He smiled. He had sensual lips and perfect teeth.

"You know who I am, but who are you?"

"I'm Kerry Fowler."

"Related to . . . ?"

"Lawrence Fowler's son."

Oh, God, someone's son. She had graduated from someone's husband to someone's son. Her aging was complete. Lawrence and Rachel didn't have any children, and Rachel was too young to be this boy's mother anyway, so he must be from Lawrence's long-ago first marriage. She found herself laughing.

"What's funny?"

"Me," Margot said.

"Are you having a good time?"

"I don't like the noise and smoke, but I like parties. At least, I always think I'm going to like them. When I was a little girl my mother always used to get me something new when there was going to be a party, a dress or shoes or something, and she would put it in the closet and say, 'Now, you can't wear this until the party.' So I'd wait and wait, thinking something wonderful was going to happen, and then the party was always a disappointment. I guess the fantasy of what would happen to me when I wore that dress was better than what ever did happen." She smiled, looking carefully at this boy, Kerry, to make sure he wasn't laughing at her. "I guess I'm still that way."

"Me too," he said. "I used to go to camp, and my parents would buy me all this stuff, and I'd fantasize about camping out in the woods and how great it would be, and then I'd always get in trouble with the counselors about breaking some rule, and they'd have to send for my parents and it would be a big hassle."

"I loathed camp," Margot said. "I'd sit in my bunk and read instead of being good at athletics, and all the other girls hated me."

"We have the same memories."

"We can't possibly have the same memories," Margot said, "you're too young."

"I'm twenty-three."

Sixteen years older than he is. But if I were a man and he was a young girl, nobody would think it was so terrible. "I'm thirty-nine."

He absolutely beamed. "That's great! You don't look it. I thought you were about twenty-eight."

"Only because at your age thirty-nine is unimaginable," Margot said. "What do you do anyway?"

"I'm a writer."

"Published?"

"I have a contract for my first novel, which is about halfway finished. It's not autobiographical."

"Okay."

"It's sort of a fantasy."

"They're the best," Margot said. "My entire life is fantasy."

"The news?"

"No, my private life. In self-defense against the news."

"Can I come with you when you go to work tonight?" He sounded so earnest, like a kid.

She shrugged. "I guess so. You can watch me type."

"I'm not much good at parties anyway," he said. "And besides, I thought then maybe you and I could go have a drink somewhere."

I wonder if he thinks I'm a celebrity. No, he wouldn't; he's been around celebrities all his life. Maybe he just thinks I'm interesting. "Okay."

His eyes were big and green, like a cat's, curious and knowing. "You're wondering why I want to be with you," he said. "But I'm wondering why you want to be with me. I think you're beautiful."

"Let's just say I think you're beautiful too," Margot said lightly, but she felt her heart turn over. I think I'm not so dead after all, she thought.

RACHEL SAW Margot King leave with Kerry and she smiled. Women just loved that boy and he loved them too. If she'd been a different type of woman she might have wanted to have a go at him herself. But she had never cheated on Lawrence in the ten years they'd been married. Even with the little sex he gave her, she had no inclination to cheat. She liked to flirt a little, she touched people a lot, lightly, innocently, but without desire. It was a part of communication to put your hand on someone's arm, to give a brief hug, a butterfly kiss. It was the language of the group they traveled with and meant no more than "How are you today?"

She sighed. They all knew so much more than she, those other women. She did everything flawlessly, but that was all she did. Margot had a job, a life, and could whisk off a young man from a party with not a backward glance, nor a forward one either. Nikki had a good job and a married life, even Ellen Rennie, who'd never done anything outstanding, was launched on a job Rachel would have been perfect for. But that was their world, and she was in hers. She wondered whether her guests envied her or whether they thought she was foolish and laughed at her behind her back, or whether she was almost invisible to them, like the caterers who made the party work so well. She wondered if any of the husbands thought of her as a woman in her own right, or just as something lovely that belonged to Lawrence and came with the house, like the Ming vase and the Coromandel screen and the Matisse.

HE THOUGHT OF IT AS Rachel's house, never Lawrence-and-Rachel's, always had, although to them he was just another guest. Just entering the place where she lived, where she had a private life, took his breath away. The specialness of her had become his

39

obsession. His fantasies concerned only her. In one of them she was in a trance, but not dead, and in his power; he could do what he wanted with her, and when she woke she would love him. Ludicrous, of course, that he had to imagine her immobile in order to possess her, when the fact that she was in his fantasy alone wasn't enough. He was always amazed that he could carry on a normal conversation with her and keep everyone from suspecting what he was thinking. It was almost as if he himself hadn't known what he was thinking until that evening, so many months ago, when he pocketed her Fabergé egg.

When he realized what he'd done he was horrified. Stealing something of that value was grand larceny. He was a respectable man. But once her egg was in his pocket, surrounded by his damp fingers, he felt it emitting vibrations of Rachel's own hand and he couldn't put it back on the table from which he'd whisked it away. He knew it was something she cared about a great deal. She had stroked it, and now it belonged to him. He had taken it home and hidden it where his wife could never find it. And after a while he realized it wasn't what he wanted at all, never had been. He wanted something closer to Rachel, something that had touched not her hand but her body.

Outside the master bedroom there was a bathroom with two doors, one leading to the bedroom, the other to a large dressing room, which in turn led to another bathroom. It was a veritable maze of luxury. He entered quickly through the bedroom, locked the door behind himself, walked through the suite, and locked the door that opened from the last bathroom to the hall. Now no one could interrupt him. Everything of her most private life was here.

One bathroom, with brown tiles and houndstooth-printed towels, was her husband's. The other, pink and white, with mirrored walls, was hers. He imagined Rachel, naked from her tub, standing reflected in all those mirrors like a kind of symbol. She was too perfect to be a woman. There should be an infinity of her, reflected and rereflected, and belonging only to him. The scent of her perfume still hovered in the damp room, and he felt dizzy from the feelings and confusion it evoked. The bath towel she had used was gone, some maid of superefficiency had removed it and replaced it with dozens of little linen hand towels. No ring in her tub, of course not. He looked around, and his breath came in rasps like an asthmatic's because he knew what he wanted now. He opened her hamper.

There, coiled on the bottom waiting for his hand, were the underpants, pantyhose, and transparent wisp of bra she had tossed in before her bath. His hand went for the bikini pants. He touched them and felt the blood rush to his groin. They were so clean it was as if she had never worn them at all. He had known that in his heart, for Rachel was no ordinary woman. Nothing about her would ever be soiled or would soil anything. He crumpled the silky pants in his fist and held them to the pain between his legs. He didn't know what to do; he couldn't walk out of here and face all those people with a hard-on, but he couldn't disgrace himself in here either. If he did it on a towel the maid would see later, and even though no one would know who had done it he would know. He didn't want to do it on her pants, not yet, not here. But why not now, here? Knowing she was somewhere in the apartment made it better.

He felt terrible afterward. It was as if he'd been crazy and had come to his senses. Why did he have these lapses? He folded the bit of sodden nylon into as small a lump as possible and put it into his trousers pocket inside his handkerchief. He was so normal, why did he sometimes get out of control like this, for her, only for her? A sharp rapping on the bathroom door brought him back completely. This bathroom was obviously the women's toilet and the other was for the men. He knew that rapping sound well enough. Some bitch in a hurry. He walked quietly out of Rachel's bathroom, through the dressing room and Lawrence's bathroom, and unlocked the door to the bedroom, letting himself out. Let the bitch suffer. He hoped it was his wife.

AT THREE IN THE MORNING Margot King and Kerry Fowler were lying in her bed. The record player had clicked off, the wine bottle was empty, they had made love, and she didn't have to get up early the next morning. She would fix him English muffins with lavender honey. Real coffee, not instant. He was everything she had suspected he would be—loving, so loving, with the perfect, beautiful body only the young had. He still had his arms around her.

"Would you like to move in with me for a while?" she asked. She waited.

"I don't know," he said finally. "I have to write my book."

"You'd keep your own apartment of course. You could write your book there. There are times I have to be alone too."

He looked at her and grinned. "For what?"

"Just for me."

"You're so beautiful." He kissed her on top of the head.

"There would be no house rules. Just honesty."

"That's a rule," he said, but she knew he was teasing her.

"I'll give you a key. I mean . . . lend you one."

"Give, lend—why are you so hung up on words? If I move in, you're my old lady."

"Old lady!"

They both laughed.

"Would you?" she asked timidly.

"Okay," he said. "As long as we both understand the real nature of this relationship."

"And what is that?"

"That I'm the grown-up and you're the kid," Kerry said.

"How did you know that so soon?" Margot cried in delight. They bit at each other like puppies, giggling. Margot felt so alive and full of joy that she thought she might die of it.

FEBRUARY

February 1975

JILL RENNIE, the older daughter of Ellen and Hank, was fifteen going on sixteen, five feet six, and weighed ninety-one pounds. At first you didn't notice it because her face still had a childish roundness, huge dark-lashed eyes, soft mouth. In a previous time she might have looked like Twiggy. But while Twiggy's little-boy look had been an accident of musculature, Jill's was the deliberate product of starvation. She had been meant to look like her mother —athletic, rangy, filled out. Instead she still looked prepubescent. Her summer uniform was a boy's undershirt and tight jeans, her winter uniform the jeans with a tight wool body sweater. She had no breasts, and she had not yet started her periods, although she lied about it to her mother. Jill wasn't really aware of what she looked like; she thought she was too fat. She wanted to lose just a little more. She knew the adults disapproved of the way she looked, however, so she never let them know she was dieting. It was easy to fool them, they thought all teen-agers were crazy anyway. She pretended to be a health-food faddist.

45

"Don't you know there are weevils in flour?" Jill would cry in horror when her mother tried to get her to eat a piece of toast at breakfast. "There are preservatives in that jam. That fruit is full of poisonous spray. I'll buy my own fruit and keep it in my room so you won't mix it up with the other."

Her mother bought fertilized eggs and raw milk. Her younger sister, Stacey, who would eat anything, finished them up. Jill existed on natural spring water, which she bought by the gallon, vitamin pills, and an occasional dried, unsulphured apricot. At meals she either rejected the food or said she had eaten. When occasionally she was forced to eat, she went to her bathroom afterward and put her finger down her throat. She was absolutely convinced that if she ate an entire meal she would change overnight to a fat person with breasts and buttocks and sexual desires, waddling around looking for release, and furthermore that if she began to eat anything she would never be able to stop.

She knew the latter was true. Although she was never hungry, once in a while she gave in, like the time her father took all of them to an amusement park. She ate ten hot dogs, six ice cream cones, two Cokes, and a whole large-sized bag of potato chips. Then she threw up in the refuse can without even having to put her finger down her throat. She was so sick and weak that they all had to go right home.

"I told you," Jill panted in the family car, looking like a rag doll flung onto the back seat of the enormous air-conditioned automobile. "There are rat droppings in hot dogs, and sodium nitrite, which gives you cancer."

"You've got to be in training to eat like such a pig," Stacey said.

"You should know."

Although they sniped at each other, she and Stacey were good friends, as good friends as a girl nearly sixteen can be with one only thirteen and a half. The little kid grasped things, she was smart. She knew about their mother's men before Jill told her. In fact, Jill wouldn't have brought the subject up, but Stacey did.

"Do you think Dad knows?"

"I don't know," Jill said. "If we know, he must know."

46

"Not if he doesn't want to know."

"How come he doesn't leave her and take us with him, do you think?" Jill asked.

"Fathers don't get custody of kids. Especially girls."

"They do if the kids are as old as we are. We could say we want to go with him."

"*Would* you want to go with him?" Stacey asked.

Jill shrugged. "You know they'll never break up, just because of us. They want us to be a family." She said "a family" with deep sarcasm born of years of watching those ridiculous soppy families on TV. Nobody's family she knew was the slightest way like that.

"Listen," Stacey said, "half the kids in my class at school their parents are divorced, and I'm not even fourteen. People are getting divorced with younger kids every day. They don't have to stay together for us."

"It's not for us," Jill said thoughtfully. "They just pretend it's for us. It's for them."

"They think we're so dumb," Stacey said.

"I never want to get married," Jill said. "Marriage is a big fake. Why get married if you're going to fall in love with someone else anyway?"

"When we grow up nobody is going to get married any more," Stacey said.

"Well, even if they do, *I* won't."

She never wanted to grow up and be like her mother. She hated even the way her face at some angles resembled her mother's. She knew her mother preferred her to Stacey because of that resemblance, and it angered her. She wanted to destroy everything in her that was in any way reminiscent of her mother and be herself, a totally separate being. She had not given much thought to what she wanted to be when she grew up. Stacey had already decided she would be a doctor. She was always taking the subway downtown to the public library and reading medical books. Jill told her not to take the subway, she could get killed. Stacey didn't care. She wandered around all over the city; once she'd gone into the Bellevue Hospital emergency room and sat there looking at all the

47

accident and assault cases for two hours before anyone even noticed her and asked her what was the matter. She had been so pleased to be able to tell Jill about the stabbings and gunshot wounds and shock, and what had been done for them, and she wasn't disgusted at all.

"Well, what do you expect me to do, take a taxi on *my* allowance?" she would ask angrily when Jill yelled at her.

"If Mom ever found out . . ."

"She's not going to find out. She's not interested in me."

Jill didn't know what to answer to that because she knew it was true. Her pain for her sister, whom she loved, made her anger at the suffocation of her mother's devotion to herself even stronger. She only loves me because she thinks I'm like her. If she only knew how much I despise her.

Her mother on the phone whenever there was a new man. Jill knew the voice her mother put on so well by now that she could even tell if it was a new man she was going to sleep with, a man she was already in the throes of sleeping with, or one of her rejects whom she liked to keep around. Sometimes she wondered if her mother really thought she was so stupid or if her mother in some strange way wanted her to know, as if to say, "*I'm* the grown-up woman around here, not you." What made her mother think sleeping with men made you grown up? As far as Jill was concerned, if she never had to sleep with a man in her entire life it would be too soon.

Her mother, the hypocrite, on the phone with her friend Margot. Margot was sleeping with a man sixteen years younger than she was. She'd been the same age Jill was now, even older, when that boy was born! But they weren't hurting anybody. Neither of them belonged to anybody else. And there was her mother, lecturing Margot, warning her, telling her she'd be hurt, that his friends must be laughing at her, that he'd leave her for a girl his own age. Jill knew her mother was probably just jealous. She'd seen her mother's last lover one day when he dropped her off at the apartment in his sports car on the way to the suburbs where he lived with his wife and children, and Jill had just been coming home. Her mother had had to introduce them. He was gray-faced and flabby, trying to look young in his sheepskin coat, driving that red Jag, and Jill couldn't understand why her mother preferred him to Dad. What was so wonderful about that old man? She bet her mother would be thrilled to have a young lover like Kerry Fowler if one would want to have anything to do with her.

IN PAST YEARS Margot had always found February the most difficult month. The New York weather had finally settled into winter, people were tired of it, short-tempered, depressed. No wonder whoever made the calendar made February the shortest month; it was almost too much to take as it was. But this February seemed too short, because she was in love with Kerry and they were living together in her apartment, and she saw the world through his eyes. Everything seemed to be happening for the first time, and in many ways it was. She had never lived with someone who wanted to be up at seven A.M. on a Saturday morning to rush down to Canal Street to buy plastics for projects. That was what little boys did! He was always doing things: building a Plexiglas coffee table (she'd had no idea how complicated that was), or making her a romantic collage called "The Sun and the Moon and the Stars," or getting tickets to a midnight rock concert, or insisting they stand on line for an hour in the afternoon in the bitter cold because he wanted to see a hit movie the day it opened. He had to see everything, they had to keep running all weekend until she was exhausted. He took her to SoHo because she'd never been, she took him to a revival of an old Humphrey Bogart movie she'd seen the first time it ran, when he'd been too young to see it, and they went to the Planetarium because neither of them had ever been.

She had gone all over New York with camera crews in the course of her work, but that had been the insider's New York, the human interest stories, the disasters. Kerry's was like a tourist's New York, taking advantage of everything the city had to offer, as if his stay was only temporary. She remembered when she had

49

been his age; she had been the same way, because everything was new, she was on her own, and at last she had some money to go places. The two of them shared all their expenses, like kids his age did, and that was good, because she didn't want to feel she was keeping him and yet she felt guilty about letting him pay for things. He wouldn't take much money from his father, just enough to get by until his novel made some money, if he was lucky.

Perhaps Kerry wanted to do everything this minute because he was young, or perhaps it was because he knew, as she did, that their love was just for now. Neither of them ever discussed that. But even at the happiest moments Margot felt sad underneath the joy. On a winter Sunday they had been ice-skating in Central Park on rented skates, and came back to her apartment just as the early dusk fell. They stripped off their wet clothes and he lit a fire in the fireplace Margot had never used before she met him because she'd thought fireplaces were messy. Outside their windows it was black, inside the warm room it was safe. His naked body was lit with a roseate glow as he kneeled over the logs setting tapers to the kindling, and she thought she had never seen a body so beautiful as his. Young, slender, perfect, like no body she had ever seen. Did young men look that way when she was twenty-three? She couldn't remember. She hadn't gone to bed with young men then, she had always been infatuated with older, married men who babied her, and then later, when she began to concentrate on men her own age in hope of finding something lasting, they had already gone to flab from their years as bachelor playboys or office drones. Kerry was looking into the fire with utter pleasure, and then he turned and looked at her with the same look of happiness, and she thought she had never been so happy in her life. At that same moment her throat closed with the beginning of tears and she had to fight them back.

Through those long, wonderful winter evenings they made plans for the summer. He wanted to take her to the Greek islands. Neither of them had ever been there. They would rent a small boat. For the first time the strange names had the ring of reality.

She would take two weeks, perhaps in July. No, he said, better make it the end of September; there wouldn't be many tourists then and he would have finished his book. She was glad he was the one who set the date farther ahead. At least she would still be seeing him in the fall. . . .

She was obsessed with his body and he seemed as obsessed with hers, or perhaps young men just wanted sex all the time. He wore her out, but she didn't care. She didn't need sleep, she only needed him. He told her he loved her and she finally let herself believe it. If caring so much made you pay more afterward, then that was a risk you had to take. She felt this could never happen again, she would be different afterward—she would have to act her age. But now there was still time to do all the things she'd missed when she was young.

There were times, of course, when the world intruded. He took her to a party to meet all his friends. He'd told her not to dress up, so she wore pants, but they were the wrong sort of pants; everyone else was in blue jeans. They were all young and skinny and long-haired, the boys and the girls dressed alike, and they were all lying on the floor on batik cushions smoking grass. Margot hated grass. Since she'd stopped smoking cigarettes, it made her just as sick as tobacco. The air stank. The kids—his friends—looked at her as if she were an intruder, some old person who didn't belong there. Nobody bothered to talk to her. She felt self-conscious and ugly. The next day Kerry took her to some store on First Avenue and bought her a pair of blue jeans that were so tight she couldn't sit down in them. He seemed to think her attire was the only barrier between her and his friends, while she knew better. It was her face and her mind and her life.

Another time they went to Sherry's to pick out wine. Kerry stood there quietly, not knowing one wine from another or caring either, while she knew all about them, and suddenly she wondered if the salesman thought the obvious and humiliating thing about them. Did they seem like a joke to other people?

"You care too much what people think," Kerry told her when she said she didn't want to go to his friends' next party.

51

"That means they do think I have no business being there."

"I don't know what they think, but I don't care."

So she went, and she saw the absolute disinterest on their faces, far more cutting than an insult. She was too old to exist for them. In self-defense she took him to places where her friends were, to Ellen's dinner party, for a winter Sunday at Nikki's in a borrowed car. If Kerry was uncomfortable with her friends, he hid it well. He was quiet and pleasant. But what was he thinking? That some day he and his friends would be old like that? He might not like it, but it was a lot better than her knowing that she would never be young again like his friends.

FOR ABOUT A YEAR NOW Nikki Gellhorn had felt that her life had stopped. She was not a person who had ever been able to put up with a static existence, she always had to be stirring things up, even if it was just a couple of harmless flirtations. She had more energy than she could cope with, but using her energy on the dreary commuting to and from her job was meaningless effort. She wanted to do new and different things before it was too late.

The feeling that she was trapped had started when the twins went away to college. She knew they would come back to visit, of course, but it would never be the same. They would never again come home to live. And although they had protested that that was not true, Nikki knew better. Last year, at the end of their freshman year, the girls were surer, stronger, looking for their own lives, talking about themselves and their futures as separate entities from the family. Nikki made herself accept it wholeheartedly so they would continue to be her friends as well as her daughters. Now, home for the midterm holiday in their sophomore year, Dorothy and Lynn were even more whole persons than they had been the year before, and Nikki knew she had lost them.

Dorothy was going to major in psychology, she wanted to work with disturbed teen-agers. Last summer she had been a counselor in a nice middle-class camp, but this summer she was going to work in White Plains in a mental hospital. It was a branch of

Payne Whitney, she said. Would she live in Wilton with her parents and commute? No, Dorothy said, the trip was too much, she would have a little room in the dorm on the hospital grounds, she was damn lucky to get it, she said, nurses got first choice. One gone, like ten little Indians, but Nikki had only two. Lynn had a boyfriend. She had been living with him almost all term. He was a senior at her college, and they were going to hitchhike through Europe together this summer. Lynn already had maps and lists of all the cheap youth hostels. She was going to be a political science major, although she would have preferred English. Lynn carefully chose her courses with an eye to getting into the best graduate school so she could get a good job afterward. How different her girls were from her at their age, Nikki thought with admiration and a sense of loss. Not loss of them, but loss of her own youth, her own best years. She had chosen to have marriage and a career; it had been a brave decision in her day, but now as she looked back on her life and compared it with the life her daughters were entering, it seemed as if she hadn't really had all of either part, the job or the marriage. She had flirted and cajoled her way through her jobs, and she had flirted and cajoled her way through her marriage. She had never dared be completely honest in any segment of her life.

There was no way she could explain this to Robert. You couldn't, after twenty-two years of marriage, turn to your husband and say, "None of this has ever been real." They had a warm, cuddly relationship that had fooled everyone, even themselves, but they had never really known each other, and now it was too late.

Sunday morning breakfast in the large, old-fashioned kitchen, with *The New York Times* spread around and Dorothy and Lynn home and Robert doing the cooking, which he liked to do on Sunday mornings, the old, deaf dog at Nikki's feet, was like old times, and yet it was temporary too, because Lynn's boyfriend was coming tomorrow to stay with them until he and Lynn drove back to school, and he would be an intruder. Nikki and Robert had decided to be modern and let Lynn and her boyfriend sleep

53

in the same room since they were living together at college anyway.

"Poor Dog," Lynn said. "Woof! Can you hear me? Mom, that dog is stone-deaf."

"He can't see too well either," Robert said. "He's going to die soon."

"Oh, that makes me feel terrible," Dorothy said. "I remember when we got him. Who named him Dog, anyway?"

"You did," Nikki said.

"Poor Dog," Lynn said again, and fed him a piece of bacon.

They had gone off to their grown-up lives and left their dog, Nikki thought sadly, hardly even noticing him, and that seemed almost worse than leaving their parents, because their parents weren't dependent on them.

"He was really your mother's dog," Robert said. "You girls never even remembered to let him out in the mornings. A dog belongs to the person who feeds him, so he's your mother's dog."

I don't want him, Nikki thought. Why do I get stuck with everything around here? The responsibilities, the leftovers, and the separations. I'm tired of being Good Old Mom. I want my own apartment in New York and my own life.

She turned to the real estate section of the *Times*. She hadn't looked at it for years, and she was shocked at how expensive the rent for a one-bedroom apartment was in New York. It would have to be within walking distance of her office, and those were more expensive still. But, so what? She had her salary, it was hers to keep, and if she had to spend every penny she made on her own life, it was about time. She wasn't leaving Robert. They would spend weekends together in Wilton as always. He could come in to New York once in a while if he wanted to go to the theater with her, or just missed her, and he could stay overnight if he wanted to. But it was important that she pay for this apartment herself so that it would be hers and nobody could ever tell her again what she could or couldn't do in her own home.

"How about a family conference?" Nikki said.

"Aren't we a little old for that?" said Lynn.

54

"You two are too old for that but I'm not," Nikki said lightly. "Robert, sit down, darling." She knew why she was doing it with all of them there instead of talking it over with Robert, because he would say no and the girls would say yes.

The three of them looked at her tolerantly. "Mind if I get another cup of coffee first?" Robert asked. It infuriated her, his attitude that something so important to her was nothing more than a form of entertainment to him, like TV, and he wanted a snack to go with it. He put the hot coffee and a slice of coffee cake in front of him and sat down.

"I have decided to rent a little apartment in New York to stay in during the week, and I'd like your ideas on the subject," Nikki said.

Robert took a sip of his coffee. "As I remember, at family conferences you're supposed to start with 'I was thinking of,' not 'I have decided.' "

"I guess I forgot," Nikki said. "It *has* been a long time. Okay, I was thinking of renting . . ." There was a knot in her stomach.

"Why?" Dorothy asked.

"Because I waste four hours a day commuting, it takes valuable time and energy away from my life and my work, and you girls are grown and don't need me here."

"What about me?" Robert asked.

"You and I hardly see each other during the week. We'd enjoy our weekends together more if I weren't so tired."

"I think you and I should discuss this alone," Robert said.

"I'd like to discuss it as a family," Nikki said.

"I think it's a great idea," Dorothy said.

"Me too," Lynn said. "Mom's never lived alone. It's great to be on your own, you really learn a lot."

"I notice you didn't stay alone very long," her father said wryly.

Lynn raised an eyebrow at him. "Mom might get lonesome and come home. But I think she should have her chance if she wants it."

"I don't know what's so unusual about this, Dad," Dorothy

55

said. "If you had the apartment in New York and Mom was staying out here in the country, nobody would think it was odd. Half the population of New York City goes away for the summer—the women and children."

"We've already accepted the fact that I love my job and I mean to keep it," Nikki said. "We have always accepted that fact. Now we should begin to accept the fact that I'm entitled to certain considerations."

"If you had an apartment, could we come to stay with you?" Dorothy asked.

"Of course! I'll get a convertible sofa in the living room."

"Great!"

"I want you to know, Nikki," Robert said, "that if you get your own apartment you'll have to do it with your own money, and I won't set one foot in it. Ever." His tone was cold and even.

Nikki felt a little chill of fear that unexpectedly turned into one of delighted anticipation. "Do you mean that?"

"I mean it. If you want your own apartment I won't stop you, but for me it will be as if it doesn't exist. I'll see you here."

"He'll change his mind," Dorothy said sympathetically.

"He might not," Nikki said. Her eyes locked with her husband's. She smiled. "If that's the way he feels, he's entitled."

THE NEXT MORNING before she went to her office Nikki looked at one of the apartments she had seen listed in the newspaper. She looked at two more during her lunch hour (which was always two hours), having canceled her lunch date. She fell in love with the third one. It was on the second floor of a brownstone in the East Fifties, in front, facing the quiet street, with a dear little balcony outside the living room windows, just big enough for a few potted fir trees in winter and some geraniums in summer. There was a tiny old-fashioned elevator that wouldn't hold more than two people, but she was used to stairs and the second floor was convenient. The building seemed clean and well kept. The apartment itself was really just a huge living room with a high ceiling and a

56

working fireplace, a sleeping alcove with a window in it, that had once probably been a dressing room, a kitchen and a bathroom. It was big enough for one person, all right for an overnight guest, and too small for two. Nikki immediately decided where she would build her bookcases. She went back to the rental agent, filled in the forms, and wrote out checks for the deposit and the first month's rent.

"You get a free paint job, of course," the agent said, "and the super on the premises will fix anything you need fixed. Here's his phone number. You'll want to get your own locksmith to change the locks, of course."

"Of course," Nikki said absently.

"Some tenants like to give the super a spare key, in case they lose theirs or they go away. But he doesn't take care of packages."

"I can get packages at my office."

"The previous tenant wants to know if you're interested in buying the bedroom air conditioner."

Bedroom? Oh, that alcove. Nikki giggled. She'd have to get used to being a city person. In many ways she was just a hick. "That rusty old piece of junk? Make him take it out, and I'll buy my own."

The agent nodded. "You're right."

"I want everything painted white," Nikki said. She would do it all in glass and chrome, very spare, in contrast to the rich oldness of the architecture. A double bed in the alcove instead of a queen-sized would give her more room. If Robert wasn't going to set foot in her apartment, then a double bed would be big enough, and if he changed his mind, then he could see that she had taken him at his word. No one was going to push her around any more.

"Send the lease to me at my office," Nikki said. It would have been nice to have Robert look it over since he was a lawyer, but she knew that was impossible. She would show it to one of the men she worked with, they were all experienced in being heads of households. And of course she would read it carefully herself. She wasn't a dumbbell. She'd been running that house in the country all these years. The only thing different about a place in the city was that it was smaller and easier.

WHEN ONE OF THE WOMEN Rachel knew asked her to join a few of them in forming a consciousness-raising group, Rachel thought it was ridiculous. Did those women think they had been *unconscious* all their lives? But when she thought over her daily schedule she realized that although all her hours were filled she was really alone all day. Her hairdresser, her manicurist, the people who waited on her in shops, none of them were actually friends. She'd always had a determination not to be one of those women who confided their private lives to their hairdresser. Rachel had never had anyone to confide in, but she hadn't thought she needed anyone, and she couldn't imagine spilling everything out to a group of women, one of whom she only knew socially and the others strangers. She, who never even made lunch dates because she'd rather sleep, and because she had to put up with enough boring women nearly every evening, was going to meet at noon on Central Park West with a consciousness-raising group? Well, why not? Lawrence always told her she ought to have women friends. She was an only child, she didn't even have a sister. So she said yes, and promised herself not to laugh at them although she was sure she would want to.

She wanted to dress properly for a consciousness-raising session, and she figured they would all be into women's lib, so she bought a pair of prefaded blue jeans, a T-shirt, and sneakers, and wore them under her mink coat. (She wasn't going to freeze to fit in.) She wore no makeup and tied her hair back in a thin wool scarf. With her big sunglasses she looked like a model again in that outfit, but it was the best she could do. She took a cab. She wasn't fool enough to walk across the park even in the daytime. The kids who mugged you today were getting younger all the time. What had happened to school?

"I'm so glad you came," Millie, the woman she knew, said when she opened the door. It was in one of those enormous West

58

Side apartments, as big as Rachel's but not elegant. There were six other women sitting in the living room, all sizes and shapes of women in all sorts of attire. The only thing they all had in common was that they seemed to have been born in Rachel's decade.

Rachel was introduced to them by first names, occupations, ages, and marital status. "What do I call you?" Millie asked her, "Housewife?"

"I don't know."

"Rachel used to be a model, now she's married. Thirty-five. No children."

The woman who lived in the apartment had set out a tray with coffee and sandwiches because the ones who worked had given up their lunch hours to meet here. Rachel, who had just had breakfast, declined and lit a cigarette. She seldom smoked, but she was nervous.

"I think it's a good idea for us to meet like this," Millie said. "I, for one, was brought up never to trust or really like other women. When we were dating, other girls were competition for the boys, then when we were all married I never trusted any of the women in the group if she fell out by getting a divorce . . ."

They all laughed. "A divorced woman took my husband away," said a large-bosomed woman, Rhoda, a psychologist. "Or at least that's what I thought until I remembered nobody *takes* someone away unless he's gone in the first place. I realized that everything I told my patients were things I believed in my head but that in my heart I was just as guilt-ridden and prejudiced as they were. Maybe more."

"I don't know why it's so important to have a husband," said a thin divorcée named Pat. "I left my husband, he didn't leave me. And there was no other man either. I just wanted to be able to think about myself for a change instead of gearing my entire life to what he wanted, to making him comfortable, to protecting him from reality."

"I think women are better able to cope with reality than men are," Millie said.

"Men and women really aren't different to begin with," said

59

Anne, a dance teacher. "But we're taught all our lives that we're different and that they're better. We ought to start here by telling all the ways we women are better than men, and then when we're feeling terrific we can figure out how to get along without them."

"Why do we have to get along without them?" Rachel blurted out.

They all turned and looked at her. "You have to be able to get along *without* them in order to get along *with* them," the busty psychologist said.

"Hear, hear!" someone said.

Rachel cringed down on the sofa and lit another cigarette. She gazed out the window at Central Park and wondered if it was going to snow. The sky was awfully gray. If it snowed, she'd never get a cab home. These women were so dreadfully earnest. Life was funny, wasn't it? You had to have a sense of humor to survive. If she didn't make fun of some people in her mind while she was lying to them and flattering them she wouldn't be able to stand it.

"My husband has never cared about what I wanted in bed," one of the women was saying. "After I told him, he tried, but he was so obviously trying to be *nice* that it made us both angry."

"As far as I'm concerned I can do it better to myself," Pat said. The other women smiled and some of them nodded agreement.

"Women are much more sexual than men," Millie said. "All the books say that."

"All my women friends say that," someone said, and they all laughed.

"You know," Anne, the dance teacher, said, "I'm so sick and tired of people putting down women who don't have a man around. I don't need a man to be somebody. I like women better anyway. You can talk to a woman, we're more loving, more understanding, and if I fell in love with a woman and she fell in love with me we'd probably have a much better love relationship *and sexual relationship* than I would with any of the men I've been involved with."

Oh, just wait till I get home and tell Lawrence, Rachel thought

60

in delight. "Did you ever?" she heard herself saying. "Have a . . . ?"

"A love affair with a woman? I'm thinking about it."

"I think we must be free to do whatever we want to, but we mustn't do anything out of anger," the psychologist said. "The purpose of our meeting here is to express our anger and get rid of it."

"What's wrong with anger?" Pat asked. "I'm mad as hell."

Some of the women applauded. Rachel looked idly at the dance teacher's body. She had probably been a dancer once, and her body was still lovely, lithe and slim. Rachel couldn't imagine wanting to go to bed with her, but it did make her think that she ought to go to the gym more often. Two afternoons a week wasn't enough. From now on she would get up early every morning and go every day.

The meeting broke at two. The sky outside the window looked dark and threatening. The women with jobs scurried out the door to get back before the weather delayed them. Rachel was about to take her coat when she felt Millie's hand on her arm.

"Let's help Barbara with the dishes," she whispered. "She doesn't have a maid. It would be the nice thing to do."

"Of course," Rachel said.

"How did you like the meeting?" Barbara asked her as they carried the plates and cups to the kitchen.

Rachel was going to lie as she usually did and say she enjoyed it, and then she decided not to. "I think if they knew what they were talking about here for the past two hours," she said, "then each one would have carried her own plate and cup to the kitchen and washed it, or at least put it in the sink."

"But I have a dishwasher," Barbara said.

They're all so damn trivial, Rachel thought when she finally was alone in the elevator. Millie had remained with her friend Barbara to continue the discussion on their own. Rachel turned up her coat collar and decided to walk along Central Park West to get some air. It was safe here, and she could continue along Cen-

61

tral Park South and then up Fifth Avenue until she got home, thus avoiding the park. It was dreary but not snowing and she needed the exercise to work off the feelings she couldn't quite sort out.

She hadn't expected anything and yet she felt cheated. She had been looking for friends, not a place to make accusations. Was this friendship? Maybe, but not the kind she wanted. She wanted a woman friend to laugh with, to feel cozy with. When she'd been a little girl back home in Kansas City she'd had a best friend, and now, after all these years, Rachel suddenly missed her, even though she knew they both had changed and wouldn't have anything in common any more. I have to find a new best friend, she thought.

Who could it be? She admired Margot King, but Margot was so busy with her TV shows, and now with Kerry, so she didn't need a new best friend. Besides, Margot had Ellen Rennie. Rachel noticed she was just passing Ellen's apartment building. Ellen and Margot even lived near each other. It was nice to have an old school friend, but she didn't have any in New York. What about Nikki Gellhorn? Rachel had always admired Nikki too. Now that Nikki had just moved into her own apartment in the city she would have more free time. Maybe they could go to the gym together! That would be a great incentive for me, Rachel thought. I'll get Nikki to come to my gym. We can go in the mornings before she goes to her office, and then we'll get to know each other better, and we can have drinks together sometimes when Lawrence is having drinks with all his men, and we can talk. Her heart leaped at the thought of having a best friend. Nikki always *enjoyed* everything so much, she would be so much fun.

It wasn't until she stopped to wait for the light to change that Rachel realized the entire street was deserted except for a man who was following her. When she stopped, he stopped at the other end of the long street and looked at her. She couldn't see who it was. If he was following her, why did he stop? If he wanted to snatch her handbag, why didn't he just come at her? She started across the street, and when she reached the other side she looked back fast and saw that he was following her again. Oh, this is silly, she thought. He's just going in the same direction. But to test him she darted around the corner and into a Spanish grocery store she saw there. Poking around among the cans of exotic foods on the shelves she glanced out the window and saw that he had stopped on the corner. He was looking down the street she had just turned into. Then he disappeared.

Rachel left the grocery and walked back to Central Park West. She felt confused. It was too easy to get paranoid about things in New York. He'd seemed well dressed, what she could see of him at such a distance. He didn't look like a mugger. Maybe he'd just thought she was a celebrity in that funny outfit. Garbo, or Jackie Kennedy or somebody. Nevertheless she waved down the first empty taxi she saw.

For one moment he thought she had recognized him. He felt the adrenaline singing through his body—panic, guilt, and then lust again. He didn't know what had finally made him follow her this morning. He had been toying with the idea for a long time, but it was too risky, and besides it was juvenile. He just wanted to know what she did all day. He could have asked her, of course, but she might have thought it was peculiar. You didn't ask a woman what she did all day; she would either take it as a put-down of her idleness or as a pass. So today he had decided to take the morning off and see for himself. He liked the bad weather because it kept people off the streets unless they were hurrying somewhere, and he could be alone with her. When he saw Rachel come out of her building in that sort of disguise he took a taxi and followed the one she had taken, and when she went into the building on Central Park West he waited for her. There were a lot of doctors in that building, and he hoped she wasn't sick. She looked so pale this morning that he wanted to take her in his arms and make her happy. He would just tell her . . . what? That he wanted to take her away from her husband? But he didn't. If Rachel were the sort of woman who would ever cheat

63

on her husband then she wouldn't be the woman he worshiped. He was convinced she was faithful. She could never turn out to be like the rest of those bitches. They were all fakes and bloodsuckers, every one of them, his own wife included. His scruples had put him into a trap. There was no way he could ever have Rachel. If he tried to have an affair with her and she gave in to him, then he wouldn't want her any more.

He'd had a new fantasy lately about her. In this fantasy he was wearing a ski mask, so she didn't know who he was, and he followed her into her apartment when she was alone and then he raped her. She fought him and was terrified. He had her, but it was entirely against her will. She was still unsoiled. He didn't hurt her, he just made her angry. But she was angry at the stranger in the ski mask, not at him. He would still be one of her friends who was invited to her home. The fantasy was highly satisfactory in one way, because it made him come, but in another way it wasn't complete. He didn't know why not, but he would wait. His life had a way of running its own course lately, showing him what he wanted without his having to understand until it happened.

MARCH

March 1975

ELLEN RENNIE'S CURRENT LOVER'S name was Jim Vector, he was an advertising executive and had a wife and three children in Scarsdale. Although her daughter Jill thought he was gray-faced and flabby, Ellen thought he was handsome, charming, considerate, and superior in bed. He always gave her so many orgasms she thought she would faint. They had been going together for a year now, and to celebrate they met for cocktails in the dim and elegant recesses of the Plaza bar, at a table by the window where they could gaze out at the park when they were not gazing into each other's eyes. He had told his wife he had to work late again, she supposed. She had told Hank she had to meet with someone from her office. It didn't matter if anyone who knew Hank saw them. Her husband didn't know anything about her job, any more than Jim's wife knew about his, she imagined. The channels of communication were so much more open with people you weren't married to.

After dinner they would go off to "their" motel—or perhaps they wouldn't even bother with dinner. Jim had wanted to be bold and rent a suite at the Plaza, but Ellen had refused, shuddering.

"Something horrible happened to me there on my wedding night," she said. "I could never stay there again."

"What, sweetheart, what? Tell me."

"No . . . I don't want to talk about it. Even to you."

Especially to you, was more like it, Ellen thought wryly. The Horrible Thing was what she always did to Jim with great mutual enjoyment. But she had been so much younger then, and so innocent, it was as if all that had happened to another person who just happened to be wearing her body.

"That's why your marriage went wrong from the start," he said.

She nodded. "That was the main reason."

"I'd like to punch him!"

She put her hand on his, gently, and then lifted his hand to her lips. "No. Forget Hank."

Tonight in the bar Jim ordered champagne. Ellen's recollections of her traumatic wedding night did not include a distaste for champagne. They toasted their one beautiful year together.

"People will think we're rich," Ellen said.

"I'll tell them you just got a promotion."

"I wish I would. I have such good ideas for publicity. I feel wasted doing what I do. But it's been only two months. They said I'd get more responsibility very soon. Funny, I was wasted in my job eighteen years ago, and I'm still being underused. Opportunities for women aren't all people say they are."

"We won't talk about the office tonight," he said. They smiled at each other.

"Tonight it's just us," Ellen said.

"I have a surprise for you," he said. "I told my wife."

Ellen felt her skin prickle. If she'd been an animal with guard hairs they would all be standing up. "Why did you do that?" she asked shrilly.

"Don't be afraid. I had to tell her. I couldn't stand it any more. I told her I love you and I want a divorce."

"Oh, no," Ellen breathed. "No."

"You're such a good, dear woman," he said. "I know you don't want to hurt her. But I can't go on like this any more. I'm not good at dissembling. I want to marry you."

He'd ruined it. What an anniversary present! How could he have done such a stupid thing? "You can't leave your children," Ellen said. "I can't leave mine. It's not their fault you and I fell in love."

"I'm willing to leave my children," he said. "And you can get custody of yours. They can come to live with us. I'd be *glad* to have your children live with us."

"You don't understand. My children adore their father. They'd be heartbroken . . ."

"Children are selfish little beasts," Jim said. "If they have two parents trying doubly hard to make it up to them they don't mind a divorce at all."

Ellen sighed deeply and trotted out her lie. "Jill, my older daughter—you know, the beautiful one you met?—she came to me just this Christmas and she said to me, 'Mommy, promise me you and Daddy will never split up. I want us to be a family.' How could I ever hurt her?"

He looked down at his glass, and when he looked up there were tears in his eyes. "Ellen, my wife . . . she . . . she cried all night. Then she said she would stay with me anyway. She knows about us and she's willing to stay with me anyway. Why are we so insensitive?"

"I'm *not* insensitive."

"I am. I would leave her even though she's willing to stay with me. She said she hoped I would stop seeing you, but she wouldn't demand it. She said she'd put up with even that."

"She sounds like a wonderful woman. You mustn't hurt her any more," Ellen said.

"Look, if I could talk to Jill. We could all go somewhere together, the zoo or something, and she could get to know me . . ."

"Sixteen is too old for the zoo," Ellen said coldly.

"All right, all right, we'll take her to the theater. To the ballet? We'll take her to the Rainbow Room."

"You are the most heartless man I ever met."

"I'm not. I only want to do the right thing."

"Then don't ask me to break my children's hearts," Ellen said. Her panic was beginning to subside and she felt in control again. He could go back and tell his wife he was willing to try again. It wasn't too late. Jim was too impetuous—it was part of his charm but it was also his downfall. She could never marry him. He might give her daughters everything in the world, but he wasn't the father they wanted. They wanted predictable old Hank. "You know how little girls are," she said. "They think their father is perfect. They don't see him the way I do. I think Hank is boring, they think he's brilliant. But you see, darling, as a father he *is* brilliant. I never want them even to *suspect* about us."

"Do you think Jill suspected when she saw us?"

"Maybe. Maybe that's why she said what she did. I think you and I ought to be more careful."

He looked around the bar. "There's no one here we know. From now on we'll go to very out-of-the-way places."

"I think we shouldn't see each other for a while," Ellen said. She saw the color drain from his normally rather pale face until she was afraid for a moment he might have a coronary.

"That's silly," he said.

"No it's not. We're too much in love with each other and we're losing our sense of reality. It's getting too dangerous."

"My wife doesn't *mind*."

"I don't want you to leave her," Ellen said. "Tell her you'll try again. Please? For me?"

"But when will I see you?"

"I don't know," she said. "I'm so confused and upset. I just had a picture in my mind of Jill's face, and . . ."

"You're so good," he said sadly. "All this time you've felt guilty. How awful it must have been for you. Why didn't you tell me?"

"I wanted you."

"I want you now."

"I want you too," Ellen said.

There were tears in his eyes again and she hoped he wasn't

going to cry in public. If he did cry it would set her off, that sort of thing always did. She felt so sorry for herself. Why was she doomed to have to make sacrifices all the time? You did one stupid thing—married the wrong man—and then you compounded it by having children, because that was what a marriage was for, and then you were trapped forever. She knew she could never see Jim any more, because he was too unpredictable, too emotional, too dangerous. All the qualities that made him exciting to her were the same ones that had made their love affair self-destruct. Why did this keep happening to her?

He paid the check and they left. They went to their motel and made love for hours. Ellen wanted it to be perfect so she could always remember it.

"I'll never give you up," he said. "Never."

"I know," she murmured, as one would to a child. They all said that.

MARCH WAS THE BEGINNING of spring and it was the beginning of Nikki Gellhorn's new life in her New York apartment. Whereas in the country she had always been rather untidy, here she was immaculate. Everything was hers and she wanted to protect it. She had a great many books from the publishing company where she worked, and she brought all the ones she liked best, plus all the ones she herself had worked on with the authors. She arranged them in alphabetical order in the bookcases she'd had built, like those in the public library, but her books were all fresh and clean. She bought a few prints and photographs she loved and had them framed in transparent plastic so they seemed to float on her white walls. She bought a small color television set for her alcove-bedroom and a white fluffy rug to put in front of the fireplace. The leather couch from Bloomingdale's was a floor model on sale, so she was doubly lucky, because that meant immediate delivery. She went to Tiffany's in a spurt of extravagance and bought four place settings of Red Dragon china. Not those

71

awful overdecorated wedding plates she had in the country and never used, service for God knows how many people she didn't like enough to invite home, and not the chipped, mismatched everyday dishes she'd acquired during the years of her childrens' growing up—these were her own dishes, for herself and her own carefully chosen friends. Meals would be served on a glass and chrome table that doubled as a desk for the work she brought home from the office. She hadn't bought sheets in years and was shocked at how expensive they'd become. Her bank account was almost down to zero when she finished her decorating. But it was *her* bank account, not the one she shared with her husband.

Robert had never seen her apartment. He remained inflexible. She tried to mention it twice on weekends when they were together, but he turned her off with a look of quiet rage. She told herself he was as entitled to his anger as she had been to hers, but in her heart she was hurt and resentful because of his attitude. He only wants to share when it's on his terms, she thought. For the first time in all the years they had been married she had no sexual feelings toward him. She knew they had vanished into her anger. While one part of her wanted to be a better wife when she was home, the other part asked her why she felt she had to pacify him all the time. Before, when they had been living together all week, she had felt free to say so when she didn't feel like having sex. Now she felt she had to do it every time he wanted to, but she couldn't respond, because it seemed so terribly important that she respond more now.

He misinterpreted her lack of passion and accused her of having a lover.

"You're crazy!" Nikki said.

"It's all so obvious," he said. "You wanted your own place, and now you're free to do as you like. You don't need me any more. You have him. You never were able to hide anything from me."

"I'm not hiding anything from you, you jackass. If I had a lover, which I don't, I'd tell you."

"You call me crazy and jackass," Robert said. "Thank you very much. Are you going to call me cuckold next?"

"You make me so mad I'm going to kill you!" Nikki screamed. Her voice seemed to echo in the room. They both stared at each other. Damn him, damn lawyer, with all his precise words. Damn his literal mind. He was probably imagining the ways she might murder him now—gun or poison? Unaccountably, she wanted to laugh, but she knew it would enrage him, so she cried instead. That always worked.

"Don't cry," he said.

"I'm so alone . . . you don't care about me," Nikki sobbed. She felt so upset at having to cry to win him over that it made her cry in earnest. She couldn't stop crying. Robert became genuinely concerned. He took her in his arms.

"Don't cry, Nikki. I'm sorry. I shouldn't have yelled at you. Do you want to come home?"

She shook her head, no. "I don't have a lover, and now you're mad at me and mean to me and I don't have you on my side any more and I'm all alone."

"I'm always on your side," he said, patting her back, stroking her damp hair. He handed her a wad of Kleenex to blow her nose.

"You won't even come to see my pretty apartment."

"I'm hardly ever in New York," he said.

"Aren't you even curious?"

"Sure," he said.

"I could give you a key."

"If you like."

"Don't you *want* a key?" she asked.

"It's your apartment, you're paying for it. It's up to you."

She had stopped crying and had become coy. "Wouldn't it make you feel like my lover if you had a key?"

"It would make me feel castrated," Robert said.

"*Why?*"

"Because you should have a key to *my* apartment."

"I do. This house."

"This is our house," he said.

"Robert, stop, stop, stop doing that horrible thing you do, being so precise. You use words like weapons. You're always look-

73

ing for shades of meaning. For God's sake can't we just feel things any more?"

"You're the one with the problem of not feeling," he said.

She didn't answer. There was nothing she wanted to say.

But when she was in New York during the week she was happy. She met friends and authors after work for drinks, she took certain business guests to dinner instead of lunch, and investigated new restaurants she'd always wanted to try. She discovered that there was one great drawback to living alone in the city; she had to have a dinner date or she got depressed. The days were busy, and it was wonderful to come home to her little apartment, take a bath, watch the evening news, change her clothes, but she had to go out. The thought of eating alone made her almost frightened. Even if she had a manuscript to read overnight, she preferred a quick dinner with a friend to sitting in bed with a container of yoghurt and the manuscript. She didn't feel like cooking for herself. She had never eaten dinner alone in her entire life. First it had been her parents, then the dormitory, then she had been married to Robert. Even on the few occasions when he'd had to work through dinner she'd had the twins for company. She associated meals with conversation and love. The television set was no substitute.

She told Margot her silly problem, but Margot didn't laugh. "Now you know," Margot said. "The greatest thing in my whole relationship with Kerry is knowing he'll be there in the morning to have breakfast with and that he'll have dinner with me every night."

"You mean I'm not weird," Nikki said.

"Not weird. Just single. In our culture, food is a social event. Breast-feeding, mama love, and all that. I did a little story on it once on the show. The thing about how old people living alone won't cook and get malnutrition. They just get so damn depressed that they don't care."

"I still buy too much in the supermarket," Nikki said.

"That's better than what I did before Kerry. I didn't buy anything. I lived on cottage cheese and ice cream."

"One night I'll take the two of you out to dinner," Nikki said. "On my expense account. You can tell Kerry I'm trying to steal him from his publisher."

"We'd love it."

Rachel Fowler called and said she wanted Nikki to try her new gym. Nikki signed up for twice a week in the mornings before work. Rachel had an enviable wandlike body, but she wasn't very graceful. Nikki had twice as much energy as she did. They signed up for the same classes anyway. Their companions were two sixty-year-old women who had been going to exercise classes all their lives and were better than they were. Nikki loved getting up early to go to the gym and care for her body instead of getting up to commute. She had become so accustomed to waking at six that she always woke up before the seven-o'clock alarm rang.

She liked Rachel, particularly in a leotard looking embarrassed because she couldn't touch her toes. "Listen," Nikki told her, "if I looked as gorgeous in a leotard as you do I wouldn't care if I couldn't touch my *knees!*"

"I'd rather be smart than pretty," Rachel said.

"I think you're both."

Rachel actually blushed.

Sometimes when Rachel's husband was working late she invited Nikki to their apartment for drinks. That still left the problem of dinner though, so Nikki asked Rachel to go out to dinner with her.

"You mean, leave Lawrence alone?"

"Why not? He's out with the boys, you can go out with the girls." Nikki giggled, a habit she'd gotten into years ago to cover up when she was being tough. "Let him know you have a life of your own. We'll have more fun without him."

"Oh, I'd really like to," Rachel said tentatively.

"Let him miss you a little."

"He wants me to have friends. . . ."

"I'm your friend. Come on. I'll be your date."

They went to a restaurant where Nikki was known. They ate fattening things, shared a bottle of wine, and split the check.

75

"I never eat like this," Rachel said, sounding both pleased and horrified. "I'm always on a diet, all my life."

"This is good for you once in a while," Nikki said, this time using her mother voice. "You're too uptight. You have the most beautiful body I've ever seen and one meal won't hurt it."

"I'm really having a good time," Rachel said. They were lingering over the last of their coffee. She glanced at her watch.

"Don't keep thinking about him," Nikki said. "You're allowed to stay out late. You're a big girl."

"I feel so guilty."

"Why? Does he feel guilty when he leaves you alone?"

Rachel shook her head, no. "I guess it's different. He's out supporting me."

"Well, let me tell you about business, my dear girl. Half those meetings are bullshit. They're together because they want to be. They could transact business in the office in the morning. But the drinking and the eating and the telling funny stories is all part of the game they invented to get away from their wives."

"Why do they get married, then?" Rachel said.

"We're convenient."

"I thought you had a very happy marriage."

"I do. It's just that I've been working most of my adult life and I know about married men."

"It's as if you and I are on opposite sides of the moon," Rachel said. "I see them when they're putting on one act and you see them when they're putting on another. The only man I've ever known who's completely honest with me is Lawrence. When he ignores me at least he's being honest."

"Oh, husbands ignore their wives all the time," Nikki said.

Rachel looked at her in some surprise. "I never really knew you before, Nikki. There's a lot of anger in you, isn't there?"

"Sometimes."

"How does your husband feel about your having a life of your own in New York?"

"He hates it."

"But you do it anyway."

Nikki shrugged and grinned at her. "If one of us is going to be mad, it might as well not have to be me."

"I really admire you," Rachel said.

She says "really" every other sentence, Nikki thought. I wonder if she's "really" as dumb as she seems.

When they got out on the sidewalk Rachel immediately looked for a cab. The restaurant had no doorman. It was a nice night, not cold. "Let's walk," Nikki said.

"Walk?" Rachel said in horror.

"Yeah, walk. You can work off some of those calories."

"We can't walk around here at night," Rachel said.

"I was planning to walk home. I do it all the time."

"Nikki, nobody walks around New York City at night."

"Who are all those people, then? Apparitions?"

"We'll walk to the corner and get a cab and I'll drop you off at your house."

Nikki thought it was funny how Rachel kept looking around while they walked to the corner. You'd think someone was going to materialize from behind a garbage can and pounce on her. They got a taxi and drove to Nikki's building first.

"I didn't know you don't have a doorman," Rachel said.

"Rachel, you may not know it, but most people don't have doormen. Most people don't have chauffeured limousines either."

"Don't make fun of me. I can't help it if I married a rich man."

"Then you can pay for the cab," Nikki said and laughed. She kissed Rachel good-night. "Tell Lawrence you had a terrific date tonight."

"I did," Rachel said. "I really did."

Nikki was still smiling while she let herself into the building and ran lightly up the flight of stairs to her apartment. Forty-two years old and not a bit out of breath, she thought proudly. She was just in time for the ten o'clock programs on television. Her favorite was on tonight, the one that Robert detested and always made her turn off if they were watching TV in bed together. There were certain advantages to living alone!

She had just started to put her key into the lock of her apartment door when she noticed that the entire lock was loose. She touched it and it moved in her hand. Her heart turned over. It had all seemed unreal, like statistics, but now . . . Someone had tried to break in and had been frightened away, or maybe had broken in. Maybe he was still in there. She was suddenly flooded with rage. How dare anyone intrude on her life, mess up her things, the things she loved? Nikki pushed the door open and entered the apartment.

No one was in the living room, nor had ever been. She went into the bedroom, the kitchen, and looked into all the closets. The adrenaline stopped pumping and her rage subsided. Nothing had been touched. What the hell was she going to do now? She couldn't call Robert, he would have a fit. She'd better call the locksmith. They had a twenty-four-hour number for emergencies.

She called the locksmith and he said he would be over in about an hour because he had to come from Queens. "You just put this lock *in*, you know," Nikki said. "It cost me fifty dollars."

"You ought to have a plate that bolts onto the door over the lock," he said. "Then nobody can tear the lock out."

"Now you're telling me?"

"I usually wait till they ask."

"Bring it," Nikki said.

She sat down to wait. It occurred to her that it was a dumb thing to do, just sit here, because the burglar might come back. He wouldn't want to waste the nice job he'd done on her fifty-buck lock. She put a cassette into her little player so he would know the apartment was occupied and poured herself a big glass of white wine. God, anybody could just walk right in. She decided to call Margot. Margot could come over and bring Kerry, then there would be a man around. But Margot's phone rang and rang. They were either out or screwing. What a pain. Who else could she call? Ellen owed her a favor for getting her the job, but she lived on the West Side, even farther away than Margot, and by the time she got dressed and came over the locksmith would be there—or the burglar. She would call Rachel. She didn't like making Rachel come out again right after getting home, but she didn't like sitting here all alone either.

"Oh, my God!" Rachel cried. "Go ring your neighbor's bell and wait there till I come."

It had never occurred to Nikki to ring her neighbor's bell. From the moment she had moved into this apartment her greatest joy had been the privacy and anonymity the building afforded. She didn't even know who her neighbors were. She drank down the last of the wine and went out into the hall. She didn't like leaving her apartment alone, she preferred staying in there and guarding it. There were three other apartments on the floor. She rang the bell of the one nearest hers.

No answer. She rang again. She heard the scrape of the peephole cover being pushed aside. "Who is it?" asked a quavery voice.

"Nikki Gellhorn, your next-door neighbor."

The door opened a crack, held to by a stout chain, but Nikki couldn't see anyone inside. Then she looked down and there was a tiny old woman, about four feet tall, about eighty years old, looking at her with suspicious little eyes like a wizened monkey.

"What do you want?"

"Somebody tried to break into my apartment."

"Ooh. Did they rob you?"

"They got scared off, but they might come back and I—"

Crash! The woman slammed her door shut before Nikki could even finish her sentence. Furious, Nikki rang the woman's bell again, hard.

"Call the police," the old voice called through the peephole.

"The police."

"Well, now I know about one of my terrific neighbors," Nikki muttered. She wouldn't bother with the other two. She would save them for something really important, like when the burglar stole her phone.

The elevator door opened. There was Rachel, her eyes shining, her cheeks flushed. She rushed over to Nikki and grabbed her in a big hug. "Oh, Nikki, I was scared to death! Why are you in the hall?"

79

"It's too long a story to tell without a drink," Nikki said. She led Rachel back inside her apartment.

"I'm so glad you called me," Rachel said. She tossed her mink coat on the couch. "I would have been hurt if you'd called anybody else."

"I did call the locksmith."

"Oh, you know what I mean. I mean I really feel that you and I are friends now."

"And what else are friends for?" said Nikki, and giggled.

She opened a new bottle of white wine. Rachel sipped at hers. "You're so calm," Rachel said. "I feel like we're having a party."

"Well, we are."

Rachel inspected the lock without touching it. "Maybe the police can get some fingerprints off it," she said. "Life is a mess, isn't it?"

"I think it's usually fun," Nikki said. "This isn't so bad. It's kind of fun. You're here."

"I admire you so much," Rachel said. "I always have."

"Well, thank you."

"When I got home, Lawrence was in his den working. He didn't want to talk. I'm glad you called. I missed you."

I don't believe it, Nikki thought. She's got a crush on me! I wonder if she's gay. I always thought half those jet set people were bisexual.

"What are you thinking?" Rachel asked.

"Nothing," Nikki said. "I'm just thinking I'm glad you're here so I don't have to be all alone." Why do I do this? I shouldn't encourage her. But I *like* that she has a crush on me. Nobody ever did before.

RACHEL WONDERED if she'd been too pushy. Having a best friend was so complicated when you were both grown-ups. The secrets you shared were different, so guarded. When she was a little girl she'd sat in her tree house with her best friend and confided, "I hate my mother," and her best friend had whispered, "I hate mine

80

too." You'd say you loved each other and swear it in blood. But now you and your new best friend had a lifetime of dissembling to keep you apart, and if you came right out and told her you loved her, she would think you were desperately lonely and would draw back.

She knew she didn't know Nikki well enough to love her, but she thought about her all the time. She would have liked to be able to see life through Nikki's eyes, to be so independent. Rachel felt now that she had wasted her life. Making Lawrence comfortable was not enough. He could hire people to do that. She should have been somebody in her own right, not just an echo. But it wasn't too late. Nikki was older than she was and had grabbed the moment. She was going to grab the moment too and become a real person. Lawrence would be glad . . . no, she had to stop thinking about herself through his eyes; *she* would be glad.

The doorbell rang and they both jumped. Nikki had put the unlocked door on the chain. "Locksmith," a cheerful male voice sang out.

Nikki let him in. He looked the lock over and lit a cigarette. "Maybe you ought to have an alarm lock," he said.

"Not with my neighbors," Nikki said. "They'd just crawl under the bed."

"Y'see, this is a good lock. He had too much trouble trying to pick it, so he just tried to yank it out. I'll give you one of those plates that bolts right through the door. Nobody can get them off—the harder you try, the more resistance you get."

"Good," Nikki said. "Do it."

"Now you're safe unless you let somebody in," Rachel said, smiling at Nikki. "You know enough not to let a stranger in, don't you?"

"I let them in all the time," Nikki said sarcastically. "I ask them right off the street. Especially the guys in the tight jeans. I may be a Wilton housewife but I'm not a hick."

When the new lock was installed Nikki wrote out a check and the locksmith left. Rachel felt drained and tired. "May I use your phone?"

81

"Do you have to ask? You saved me."

Rachel called the limousine service and told them to send a car right away. Nikki was looking at her with amusement. Maybe it *was* silly, but it was late, and that was the way she lived. She told them what apartment the driver should buzz when he arrived.

"What did your husband say when you dashed out of there?" Nikki asked.

"I left him a note on his pillow with your phone number. I said you were having an emergency. He probably thinks it's something emotional. I'm not the type people call when they have a real emergency like a burglary."

"I don't know why not. I'll refer you to all my friends."

MARGOT TOOK THE PHONE out of the closet and turned the bell back on. She would call her service another time. Kerry was standing over the dying fire. He turned and looked at her. "Another log, love? Or do we go to sleep?"

"I hate to go to sleep," she said. "I feel as if I'm missing all those hours when I could be with you."

"You *are* with me."

"I know, but I'm asleep, so I don't know it."

He yawned. "I vote for sleep."

We used to stay up all night and talk, she thought. She felt the smallest warning. They'd had almost three months together. She was hopelessly in love with him. But he couldn't be tired of her, not so soon. She was resigned to it happening some day, but not this soon. He probably really was tired. She wouldn't be surprised, the way he used up all that energy and the way he hardly ate anything. She went out of her way to go to gourmet shops to buy him wonderful treats and then he had no appetite. That was why he had such a beautiful body. It wasn't just youth, it was the way he lived. Or maybe he loved her as much as she loved him. She had very little appetite now too. Sometimes he would wake

82

up in the middle of the night and look at her, and hug her, and say, "Oh, Margot, I love you so much."

Moments like that she carried with her for days, until they happened again. Sometimes lately she could even go through a whole day with a feeling of safety, that he wouldn't abandon her, that together they could stop time. She would give anything for that, do anything, if only she knew what to do.

APRIL

April 1975

JILL RENNIE KNEW her mother was on the prowl again. She had broken up with the gray-faced man, and he phoned often, at dangerous times, when the whole family was home. Jill had answered the phone a few times and had been sorry for him when she recognized the desperation in his voice. He was a gray mouse, that was what he was.

"For you, Mom," she would say cheerfully.

"Who is it?" her mother would ask.

"I don't know," Jill would lie. Then she would go into her room and listen on the extension. They had a lot of push-button phones in that apartment. One number was for her parents, the other was for Jill and Stacey to spend hours talking to their friends. Her father liked push-button phones and he also liked the kind where you pushed little square buttons instead of dialing. Her mother said they were too expensive and they couldn't afford them any more, but her father insisted. Jill thought that was great. She loved gadgets.

She had lost six pounds and was down to eighty-five. People had begun to notice. First, of course, it was her sister.

"Jill, you look horrible," Stacey said. "You look scary. How much do you weigh?"

"What difference does it make if I feel all right?"

"Do you know what happens when you starve? Your body starts eating its own protein. You're eating your muscles. Then you'll eat your spinal column, and then you'll die."

"Where did you read that crap?"

"Jill, don't you even feel hungry?"

"I eat."

"You can fool them, but you can't fool me. You don't eat."

"All right, I'm not hungry."

"If you get any thinner they'll have to put you in the hospital and force-feed you," Stacey said.

"I'd just throw up," Jill said calmly. "You know I throw up if I ever have to eat something I don't want to."

"Then they'll put you on I.V. They'll stick needles in your veins. Aren't you a little bit concerned about that?"

"Nope," Jill said cheerfully.

"I looked up your symptoms in a medical book at the public library," Stacey said. "You have adolescent anorexia nervosa. They can't cure it. Only you can cure it. Either that or you die."

"Well, we'll worry about that later," Jill said. "Why don't you go out and play doctor with some nice little boy?"

"They'll put you in Payne Whitney," Stacey said. "They'll have you committed. They'll put you in the psycho ward."

"Do you mind getting out of my room? I have to study for a French test."

Stacey stood there, sturdy and adamant, her hands thrust into the pockets of her faded jeans, but her eyes were scared. "I don't want you to *die*, Jill. You're the only sister I've got."

"Be a good girl and make me a milkshake, Stace. With the raw milk and one fertilized egg, and *no sugar*. Okay? You can bring it in and I'll drink it while I'm studying."

Stacey came back in a little while with the foamy milkshake. "I'll just wait here while you drink it," she said suspiciously.

"You don't trust me?"

"No."

"Well, help yourself to a chair." Stacey set the milkshake on the table beside Jill and sat down, waiting. Jill read her French book and every few minutes she took a little sip. She couldn't drink it faster, but if she waited too long it would get into her body. She finished the whole milkshake and forced a smile. "Okay? Now take the glass away and wash it, please."

The minute she heard Stacey go into the kitchen Jill bolted for her bathroom and threw up. She was getting quite good at it, she could almost throw up at will. She flushed the toilet, brushed her teeth, and came out of the bathroom feeling her old healthy self again. Stacey was standing in the doorway.

"I knew you'd do that," Stacey said.

"I didn't do anything. You're crazy."

"Who is it you hate so much?" Stacey asked, and she looked as if she was going to cry. "Is it Mom? Is it yourself? Is it me?"

"I don't hate you, baby. You're the only sister *I've* got."

"Then who is it? Answer me!"

"I would if I knew," Jill said.

"Well, I know."

"Then you tell me," Jill said lightly.

"I can't," Stacey said. "First place, you wouldn't listen. Second place, you're supposed to find out for yourself. Third place, I'm not a doctor. And fourth place, *I'm only thirteen years old and I don't know how to handle this.*"

"WE HAVE TO HAVE A TALK, you and I," Ellen said to Hank. She saw the look of caution cross his face, first fear and then the bland mask she was so used to. He had to know about all those phone calls from her last ex-lover, and now he was afraid she was going to say something about them. He would never really know her. As for the calls, she would have to put a stop to them some-how. None of her other former lovers had ever been so recklessly indiscreet as Jim. Poor Hank. Maybe he was afraid she was going to say something about the terrible state his finances were in. About the ever more frantic calls from his office. That spring was here and nothing had changed. He should know her better than that. She had put her paychecks into their joint checking account without a word and let him handle all the bills as usual. But lately she couldn't even ask him to sit down and have a talk with her without seeing that look on his face.

"All right," Hank said.

"It's about Jill. You've noticed how skinny she's gotten."

"I thought all the kids wanted to look like that."

"Hank, she's emaciated! None of the other kids look like that. Jill's starving herself, and I don't know what to do about it."

"Tell her to eat," Hank said.

"Don't you think I have? I've nagged her, ordered her, tried to cajole her, even offered her a car next year if she got up to a hundred pounds. A hundred pounds is not too much to ask. She just kept wiggling out of the discussions. It's as if all Jill's life and energy have gone into this kind of secret thing she has."

"Should I talk to her?"

"If you think it would help."

"Maybe she's sick," Hank said. "Did you take her to the doctor for a checkup?"

"She went five months ago, he yelled at her and told her to eat, she promised to try, and then she lost six more pounds. She'll say anything to please what she thinks of as the enemy."

"Well, what did the doctor say to you?" Hank asked.

"He said if she doesn't grow out of it she ought to go to a psychiatrist."

Hank looked aghast. "We don't have the money, Ellen."

"Maybe she could go to a clinic."

"Why didn't you tell me all this before?" he said. He seemed angry.

Ellen shrugged. "I don't think she needs a psychiatrist. I

thought I could handle it myself. Maybe you'll have better luck."

"I'll talk to her tomorrow," Hank said.

"Why can't you talk to her tonight?"

"Because I don't know what I'm going to say yet. You just sprang all this on me."

"You have eyes. You could have noticed."

"I guess I did notice, but I have more pressing problems, in case you forgot, Ellen. I have worries about my business."

"I know that."

"Girls . . . I leave girls to their mother."

"Terrific," Ellen said. "Just terrific. Another one of those archaic ideas you got from your father."

Hank chose to ignore that. "Maybe Jill's scared of boys," he said thoughtfully. "She never dates. I never see any boys around here. Maybe she's just at the age where girls are afraid to turn into women."

"She's nearly sixteen," Ellen said. "In case you don't know, that *is* a woman. Jill's a beautiful girl—why wouldn't she want to grow up and date? It's the ugly ones who are afraid."

"Well, maybe we just don't know her very well," Hank said. "I sort of don't know her. Kids keep a lot of things inside them. Everybody does. We all have little private problems."

"Maybe she'll confide in you. God knows, she's being suddenly very difficult with me."

The next evening, after Ellen prodded him, Hank went in to Jill's room and had a ten-minute talk with her. "Well?" Ellen said.

"She says she doesn't have any problems."

"And . . . ?"

"And she said she eats organic food at the health-food bar near her school and she isn't hungry when she comes home. She said the only reason she looks thinner is she's growing."

"She's not growing," Ellen said savagely.

He looked at his hands, large and white, blond hair on the backs, powerful hands, now so powerless. "I asked her about a psychiatrist and she said we can't afford it. She's right."

"Did she want to go?"

"No. She said it was silly."

"Did you talk to her about boys?" Ellen asked.

"*Me?*" Hank sounded horrified.

"It was your idea."

"But you're her mother. You talk to her about boys."

"You were a boy once. Why can't you do it?"

Hank looked at her as if he wanted to hit her. Ellen had never seen such rage on his face in all the years she had been married to him. "Because I can't do it," he said. He sounded as if he were choking. She was suddenly, for the first time in her life, afraid to pursue the discussion further with him for fear he would lose control and do her some violence. She had never thought Hank had it in him. She wondered if this dark flame had always been waiting in him or if it was the result of all the strain he'd been under. No matter what it was, she wouldn't want him to start on her with those big hands. She gave him a conciliatory smile and got up and left the room.

They did not discuss Jill again. Ellen thought of calling their family doctor and asking him if he knew any psychiatrists who would take Jill for a reduced fee, and then changed her mind. She couldn't debase herself in front of the doctor, admit she couldn't handle her own daughter. Maybe Jill just needed to meet a nice boy. If Jill became interested in someone and he told her he thought she should gain a little weight, maybe she'd do it for him. When she had been Jill's age all she thought of was making herself attractive for boys. There were boys in Jill's school. All she needed was one.

When the phone rang Ellen at first didn't want to bother answering it. Then she thought it might be important, so she did.

"Can you talk?" It was Jim Vector, already in her past, still clutching onto the present as if he had a share in it.

"I think you have the wrong number," Ellen said.

"When can we talk?" he whispered. He sounded hoarse. "I have to talk to you."

"Please don't call here any more," Ellen said.

"You won't talk to me in your office. I have to talk to you."

"No, Jill dear, it's just a wrong number," Ellen sang out, and hung up.

She felt as if everything were closing in on her. They all wanted more of her than she could give. She was so nervous she thought she might burst out of her skin, and smiled wryly at the thought of bits of herself scattered all over her already messy kitchen. Where's your mother? Oh, she fell apart—everybody wanted a little piece of her and it was the only way she could manage it. Ellen clutched her arms around her body to still the trembling. She needed to get away again, the only way she knew how, the only way that worked. She needed someone new.

She felt the same way the next morning and was distracted at the office, and when lunchtime came she decided to go to the delicatessen in the neighborhood and buy something to take back to her desk. She'd let the work pile up all morning and had made mistakes, gazing off into the distance, hardly aware that her fists and teeth were clenched until she felt her nails digging into her palms and realized her jaws hurt too. Maybe she ought to buy some tranquilizers. She'd eat a sandwich and finish what she had left undone before she ruined the whole afternoon too.

The delicatessen was crowded, and Ellen was going to leave without buying anything when she saw Kerry Fowler. He was wearing a turtleneck sweater and jeans and he looked gorgeous. She had never realized before how beautiful he really was.

"Well, hi," he said with a big grin. "Are you going or coming?"

"I don't know," Ellen said. She smiled back at him. "I didn't have anybody to eat lunch with so I thought I'd buy a sandwich, but it looks as if the whole world had the same idea."

"I live around the corner," he said, gesturing with a hand that had a filled paper bag in it. "I finished a chapter just now so I thought I'd take a break." So that was where he kept his own apartment.

"How is it going, the book?"

"Today was good."

"You should celebrate," Ellen said. "It's not every day a person can say something good happened."

"You sound down."

"I just have too much work. I'd like to forget it all for an hour."

"Well, listen," Kerry said, "I have enough here for two, and nobody should have to eat lunch alone. Why don't we go to the museum and eat in the sculpture garden?"

"It's too cold," Ellen said. "I'd like to get a bottle of wine and go someplace warm and quiet."

He looked at her and she was aware of those catlike eyes. He seemed able to look right through her. Did he do that to everyone? If he could see through her he'd invite her to his apartment "around the corner." He was Margot's. She shouldn't be doing this. She hadn't done it.

"If you don't mind a mess, we could go to my place," Kerry said. "There's even a liquor store on the way."

"Terrific," Ellen said lightly. "If you play your cards right I'll pay for the wine."

Ellen was astonished at the perfection of Kerry's small apartment. It was immaculate, even the stacked pages beside the typewriter, and as carefully thought out as if a professional architect lived there. It was in a brownstone that was more like a semi-tenement than a town house, but he had scraped the old walls down to the brick, built cabinets, lowered the ceiling so he could hide lights behind it under smoked glass, and he even had plants. His apartment obviously meant a lot to him. No wonder he didn't want to give it up when he went to live with Margot. It was personal, a work of art.

"I can't get over your apartment," Ellen said in awe.

"I'm thinking of getting rid of it," he said.

"And live with Margot?"

"No, of course not. I mean get another apartment. This one only interested me when I was restoring it. It was like a hobby. But now that it's finished I'm bored with it."

94

"I think you're in the wrong profession," she said. "You could be an interior designer."

"It's just a hobby. I have a lot of hobbies. Would you like to see my drawings?"

She smiled, thinking about the old etchings joke, and then she realized that of course he was too young to know anything about that. *She* was almost too young. He took a large scrapbook down from one of the shelves and opened it on the coffee table. His drawings were in pen and ink. Some were of mechanical contraptions and others were of anatomy—arms, legs, torsos, necks, and a few sketches of a man's face.

"They remind me of the sketches of Leonardo da Vinci," Ellen said. "Did you study art?"

"No," Kerry said. "The model for all the anatomy was me."

"The face did look familiar," Ellen said.

"Well, the rest would too if you knew me better." He smiled. "Shall we have lunch?"

He put away the scrapbook and put place mats and plates on the coffee table. Then he unloaded the paper bag: cold cuts, fresh bread, coleslaw, pickles. Ellen had bought the wine already chilled, so she opened it and found two glasses in his tiny kitchen. Even his dishes and glasses were perfect.

"That's going to be too much food," she said.

"It'll keep." He sat on the floor beside the low table and she did too. His rug was very soft. He sipped at his wine and looked at her with those eyes that knew everything.

She sipped at her wine too, and neither of them made a motion to take any of the food. Ellen hated the smell of garlic pickles and couldn't figure out why he'd gotten them until she remembered that of course he'd bought all this food before he ran into her. The garlic pickles on the table in front of them made the lunch seem somehow very innocent. She wasn't going to do anything Margot could hate her for. Nobody was going to be hurt. But her heart was pounding wildly.

Kerry reached over and snapped on his hi-fi, a contraption with reels of tape and all sorts of things Ellen didn't understand. Soft

95

music came from the walls. The sort of thing Jill played. But here it sounded completely different. She tried to think of something appropriate to say to show her knowledge, but he seemed so relaxed that it didn't seem necessary. For the first time in her life Ellen found herself on the battleground of the adversary. She was not going to be able to win him with the wit and wisdom of Ellen Rennie. This boy was a generation away from all that. He saw directly into her need and was neither frightened nor thrilled by it. He absorbed it into his being the way he absorbed the music and the wine, and he waited, looking at her, until her hand began to shake and she had to put the wineglass on the table.

He moved to her with the same ease with which he had snapped on the hi-fi and kissed her, lowering her to the rug. His lips were soft and sensual and he kissed her for a long time, slowly, and Ellen remembered those hours in those cars twenty years ago and was filled with unbearable excitement. His hands moved over her, taking off her clothes, touching her, taking off his clothes, kissing her the entire time, while the music never stopped, and she came under his hand the way she had so many years ago with hands she'd forgotten, and then she came under his mouth, and then he entered her and she came again and again until she thought she would die of it. How did he know what she liked?

They lay there on the rug afterward and he kept tracing the line of her body with his finger like a sculptor or a painter. Ellen wondered if she was going to end up in his sketchbook. He had a lovely body, much nicer than hers. She ran her fingers over it and he immediately began making love to her again. She had no intention of going back to the office this afternoon.

At half past six Ellen took a shower in Kerry's plant-filled bathroom, being careful not to let her hair get wet, and prepared herself to go home. When she came out of the bathroom he had cleaned up the living room, put away the uneaten food, and washed the glasses and plates. It was as if she had never existed. She supposed he had to go meet Margot for dinner. She was surprised at the force of the jealousy that hit her just when she should have been feeling the most guilty. She had gone to bed with Margot's lover, not just once—which might have been rationalized as an accident—but over and over for hours. What good would it do to say that she had been driven to this by pressures in her unfortunate life? She could have chosen a dozen other men, not Margot's man. Still, Ellen felt more resentment than guilt, because she had the feeling that Kerry didn't care about her. He liked her enough, he'd enjoyed this afternoon as much as she had, but she didn't mean much to him. He wasn't in love with her the way all the other men always were. She felt enraged and in pain, a pain that was very like love.

He had found the way to get to her again. He had been unerring about her from the moment they met today. He had read her sexuality and her need, and he had fulfilled them, and now he read the secret of her insecurity and had chosen not to help her, and so she felt as if he had conquered her. He's a horrible person, Ellen thought. He's going to hurt me, break my heart. I don't want any part of him. She wanted to cry. He had no right to take control. The control had to be hers, because she had the most to lose, the husband, the family, while he had nothing but Margot, whom he obviously didn't care much about anyway. He was utterly free, he could take her or leave her.

He put her coat on her, buttoned it up as if she were a child, and kissed her forehead, her cheeks, her lips. "We must stop meeting like this in delicatessens," he said in a foreign accent that she took to be Transylvanian. "People will find out."

Despite herself, Ellen smiled. She hugged him. He felt fragile in her arms, like a young boy, but strong. Did he mean he wanted to see her again or not?

"What are we going to do?" she asked.

He did not drop the accent. "I will send you a message," he said.

"I don't want anybody to suffer," Ellen said. "I have to think about this."

"Of course."

97

She went down to the street and found a cab. This afternoon had been a mistake. She would have to keep away from him. One of the people who could easily suffer the consequences would be herself.

MAY

May 1975

THE WINTER WAS really over. Since New York has had no real spring for many years, people were planning for the summer. Cars were rented for forays into Connecticut and the Hamptons to look at houses to rent. Children were told how much they would enjoy camp. Teen-agers worried about the shortage of summer jobs. Apartment buildings with air conditioning sent handymen around for the annual changing of the filter. The poor had no such problems; they only hoped this year would not be as hot as last, that prices would stop rising, that no one would steal the Social Security check again this month, that the landlord might fix the broken window, the leaking ceiling, the broken toilet. The middle class worried about prices and crime too. The rich discussed these problems, but they did not worry, except those who depended on the stock market for their income. They worried a great deal.

The Lawrence Fowlers were rich enough to be able to ride out any temporary economic fluctuation. They had owned their own home in East Hampton for many years. They kept year-round servants there, to prevent robberies in winter and to be available in summer. In past springs Rachel's main concerns had been shopping for her summer wardrobe and getting Lawrence to set the date of their annual May trip to London, Zurich, and Paris, so that she could arrange their New York social calendar accordingly. This spring was different. She had decided to go back to college in the fall.

She wrote to her high school back home for her academic records, sent for brochures from Barnard, NYU, and Columbia, and decided to apply to all three. She'd had good marks in high school, but no one in her family had thought it necessary that she consider going to college. She had already done some local modeling, she was the model type, and they had very little money, so they agreed with her that she try New York, try to be a cover girl, maybe land a rich husband. Although she was an only child, her parents were not protective. They felt her looks were a godsend; she could become rich and successful with those looks. The only stipulation her parents made when Rachel left for New York at the age of eighteen was that she stay at the Barbizon Hotel for Women. She did—for two weeks.

Then she began making her own money and moved into an apartment with three other girls. Shortly afterward she moved in with the son of a rich man. He said he would marry her. He didn't marry her, but he taught her how to read menus in French and Italian restaurants, how to play tennis, and he paid for her abortion. After he lost interest in her she moved in with a young man who had made his own money, who said he would marry her. She was now using birth control. She got pregnant anyway, which was very strange, but the young man she was living with paid for her abortion and managed to have it done in a good hospital instead of the sleazy place she'd gone to the first time. When she got out of the hospital the next day Rachel discovered that her fiancé had closed his apartment and left town for an indefinite period. She couldn't get any of his friends to tell her where he had gone. By then she decided she had learned more in three years without college than most girls learned in a whole lifetime, and she began to devote herself wholeheartedly to the development of whatever it took to find a rich man to marry her.

Whatever it took, Rachel did everything wrong. She enchanted phonies who passed bad checks, gamblers, men with divorces that were not final, liars, and several genuinely rich young men, one of whom wanted her to spank him with her hairbrush and another who wanted to try on her clothes. When she met Lawrence Fowler she was twenty-four, had her own apartment, was recovering from her third abortion, and hated men.

He was twenty years older, which was not ancient, but she found herself thinking of him as a father image. He didn't want anything from her. He was very nice to her, but he didn't try to keep her or change her. He mentioned that he was getting divorced, but she didn't pay any attention because she'd heard that one before. After she had been going with him for a year he told her he was going to marry her. She was sick and tired of hearing that one. She insisted on telling him all about her past. He was not shocked, but he was very angry at all those men who had undervalued her. He told her to forget the past. He said he just wanted her to be with him, and he would make it up to her.

It was after she was safely married to Lawrence Fowler that Rachel allowed herself to fall wholeheartedly in love with him. She stopped being afraid of things. He said he didn't want children, since he already had one son, Kerry, and he wanted to be able to travel with Rachel, to have her all to himself, he didn't want to start all over again with babies. She discovered she couldn't have any more anyway, so that was fine. She decided everything that had ever happened to her had been for the best.

It was only during this past year that Rachel had discovered her happiness was not enough. It was satisfaction but not joy. She had been lying dormant. She knew you could never go back and do everything all over again, but you could make up for things you hadn't done. She didn't know exactly what she expected to get out of college, but she knew it would make her feel less different, less inadequate. The fact that being a thirty-five-year-old freshman would make her very different didn't matter.

On one of her gym mornings she got up earlier than usual so she could catch Lawrence before he left for his office. He looked up from the breakfast table and his newspapers in amazement at the sleepy figure trailing into the dining room in a misbuttoned robe.

"Well, what is that?" he asked, amused.

"It's me." She sat down across from him.

"I'll get you some tea."

"No, coffee's okay," Rachel said. She let him pour her a cup of it. "Can we talk?"

"Of course."

"I want to go to college."

"All right. But we're going to Europe, and then we go to East Hampton every weekend. Summer school might be too much."

"I mean real college. I want to start in the fall."

He raised his eyebrows. "You're leaving me?"

"No, I'll go in New York of course. What do you think?"

"I think it's a good idea."

"You don't think I'm too old?" she asked.

"Not at all. Nobody's too old for education."

"Will you pay for it?"

"I don't expect *you* to," he said with a smile.

"You really don't mind? I'll be busy doing homework, there'll be things I can't attend to around the house . . ."

Lawrence shrugged. "If I need a social secretary I'll hire a social secretary. I thought you enjoyed doing those things. If you'd rather go to college, that's fine."

Rachel took his hand in both of hers. "You're really good, do you know that? You didn't even ask me what I want to be when I grow up."

He laughed. "What do you want to major in?"

"I want to take history, government, and banking."

"Banking!"

"I want to know what you do," Rachel said seriously.

"Why do you want to know what I do? It's boring."

"You don't think it's boring."

"Okay. If you want, I'll help you. We can have talks."

"Oh, I'd love that!" Rachel said. "I'd really love that."

"Which college are you going to?"

"The one that takes me."

"I hope they all take you," he said. "If you want any help in applying, ask me. I have a few friends."

"I've already applied."

He looked annoyed. "Why didn't you tell me? I could have helped you."

"I want to get in on my own."

"You're so stubborn," he said.

"Why do you sound so angry?"

"Because I don't want you to be hurt."

"You think I won't get in."

"I didn't say that."

"But you're afraid of it," Rachel said. "You think I'm too dumb. I know it. I want to show you I'm not too dumb."

He patted her hand. "It'll be all right." But he still looked disturbed. Rachel had the disquieting feeling that Lawrence was going to investigate all this, maybe pull a few strings. She didn't want to tell him she suspected, because then he'd get angry and not help her at all. She didn't know what she wanted. She had grown so used to having him make everything easy for her. She wanted so badly to get into college that she hoped he *would* help her—now that he'd mentioned it and made her insecure again. Oh, if she could only do one thing on her own! But even if he helped her get in, she would still have to do her own work. If she was too lazy or too stupid they would throw her out. She hated the way she felt, so easily manipulated, so easily made insecure. All Lawrence wanted was the best for her, not to have her get hurt any more. She ought to be grateful. Why, then, did she feel so disappointed that he had taken her hand and walked into her dream?

"Why do you look so sad?" he asked. He smiled and kissed her. "Be happy. You're going to go to college."

105

On a hot day Rachel went to Bloomingdale's to buy a typewriter. She had been too poor to own one in high school, and afterward there had been no need. Now that she was going to go to college she would teach herself to type. That would be her summer project. It occurred to her that perhaps she should have gone to an office-supply place, but Bloomie's was one of the stores where she had a charge account. She walked right into the middle of the lunch-hour crowd.

She had never seen so many people milling around. Some were there to buy, some to look, others just to get out of the heat into the air conditioning. This was her morning; it was their noon. She was aware that her daily rhythm was different from most other people's, and so was her life-style, but being buffeted around by all this humanity made her more aware than ever. At least nobody else seemed to want to buy a typewriter today. She bought a portable, had it sent, and went down on the escalator.

It was strange about crowds: usually they didn't bother her, but today somehow she felt touched and prodded, as if someone was personally brushing against her, the light flick of a damp hand on her hip. She didn't like it. She turned around twice to see who it was, but there was no one she could pick out as a possible public feeler. It was probably just her mood. Still, her mood was getting worse, and she escaped into the street. The crowds there were thicker. These people were all so anonymous, each concerned with getting somewhere, but Rachel kept feeling that personal force directed against herself. She actually felt eyes on her, someone watching only her, but when she looked from side to side, there were only the self-absorbed strangers. She got into a taxi and went downtown to NYU.

The university area looked nice in the springtime. All the trees in the park were trying their best to flourish. Rachel went into one of the buildings and walked around, imagining herself a student here. It was quite empty. The students were either in classes or outside in the sun. This was certainly a big place. She could disappear here when it was filled with students, and nobody would think she was too old. She read the hall bulletin boards with amusement, trying to understand the world of these young kids, a generation removed from hers. A lot of them seemed to have their own apartments. There were handwritten cards advertising Village sublets wanted and available, furniture for sale, even kittens. Flute lessons. French books for sale. Roommate wanted. It was too bad she couldn't live her eighteenth year all over again knowing what she did now. She would have handled everything differently, all the way through, until she met Lawrence. Of course there had to be Lawrence in this second chance. She couldn't imagine being happy without him. But would he have wanted her if she were different? Would she have found him such a savior, or would she have been contentedly living with a group of her contemporaries, not vulnerable, not in pain, not bitter? Had he been drawn to her need and her dependence as much as to her looks?

She heard a sound and saw a door open a little and then close again, but not all the way. It seemed to be some sort of utility closet. There was no one in the hall but herself. Rachel walked to the water cooler at the end of the hall and leaned over to drink, watching the partly opened door. It moved again, just a bit. Maybe some student, stealing something. This was a college. Colleges were safe, not like the street, not like the real world. It couldn't be someone watching her. Why would anyone want to watch her here? Still, she had that eerie feeling she'd had in the crowd in Bloomingdale's, and she walked away from the corridor and down the stairs to the street. She felt safer in the sunlight.

She had to get herself under control. This was probably just some psychological reaction to the nervousness of starting a new life. Instead of facing it she was imagining invisible enemies. That had to be all it was. So okay, she was scared about getting into college, scared about keeping up, getting good marks, passing exams. That was natural. If she would face it, she would stop imagining bogeymen in closets and eyes in crowds. She walked to Washington Square Park, through it, and then took a cab uptown. College faded from her mind as she concentrated on

what she and Lawrence were going to do that evening with the
grown-ups.

HE WAS GETTING braver. For a moment in the hall he thought she
had noticed him and his excitement almost exploded him into
his fantasy. He could have come out of the utility closet and con-
fronted her. She was alone, and so close. He had been following
her all day, to the store, to the university, getting closer and more
reckless in the noonday mob. It was getting harder for him to
separate his fantasies of her from the real thing because his secret
encounters with her were so like fantasies. He had even started
dreaming about her at night, and these dreams mingled with his
daytime imagining. Sometimes he worried that he was losing his
mind. The important thing was control. There were too many
things to worry about during the normal day, to keep control
over, without trying to hold down these lapses too. A man had
to have somewhere to blow off steam. You couldn't hold everything down forever. There was an image to keep up—a job, a life,
a family—and then there was his feeling about Rachel. It was all
so carefully held in check, but once in a while something opened
up a crack and he knew something very dangerous was going to
come out. He didn't want it to happen at home or at work; those
areas had to be protected. It was why he had let himself follow
his needs in this secret obsession with Rachel. He didn't think he
would ever hurt her. She was one of the only people in the world
for whom he felt absolutely no hate. To her he was just another
one among her large group of friends and acquaintances. He
wondered why he didn't resent more being so unimportant to
her. He ought to hate her for it. Maybe one day he would find a
way to test her.

THE PEOPLE on Margot King's television show, like all the news
shows lately, put on a great public display of their friendly rela-
tionships. They teased each other on the air, they laughed, they
had fun. With the arrival of the good weather, there were base-

ball games in the park against the staffs of other news shows. But after all of this was over, they were like the people who worked in any office anywhere in the city; some were friendly, most went their separate ways. The commuters dashed home, those who lived in the city had errands to do, friends to meet. Enough was enough, they all seemed to feel. Margot, in particular, had always been a loner. While reporting the news she had been totally isolated in her own world. If their appearance on television made all of them more visible than most people, they had to try harder to keep to themselves the part of their lives that was private. One of the women on the show was pregnant and the world saw it, when she was absent because she was having her baby the world knew it, and cards and little presents came flooding in. But she never invited Margot to come home with her and see the new baby, and Margot didn't expect her to. She mentioned on the air that the baby was a boy, but she didn't say what his name was, nor did she tell anyone that the name she used professionally was not her married name. There had been a kidnap threat. It was obviously from a lunatic, but it had been handed over to the police and was not mentioned on the show. Being a public person had dangers.

Margot was used to receiving crank letters. She got fan letters too, even proposals of marriage from strangers. She wondered what kind of lonely people sat around writing to total strangers. The hate mail was the most perplexing. When the members of the show were photographed for a newspaper ad, people cut out the photograph and sent it to their favorite hates, writing on their faces. Margot got six pictures of herself with penises drawn on her body, one with a moustache, one with a big nose, and one with swastikas all around the margin. She was called bitch, cunt, whore, fascist, and communist. One letter said: "You believe in abortion, you will die." She kept all the crank letters in a folder in her file cabinet, just in case someone killed her. It was probably paranoid, she was aware that people who wrote crank letters seldom went further; but by the same token, she knew that anonymous people who sprang to prominence by killing a celebrity had

109

been known to write crank letters that were ignored. She had an unlisted number and never discussed her personal life on the show. She never answered letters unless they were from schoolchildren who seemed sweet and bright. Even then she kept her letters brief and typed them on office stationery. She felt no warmth toward her public. She had often heard celebrities gushing on talk shows about how much they loved their public, and she wondered if it were possibly true. You needed your public in order to remain popular and employed, but how could you love them when so many of them obviously hated you for no reason?

She thought of herself as a reporter, not a personality. She did her own hair, even though expenses for a hairdresser were tax-deductible. She had it professionally cut every three months. Her clothes were simple, and while she was careful not to wear the same thing twice during the same week, because that too brought angry letters, she also repeated her wardrobe in order not to antagonize the have-nots who wrote in asking for her old clothes, money, and her head on a platter. She thought how ironic it was that while she was not really famous she was visible enough so that some strangers felt she should also be accessible.

Her life centered around Kerry. Her schedule was erratic and difficult, but so was his. This worried her. She had to be on call for her job, but when he didn't come home he was wherever he was by choice. During the past few weeks his hours had become more unpredictable. She always told him where she would be that day, and he told her he didn't know where he would be. She had to accept that. He liked to wander around the city, see friends, do things on impulse. She was afraid to phone him at his apartment during the hours she thought he might be writing. But when he knew she had prepared dinner and was waiting for him, and he did not arrive, then she did call, and when he wasn't in his apartment she felt a chill go through her. Whenever he showed up he always had the same innocent excuse, he had met a friend, he'd forgotten what time it was. He didn't even bother to make up something melodramatic, so Margot had to accept what he said as truth. She was less important to him than his moment-to-moment life. She hated that, but she had to take it. She wished she had been the kind of person who had a life like his, who met friends in the street and wandered off with them for hours of talk, who didn't plan, who forgot meals. The only thing Kerry planned for was their fall vacation in the Greek islands. That, at least, still existed, and she held on to it whenever she became nervous or frightened. She wished she could think of a way to make herself more important to him now.

She brought the folder of crank letters home. She showed them to him. She wasn't sure what reaction she expected them to evoke, probably his wish to protect her. She was totally unprepared for the reaction they did evoke.

"These are fantastic!" Kerry said, delighted. He was sitting on the floor, her hate mail spread all around him. "These are the most incredible social document! The neurosis of our time . . . they're a book. Did you ever think of making a book out of them, love?"

"You're joking, I hope," Margot said.

He looked at her with eyes that were clear, innocent, and enthusiastic. "No, I'm not kidding. It could have photographs of nice, ordinary people, mowing their lawns, having supper, walking their dogs, kids doing homework, housewives ironing, people in front of TV sets in sleazy hotel rooms and nice apartments with crocheted things on the arms of chairs—you know, those old things my grandmother used to have."

"Antimacassars," Margot said coldly. She did not like being put in the memory bank with his grandmother.

"Right. And then you'd have the letters. You'd have a little girl on the swing in the park, having a great time, and then you'd have the letter that says you're a cunt and a whore."

"Those were written to me," Margot said. "*Me!* Don't you realize that? They're not for your entertainment. Some real people out there somewhere wrote those letters to *me.*"

"Then they belong to you," Kerry said. "They're not signed. You can publish them as a human document and make some money."

She scrambled around the rug, furiously gathering up her hate mail. "I'd just get more."

"Those people don't read books," Kerry said pleasantly.

"I'm glad I never wrote you any love letters," Margot said. "You'd probably publish them if you thought they had any commercial possibilities."

He smiled. "You're angry."

"No, I'm hurt."

"Why are you hurt?"

"I guess I thought you might be concerned."

"I guess I'm different from you," Kerry said.

"Not where it matters," Margot said quickly.

She took the letters back to her office that evening and locked them away in her file. Had she made a fool of herself? No, Kerry thought she'd brought the letters home to amuse him. She hoped he didn't know she had been trying to get him to pay more attention to her. He would accuse her of crying wolf. She knew you couldn't make someone love you by making him sorry for you. When she'd been young and in love with married men, they had always said they were sorry for their wives, sorry for their children, but she had finally realized they were only saying that. Their wives and children were their protection from young girls like her who wanted to marry them. Their families did deserve sympathy, but those men were the last ones in the world to realize it. Pity was a burden. She would never again try to make Kerry feel sorry for her. She was glad she was old enough to know some tricks of her own—the most difficult of which, and the most successful, was self-control.

ELLEN RENNIE, for the first time in her life, was getting a lesson in self-control. Every day in her office she jumped whenever the phone rang, hoping it would be Kerry, and it never was. She got to work promptly at nine and stayed until six, hoping he would call, but finally she realized it was useless. He wouldn't call, ever. She had been a moment of gratification to him, nothing more.

Maybe even less—maybe he thought he'd done her a favor. That thought panicked her. He *had* done her a favor, that was what was so humiliating, but instead of being grateful that he had found her, as all her other men were, he probably felt like a boy scout who had helped an old lady to cross the street. She would never, never go to bed with a young boy again. Sex was too easy for them. She needed a man who would find her important, valuable. A man who was well married, who seldom cheated, who would find himself overwhelmed by passion and guilt, but not so overwhelmed that he wanted to stop. She wanted to be someone's great love. She needed it. No matter how often Ellen had choreographed her great romance in her mind, it always happened as something fresh and new.

She looked around the company for the first time, seeing the editors and authors in a new light. There wasn't much to her taste. The man she was looking for had to send a particular kind of tingle through her. He didn't have to be of any particular type, but he had to have the chemistry. Ellen was so angry at Kerry that he no longer seemed sexy to her at all. She wanted someone totally different, starting with Considerate and Kind.

When she walked into Reuben Weinberg's office Ellen knew he was the one. She wasn't really sure whether it was the way his thick, dark hair curled over his neck or his wife's picture on his desk in a Kulicke frame. *She* had put it there, not he, and it was an old picture. Ellen had once seen his wife. It had been a long time since this man had cared about looking at his wife's picture on his desk, but he obviously felt he had to keep it there. Ellen looked at Reuben Weinberg with new interest. He was the executive editor and a vice-president. Some of the women in the office had crushes on him, but he had never been involved with any of them. He had power in the company, he was sweet, he was four years older than she was, and he was Jewish. He had just the right amount of guilt.

"I came to ask you," Ellen said, "if that Russian of yours is taking his interpreter on tour with him."

"He always takes her," Reuben said. He smiled, because the

113

interpreter was a pretty young thing and the Russian author spoke quite good English.

"Should I get them a suite or are we being proper?"

"I'm sure he'd be thrilled to have a suite. With or without her."

"I'll book them a suite," Ellen said. "It makes him look successful for the interviewers. It doesn't cost any more than two rooms." She sat comfortably on the edge of his desk and gave him a long calm look. Slightly crooked teeth—that meant his parents couldn't afford to have them fixed. A hint of acne scars on his cheeks, not enough to be unattractive, but it meant that he'd probably had an inferiority complex as a teen-ager. Pimples, no money, and bookish, just when he had been at his horniest. Married young, probably for sex. Just at the age now when he realized all he'd missed. Nice body, what she could see of it. Not too tan—that meant he wasn't a tennis or a golf freak. A man shouldn't have too many outside interests, they siphoned off his interest in cheating. He blushed slightly under her gaze. She looked into his eyes and smiled, and then she looked at his mouth. When she knew she had made him uncomfortable enough she eased off his desk and walked casually to the door. When she got back to her office her phone rang.

"Maybe you should get two rooms," Reuben said. "Alexi's married."

"Who isn't?" Ellen said.

"Of course, his wife's in Maine and speaks no English."

"She sounds perfect," Ellen said.

"You're frisky today."

"No more than usual."

"I had a lunch date canceled on me," Reuben said. "If you want I'll buy you a sandwich."

"Terrific." She replaced the receiver gently and ran her hands over her breasts and down her slim waist. She would go slowly with him. He was going to be easy. She felt better already. It was going to be a marvelous summer.

JUNE

June 1975

FOR THE FIRST TIME in her life, this summer Nikki Gellhorn felt like one of her own daughters. They were setting off on their own adventures, she on hers. College over for the summer, Lynn and her boyfriend flew to London, the first leg of their European summer. Lynn had her knapsack, her passport, her traveler's checks, her map of the London subway system, her map of the French wine country, her list of youth hostels, her birth-control pills, her blue jeans, her paperbacks, and (under protest) was wearing her silver Medic Alert bracelet that said she was allergic to penicillin. She and her boyfriend had not even bothered to buy wedding rings in the five-and-ten, a suggestion Nikki had tentatively offered, which was met with hoots of laughter.

Dorothy was working at the suburban mental hospital. She loved it. "They're not violent, Mom," she assured Nikki. "The violent ones get locked in another wing. I get the spoiled teenagers whose parents want to get them off pills and dope at a hundred dollars a day—the hospital, not the habit." She had her uniforms, her name tag, and her tennis racket. She played with the patients and the other aides. She'd already met a medical student there she liked. Nikki doubted if Dorothy would ever favor her parents with a weekend visit, even with the medical student. A house in the country wasn't that interesting. Nikki didn't enjoy the weekends there any more herself. She and Robert were pleasant enough to each other, and they went to barbecues and picnics and gave a brunch, but she was always glad when Monday morning came and she could go back to New York. Going back Monday morning instead of Sunday night was her concession to Robert's ego, although she found it very inconvenient.

At her office they were working on books for next year. The summer was a more relaxed time, though, because people took their vacations, and that seemed to demoralize the ones who were left. The building never seemed to give them enough air conditioning. On Monday mornings they compared tans. The summer bachelors whose wives were in the Hamptons or on Fire Island had set up housekeeping with their girl friends. One afternoon the whole office went off to a screening of one of the Heller & Strauss books that had been made into a movie. Ellen Rennie sat with Reuben Weinberg and when the screening was over they went off together. Nikki didn't give it much thought.

The next day Ellen came into her office. "Busy?"

"The usual," Nikki said, putting down a manuscript she had been reading.

"I had to tell you," Ellen said. "Can you keep a secret?"

"Sure."

"I'm in love."

"No kidding. Who are you in love with?"

"Reuben," Ellen said.

Nikki knew something of Ellen's past from Margot, but she had always imagined the men as irresistible somehow, not like Reuben. She couldn't picture a woman jeopardizing her marriage for Reuben.

118

"I had to tell somebody," Ellen said. "I've never been in love like this before. You never know who it's going to be, do you?"

"No, you don't," Nikki said.

"I fought it," Ellen said. "After all, I have to keep my home together. It's not easy. And Reuben's married, so that's trouble too. But I just couldn't resist finally. He's so incredible. But you know him, of course."

"Not the way you do," Nikki said with a smile.

Ellen sat on the edge of Nikki's desk and stared off into space with a faraway gleam in her eye. "Such incredible sex . . ." she said.

"Haven't you told Margot?"

"Of course," Ellen said. "I tell Margot everything. We're life-long friends."

"Well, I don't think you should tell anybody else in this office besides me," Nikki said. "There's a lot of gossip around here."

"Oh, I wouldn't dream of it. I only told you, Nikki, because you're my best friend here and I know I can trust you."

"You can." She wondered how many other people Ellen had told already. Ellen seemed too eager to confide, she seemed almost disappointed that Nikki wasn't pressing her for details. Is it the idea of the affair she likes, Nikki wondered, or the affair itself?

"It's not easy to be in the same office together," Ellen said. "Luckily his wife and kids are on Fire Island for the summer, and he goes there only weekends. We use his apartment during the week."

"Don't you have to go home?"

"Oh, I mean lunchtimes and after work—you know."

"I don't know," Nikki said. "I'm very boring, I never had an affair."

"*Never?*"

"I never had time."

"You must have a very happy marriage," Ellen said wistfully. "Mine is a nightmare. However, one does what one can to survive. Stolen moments."

119

"That sounds like the title of a silent movie. D. W. Griffith."

"No wonder you're an editor," Ellen said.

I'm just like Robert, Nikki thought in horror. I do that thing with words he does. Maybe if you live with someone long enough you become identical twins.

"Believe me, Nikki," Ellen was saying, "if you had a bad marriage you'd have time to have an affair. Men are always after married women. It's *too* easy for us."

Nikki thought back. There must have been at least a dozen men in her life who'd made serious offers. She'd put them all into her mind as if she were holding a dance card and laughed them off. An advance was as good as a *fait accompli,* she'd always thought. And a lot safer. And after all her goodness, there was her husband accusing her of playing around. It certainly was ironic. "Does your husband suspect?" she asked Ellen.

"Hank? Never. Or if he does, he doesn't want to admit it to himself. People are very self-protective."

"I guess so."

Ellen went back to her office and her dream world and Nikki went back to her manuscript. She wondered if her daughter Dorothy was doing it with that medical student. Wouldn't it be funny if both her daughters ended up marrying doctors? Her mother would be so thrilled. God, I've got to stop thinking marriage, Nikki thought. Girls don't get married any more just because they're sleeping with somebody. Or because they want to. They just play around. And their mothers play around. I'm not that much older than Ellen. She looks older than I do. "Too Old" is a trick our mothers invented to keep us in the seraglio. First we're Too Young, then we're Too Old. Not that I want to do anything, but if I ever do I'm not going to let being forty-two scare me away from adventure.

Her secretary, Elizabeth, rapped on the doorframe. "Nikki, can I borrow ten dollars till payday? I got mugged last night."

"You're kidding!"

"No, really. Ripped off. I was coming home from shopping— the stores were open late last night—and some guy cut my shoulder bag right off me with a pair of scissors. Whack, it was gone. I turned around and saw him taking off for the subway entrance, and I wasn't going to follow him there."

Nikki looked at the pretty Chinese girl, twenty years old, long, thick, straight hair, blue jeans, no hips, and thought she was lucky she was only robbed, not raped. "What did you do?"

"Well, luckily I'd spent most of my money. But what really bugged me was there was this skirt I wanted a lot, and I told myself I was too extravagant and it would be good for my soul if I didn't give in for once, so I didn't buy it. And then this junkie takes my money. I was so mad!"

"Look at it this way," Nikki said, "you could have bought the skirt and then he could have taken *it*."

Elizabeth laughed. "Can you spare ten? I hate to ask."

"Of course." Nikki dug into her bag and found her wallet.

"You carry all your credit cards?" Elizabeth said.

"Sure, why not?"

"And your money, and your keys? Some guy could rip you off and get to your house before you do."

"I doubt that's going to happen," Nikki said. She remembered her would-be robber and felt a slight chill. "What happened to your keys last night?"

"I keep them in my pocket."

"How can you *live* like that?"

Elizabeth shrugged. "He didn't get them. That's the main thing."

"Does everybody live like you do?"

"No. Most of my friends don't care. But I got mugged once before and it really made me mad. There's this horrible feeling of invasion, and rage, and helplessness. On the other hand, my boyfriend carries around what he calls 'mugger's money.' It's twenty dollars so the mugger won't get angry and beat him up or anything. I guess these bastards expect more from men. I mean, if a secretary has only thirty-five cents on her they figure okay."

"You certainly are cynical for a girl your age," Nikki said. She gave her the ten.

"Thanks. I'll pay you back next week."

"Don't worry about it."

Elizabeth grinned and tossed her long hair. "Cynical is better than innocent, believe me."

"I'll continue to live dangerously."

After her secretary left, Nikki looked at her handbag for a long time. She remembered the time ten years ago when she'd been working late, alone in the office, and coming back from the ladies' room had surprised a young man taking her wallet out of her purse, which she'd left on her desk. She had been so filled with rage that she had chased him all the way to the elevator screaming, "Give me back my wallet, you!" He had been a small, scared young man, and she had trapped him at the elevator. He had dropped the wallet at her feet, the money intact, and fled down the fire stairs. When she had told the other people in the office the next day they had laughed. Now people locked their offices when they went out, or took their money with them. Nobody worked late alone. The glass doors to the reception room were locked at five o'clock and employees had keys. There was a guard in the lobby at night and a sign-in book. Things had changed. Even she had changed in little ways. She had become street-wise in the office, but not in the street. She resented having anyone take her freedom away. You could live in a prison of fear in your own mind, and maybe that was just as bad. She wasn't sure.

THE ONLY PEOPLE who knew it was Ellen Rennie's fortieth birthday were Ellen's family, Ellen's lover Reuben, and Margot. On their birthdays Ellen and Margot always took each other to lunch and gave each other expensive presents. It was a tradition they had started in college. This year Margot took Ellen to lunch at Madrigal and gave her a Gucci handbag.

The restaurant was all yellow and white, as if bathed in sunlight. On the walls were murals of eighteenth-century French troubadours, and on each table there were yellow and apricot roses in large brandy snifters. Set out on display were boxes of fresh raspberries, scarcely to be found in the city, and in back of the room you could see a small garden drenched in vines. They both drank several glasses of wine, each for her own reasons.

"How does it feel, being forty?" Margot asked.

"To tell you the truth, today feels exactly the same as yesterday. Except for the fuss everybody's making. The kids insisted we have a birthday dinner. They're cooking it themselves. I had to promise I wouldn't come home until six o'clock, which turned out to be convenient, because I'm spending the afternoon with Reuben."

"Just another day," Margot said, smiling.

Ellen wasn't sure it was just another day. She had awakened this morning to a feeling of dread, as if a clock had chimed: half over. She had to admit her life *was* half over, and that made her beginning middle age. There was no way to get around the logic of that. And if she didn't live to be eighty, or if she became senile or something, that meant now she was well into middle age. She didn't feel any different, she didn't look any different, and it wasn't fair. Well, say the first ten years she was just a kid learning things, and the next ten were the time of trial and error, so she'd only had twenty years of a real life, and it had all gone by so fast. A lot of it had been unhappy. Some of it had been exciting. But it was gone, and now what was left seemed invested with too much importance because for the first time Ellen was aware of how limited time was.

"Don't look so depressed," Margot said. "It's your birthday. I get to have mine in a few months. You're scaring me."

"It makes you wonder . . ." Ellen said.

"What?"

"I wonder what I've ever done with my life that was memorable. If I'm this depressed now, how will I feel at fifty? I'll probably lock myself in my bedroom with a bottle of gin."

"More likely you'll be in someone else's bedroom with a bottle of champagne. Another scalp on your belt."

"Oh, Margot, how can you say that? I never took advantage of anyone! They were never scalps."

123

"Maybe if *I* got married to someone Kerry would like me better."

Ellen felt her heart turn over and she hoped she hadn't gotten pale. Was Margot digging at her? Maybe that little fink had told her. He wouldn't dare. Margot would have told her directly, she would have thrown a fit, and they certainly wouldn't be having this nice birthday lunch. Just when she thought the whole embarrassing incident with Kerry was over and gone, it had to pop up like this. But Margot looked totally innocent and self-absorbed.

"The next man you fall in love with you should marry," Ellen said.

"Good old mother Ellen. You're a fine one to talk about the glories of marriage."

"*You* should be married," Ellen said. "You need one man. You need love and security."

"I think I'm too set in my ways to get married," Margot said. "I really don't like to share things."

"That's a crock," Ellen said.

"I don't see any happy marriages around me, do you?"

"You would have one."

"Nope, it wouldn't work. If it worked I'd have married someone years ago, anyone. I can accept myself now. I admit I never wanted it."

"Second marriages work better," Ellen said. "If marriage was such a dead loss, how come most of the people who get divorced at our age get married to someone else?"

"Or just live together," Margot said.

"I'm not the 'living together' type," Ellen said. "If I ever divorced Hank I'd only do it to marry someone else."

"Anyone special in mind?"

"No. Just having the birthday blues. It's very depressing to be forty and married to Hank."

Margot laughed. "*That* I can believe."

"No, seriously, Margot. Tell me the truth. Do people look at Hank and me and think: I wonder what she ever saw in him?"

"I do."

"Not you. I mean strangers, casual acquaintances. Do they think Hank is a loser?"

"It depends on whose friends they are, yours or his."

Ellen sighed. "I don't know why I asked. I know the answer. Even *his* friends think he's a loser. God, how can you know at twenty what's going to happen when you grow up?"

"Why don't you divorce him?" Margot said. Her eyes were serious. "You're not too old. Get out while you still have a chance. You have the girls for company. Wouldn't you love to live in your own apartment with Jill and Stacey? No Hank—think of it."

"What would he do without me?" Ellen said. She couldn't understand why Margot didn't see the inescapable logic of it. "I'm the one bringing in the money in this family."

"Then you wouldn't have to feel guilty leaving him," Margot said with her own brand of logic. "He won't have to support you."

"I can't kick him when he's down, Margot. Hank loves me."

"He certainly must. You've always been very sloppy about covering your tracks."

"I know," Ellen said. "Hank isn't a curious person. Strange, but not curious." She laughed. "Let's not be bitchy about my poor husband. He's the only one I've got."

It was so nice to be here with Margot, just like the old days at school, dishing the boys. It was almost as if Hank were just one of her faithful puppy-dog dates, someone she could laugh at and get rid of when he bored her. Ellen wished it were true. If she could just disappear into the past like Alice down the rabbit hole. If she had it all to do over again she would pick an intellectual, like Reuben, someone who loved books and talked books and had power, who knew interesting people, who was creative, and who made love so gloriously, as if he had just discovered sex for the first time and couldn't get enough of it. The poet of the bedroom, she had told him one day.

"Would you like to live your life over again?" she asked Margot.

"Yes," Margot said. "Provided it was different."

"Well, that would be the only point, wouldn't it?"

AFTER LUNCH Ellen went directly to Reuben's apartment, which happened to be on the West Side, not too far from her own. He had taken the afternoon off too, in honor of her birthday, and was waiting for her there. The doorman knew her by now and didn't stop her to ask where she was going, and Ellen wondered how many doormen all over the city were nodding courteously to women who were going to visit men whose wives were away for the summer.

Reuben opened the door the moment Ellen rang his bell, and they kissed and hugged as if they hadn't seen each other for a month. One of the things she most loved about him was that he was so affectionate. She had asked him once if he was an affectionate father as well as lover (she didn't say "husband") and he had said yes, he always hugged and kissed his two little boys, because his own father had been cold. He had then added, with a gleam in his eye, that perhaps he wasn't as affectionate a husband as he ought to be. He was so perceptive, and so kind. He knew when she wanted to ask something and hadn't, and he always answered.

"Wait till you see what we have!" he said happily and pulled her into the living room. It was the first time Ellen had ever seen the living room without all the furniture covered with sheets. Reuben's apartment always amused her because his wife had covered everything, even the lampshades, just like an old woman, so it wouldn't get dusty during the summer while she was away. Never mind that poor Reuben had to live there during the week. The only place she'd left for him was the bedroom and the kitchen.

He had put out a cooler with ice in it, and in the ice was a bottle of Dom Pérignon. Beside it were two tulip glasses chilling. On a silver plate was an open jar of Beluga Malossol caviar, Ellen's favorite, and a plate of toast he'd obviously made himself. He had

126

even cut it into little squares and trimmed off the crusts. And the final touch was a small box from Cartier.

"Happy birthday, darling," he said.

"Oh, Reuben, this is the best birthday I ever had!"

He produced a wrench and opened the champagne with a satisfactory pop and sizzle of frosty steam but no overflow. Ellen applauded. "I learned that trick from a bartender," he said. "My hands aren't very strong."

He poured the champagne, they toasted each other and drank, and then he made her eat caviar although she wasn't hungry. Then he gave her the present. She opened the box and saw a small, delicate gold chain that would just fit around the base of her throat.

"Oh, put it on me," Ellen said. He did, and kissed her neck above the chain. "I'll never take it off," she said.

"I thought perhaps I shouldn't," he said. "But I do love you. And you can make up something in case he asks, can't you?"

"Of course. I'll say I got it from Margot." She thought of the Gucci bag. Reuben hadn't even noticed the box, or if he had he had already forgotten it. So she could just put the bag in her closet, and when she started using it Hank would never give it a thought.

"Two presents?" Reuben asked. "Your Margot is a big spender."

"You never lose your capacity to surprise me," Ellen said.

"I hope I never do."

She wore the necklace while they made love on the bed, and she thought that now it really was his gift to her because it had the touch of his skin on it, and, she imagined, even the scent of his skin. Even though she would wear the necklace in the shower and in the world outside it would still be a part of the two of them making love. She liked the idea. She also liked that he had taken the sheets off the living room furniture and had entertained her there, so she would not feel like a summer interloper. He really was a very thoughtful man. She supposed that when fall came he would find another place to take her where they could both feel safe and comfortable. She didn't picture Reuben in a

127

motel somehow. He was much too naïve, too idealistic. He would probably have a close friend with a bachelor apartment.

"I love you," he was saying over and over. "I love you, I love you."

That was so nice. She could listen to that forever. "I love you too," Ellen said.

STACEY HAD SPENT the entire afternoon baking a birthday cake. She had also bought her mother a bottle of perfume. Jill had bought her mother a book she herself wanted to read anyway, and spent the day reading it, very neatly, and then wrapped it up again in its gift paper. Of course she could have waited until her mother was finished with it and then borrowed it, but it gave her a special, secret pleasure to have it first. Jill was a fast reader. Now that the book was all hers, safe in her mind, it was nothing but a shell, like an old squeezed orange, a perfect birthday present for her shell of a mother.

Stacey finished the last laborious icing decoration. "There! Just like the store."

"It's too good for her," Jill said.

"Like Mom says, no point in doing something if it isn't perfect," Stacey said cheerfully. "It's time to put the chicken in. Did you wash the salad?"

"Not yet."

"Jill! I can't do everything."

"It was all your idea."

"But you said you'd help me," Stacey said.

"Don't whine."

"You don't understand, I'm doing all this because I like doing it. The party is just an excuse."

"Then why didn't you have a party for your friends?"

"She would have said it was too expensive. This is one of our big Family Charades. You'll see, she and Dad will be thrilled."

Jill sat down on the kitchen chair. She had been feeling faint

128

lately, spots in front of her eyes, periods of nausea and lassitude. She didn't like the way she felt, not at all.

"You look kind of green," Stacey said. "Are you all right?"

Jill bit her lip. "It'll pass. Get me a glass of bottled water from the fridge, please."

Stacey brought it at a run. Jill drank a little and felt like throwing up. She felt cold sweat breaking out on her face and running down her sides. "I'd say it was something you ate," Stacey said, "but seeing as it's you, it's probably something you didn't eat."

"I wonder if I have cancer," Jill said.

"Cancer! It's either the twenty-four-hour virus or starvation. Or both."

"The family doctor."

"If you can just make it to Halloween, kid, we can send you out trick-or-treating as a skeleton."

"Har-de-har-har," Jill said. She was feeling a little better. She wiped her forehead with the back of her hand and was surprised to find her hair was wet. Her forehead felt cold, no fever, far from it. Her hand was cold too. Her fingernails looked bluish under the fluorescent kitchen light. She hoped she could make it through dinner. The kitchen clock said a quarter past six. Her mother wasn't home yet, and her father was taking a shower, planning to get all dressed up. Stacey had started washing the salad greens, casting Jill anxious looks.

"You look lousy," Stacey said. "I wonder what your blood pressure is."

"Don't you have a little set in your room?"

"I bet your blood sugar's low too."

"Well, I'll tell you what, Stace. When I die you can do the autopsy."

"I'll use this," Stacey said, waving the kitchen knife and grinning. "But wait till after dinner, I need it."

Their father came into the kitchen dressed in clean slacks and a clean sports shirt and smelling of pine. He beamed at the two girls. What a domestic scene, Jill thought in disgust. Stacey's ass-kissing, I'm dying, Dad's putting on his act, and Mom's out with her lay. I wonder if she'll even remember to come home for dinner.

Ellen came home at half past six. She went directly to her bedroom, then to the bathroom, took a shower, and came into the kitchen in her bathrobe. "What are we wearing tonight?" she asked cheerily. "Well, Hank, don't you look nice. I guess I'll wear pants, then," and she went into her bedroom without waiting for anyone to answer her.

Hank mixed some Bloody Marys and took one to the bedroom for Ellen and one for himself. Jill was still sitting on the kitchen chair like a lump. She didn't think she could work up the strength to stand.

"I'm going to change my clothes," Stacey said. "Jill, will you watch the chicken? Take it out when the timer rings. Jill?"

"I heard you."

"If it burns, it's your fault. If the timer doesn't work—and it sometimes doesn't—take it out at seven fifteen. Jill?"

"Yes."

"When the little hand is on the seven and the big hand is on the three."

"Up yours."

"I'll hurry, and then you can get dressed. Unless you plan to remain like that."

"Stacey," Jill said, "I can just see it now. You're going to grow up to be somebody's mother."

"Up *yours*."

"I haven't got one."

Jill heard Stacey's radio playing her favorite country music and wondered which of her sister's collection of T-shirts with things written on them they were going to be honored with tonight. The sound of the music kept going in and out. She felt as if the chair was very gently rocking. Her body felt very heavy, endlessly heavy, so heavy she couldn't move it, drawn inexorably toward the ground. She weighed a thousand million pounds, a stone body, paralyzed. When she hit the floor she didn't even feel it.

SHE CAME TO in what felt like a car, but she fell asleep, and when she came to again she was lying in a bed in a strange room. One of her arms was strapped to a board and there was a needle taped into the big vein in the arm; tubing ran from the needle to a big bottle hanging above her on a steel stand. Her arm vein hurt like hell. There was a buzzer taped to the pillow. She rang it with her free hand. Hospital. Now, which hospital, and where?

A nurse came in and smiled when she saw Jill was awake. "How do you feel?"

"I have a headache."

"Well, you hit your head when you fell. You had three stitches, but the doctor says there won't be any scar. You're a lucky girl."

Jill felt her head with her free hand. There was a bandage going diagonally across her eyebrow. "Where's my family?"

"They're waiting outside. I'll send them in."

"What hospital is this?"

"Payne Whitney."

"The *nut* place?"

The nurse never lost her plastered-on smile. She looked like the girl on the Burger King commercial. "Now, you don't think you're a nut, do you?"

"No, I don't. So why am I here?"

"You're very lucky to be here," the nurse said, and strode out of the room, returning quickly with Jill's parents and Stacey. Ellen looked as if she had been crying, and she rushed over and hugged and kissed Jill, which made Jill cringe. Her father gave her a fake hearty smile and took her hand in his big nice hand. Stacey of course was inspecting the paraphernalia that they'd attached to Jill while she was asleep.

"You have a catheter," Stacey said triumphantly. Jill followed Stacey's glance to the floor where a bottle stood, partly filled with urine, with a tube coming out of it which—she discovered with a twinge when she tried to move—was attached to her insides. She felt like a piece of meat. Her eyes filled with tears.

131

"Now that you're awake we can take that out," the nurse said cheerfully. "Would you turn around please, Mr. Rennie?" Her father turned his back and the nurse whisked the tube out of Jill and collected the bottle. "But, Jill, you have to use the tin cup in the bathroom, not the toilet, because we have to measure everything that comes out of you. Ring for the nurse whenever you have to go to the bathroom. Don't go by yourself. You might fall down."

Jill looked at the bottle on the stand attached to her arm. "What about that thing?"

"Oh, it goes with you. On wheels."

"What do you mean, 'goes with me'? For how long?"

"Until we get you up to eighty-five pounds or you start to eat by yourself, whichever comes first."

"Oh, my God. It's the Chinese water torture."

The nurse directed her endless smile to the other members of the family and left the room. Ellen was stroking Jill's head. Jill wished her mother would take her paws off her. She wondered how long she had been here. It couldn't have been long, there weren't any flowers in the room, also no TV, and her father was wearing the same outfit he'd had on for her mother's birthday dinner. Oh, God, the birthday dinner!

"Gee, Mom," Jill said, "I must have spoiled your birthday."

"What birthday?" her mother said cheerily. "I'm still thirty-nine."

"I'm sorry I got sick."

"You just get well," her father said. "That's all we want."

"How long do I have to stay here?"

"A couple of weeks," her mother said.

"Well, we can't afford it," Jill said. "I'll eat at home."

"Nobody trusts you any more, Jill," her mother said.

"Thanks."

"This time you're going to get well," her mother went on. "Your father and I have all kinds of health insurance. In fact, since you have to be in the hospital a couple of weeks, we were lucky enough to get you transferred to the Payne Whitney branch in the country. It's very pretty there, just like a college campus. They have tennis courts, and trees—"

"Who do I play tennis with, other loonies?"

"There will be a doctor to talk to you every day and find out why you have this obsession with being thin. You'll work it all out. You'll see, everything will be fine."

"We'll visit you all the time," Stacey said. "It's near."

"And," her mother finished triumphantly, "I had a plastic surgeon sew up that cut. You won't even be able to see the scar."

I'm sure that was the first thing she thought of, Jill thought. Don't let my beautiful daughter have a scar on her face. Anything that came out of me has to be perfect.

"My arm hurts," Jill said. "Make the doctor take this thing out. It really hurts."

Her father looked for a moment as if he were going to lose his composure entirely and burst into tears. Then he collected himself and rang the buzzer. When the nurse finally came he said, "My daughter says she's hungry."

"Wonderful!" the nurse said. She scooted away and returned with a tray on which were a little paper cup of custard and a spoon. Just like room service. She cranked up the bed and put the food on the bedside table which she pushed across Jill's lap.

"I am left-handed," Jill said. "I can't eat that unless you take the splint off my arm."

The nurse peered at her suspiciously. "She is left-handed," Jill's mother said.

"I'll have to ask the doctor."

"So ask him," Jill said.

"You're bargaining with me," the nurse said.

"What's the difference?" Jill said. "If I eat we both win."

The nurse left the room and returned carrying a tray with Band-Aids, cotton, and something in a bottle that looked like alcohol. She unhooked Jill from the torture machine, swabbed her arm, and slapped a Band-Aid on the hole. Jill could see a bruise even outside the bandage. She shook her left hand, which felt weird, and took the spoon. They were all watching her. They

133

looked like a bunch of idiots. She took a spoonful of the custard, which was surprisingly tasteless, and swallowed it. She nearly gagged but suppressed the feeling until it went away. This isn't food, she told herself. It doesn't look like food. It certainly doesn't taste like food.

They all hung around until she had finished the custard and drunk a glass of water, and then they hung around some more to make sure she wouldn't throw up. Jill had no intention of throwing up. She was going to be a saint in this hospital and also in the loony place in the country, and as soon as she got to be whatever they considered well, they would let her out. The doctors wouldn't let her blow up into an enormous freak, a fat balloon. She'd be safe. Then she could be free to resume her normal life. She would tell the doctor whatever he wanted to hear. Maybe she would tell him she wanted to be a model. He would believe that. And he would have to let her out while she was still slender. Nobody ever heard of a fat model. She wished she was old enough to get her own apartment, to make some money. It was hell to be trapped with your family, at their mercy. They were trying to take over her last private thing, her own body. She would never let them have it. She was smarter than they were, even though they had the power. Jill knew she would win.

For the second time that week Kerry didn't come home for dinner. Margot had rushed back to her apartment from the studio the minute she got off the air, started cooking, bathed, put on something nice and sexy, and then waited. She played his favorite records, drank a few glasses of wine, called her answering service twice more in case they'd made a mistake the first time when they said no one had called, and waited. She phoned his apartment. No answer. She turned down the heat under the blanquette de veau so it wouldn't get overcooked, phoned Kerry's apartment again, and finished the bottle of wine. She hated stew, she was making it only because it was the one thing she could think of that wouldn't get ruined if he was late. She could have made a

134

steak, of course, but it smelled up the apartment and that wasn't very romantic. She had the air conditioners on in both rooms and was burning scented candles. Lily of the valley, because it was June. It smelled like cheap lollipops, and she blew out the candles.

She wanted to call someone, to have someone to talk to because she was lonely and frightened, but she didn't want to tie up the phone. Why the hell hadn't she gotten two lines? Too cheap, that's why, knowing her friends could call her at the office where there were a million lines, all free. Even through all these years of being self-supporting she had never quite gotten over the first fear she'd had of being broke. It had amazed her to be making what her father proudly called "as much money as a man," but she kept worrying that her luck would go away. So one minute she was extravagant, giving Ellen that Gucci bag for instance, at over a hundred dollars, when Ellen would probably have preferred a gift certificate to a gourmet shop so her family could at least eat. And the next minute she was stupidly economical, not getting two phone numbers. She was trapped here, waiting for Kerry to appear or to call, and knowing in her heart he wouldn't call, that he would show up when he was ready and not a minute before. There was no point in being angry about the phone, she should have been angry about her choice of man.

Margot was getting furious. She opened another bottle of wine. She'd lost weight from nervousness since knowing Kerry, so she could drink as much as she wanted to tonight. If she got drunk maybe she would tell him exactly what an inconsiderate little pig he was. He had no right to treat her as if she were nothing. Who was he anyway? Just a kid, with an unpublished novel he'd never even let her read. Maybe it was callow, narcissistic, like its author. She was sure it was. His influential father had probably gotten the publisher to give the kid a contract and a token advance as a favor. The publisher probably thought Lawrence Fowler would buy ten thousand copies and warehouse them, give them away for Christmas presents; he could afford to. Little brat. Why didn't he come home? He knew damn well she was doing the eleven o'clock news all next week as well as the early evening news and they wouldn't be able to have a decent evening together. This week was supposed to be special. He could fool around next week. Where was he that was more important than being here?

It was half past ten and Margot was pacing around the apartment like a caged animal. She wasn't even hungry, just high and furious, but not so drunk that she wasn't still in control of herself. She wouldn't yell at him, she would just tell him calmly what her needs were and why he was being unfair. He would apologize as he always did, but this time she wouldn't let him win her over. She would make him know how she felt. He really didn't have any idea, his apologies were just part of his easy charm.

A quarter to twelve. She heard his key in the lock and her heart turned over. She had been afraid he was dead. She remembered when she'd been a little girl and her parents had left her alone at night with the maid, or a cousin, or some adult they could scrounge up. Margot, the good little girl, had lain in her bed as still as a mummy, in a sweat, sleepless, until the moment she heard that key in the lock. It had sounded as loud as a shot, echoing through the entire silent apartment. She had sighed blissfully at the first murmur of her parents' hushed voices, and was asleep before they even got into her room to look.

"Kerry!"

"Hello, love." He looked calm and fresh, not even sorry. "I smell something burning."

"The veal," she said dully. She just didn't want to be alone. How could you say that to someone? It was the worst thing you could say, because then he'd tell you to find someone else.

He went into the kitchen, peered into the casserole, and turned off the flame. "It's saved," he said. "We just won't scrape the bottom. Sorry I'm late."

"Oh, you noticed."

"I'm sorry. I was helping a friend move into his apartment. I know I should have called, but he didn't have his phone yet."

"I don't believe you."

"You don't have to," he said sweetly. He hung his jacket in the bedroom closet and then came over to her and rumpled up her hair. "You look cute."

"I'm very angry," Margot said. "You are very inconsiderate and I don't like it."

"Oh," he said. "I guess I am. You know what I'm like, I forget normal things. I'm not good at domestic arrangements. Is there any wine?"

She gestured to it instead of rushing to pour him a glass, the way she usually did, his geisha. "It's quite good," she said. She was afraid to carry the fight further, but she wasn't ready to make up with him either.

Kerry poured himself a glass of wine and came to sit down next to her on the floor. *Not good at domestic arrangements,* she thought. He doesn't even need a chair. He doesn't need food. He doesn't need me. He sipped the wine and gave her a sad, sweet smile.

"You're so angry, aren't you, love?" he said.

She shrugged.

"I have to tell you," he said. "I want to move back to my own apartment. I have to be free. I want to see other girls. Other people. I want to be alone."

She felt as if all the little cuts from all the years of hurts inflicted had opened up again. She'd thought they were healed. They were as fresh and burning as if no time had passed at all for mercy. She could hardly breathe.

"We'll still see each other," Kerry went on. "We'll date every so often—I do love you, you know, and I want to keep seeing you."

"Date?" Margot breathed. She wanted to punch him in the mouth, to draw blood.

"We're friends, aren't we?" he said.

"Friends? You wouldn't know what a friend is!"

"I'll be a good friend, you'll see." He smiled at her, that old winning smile he was so sure of. "I'll build you new bookcases."

"When did you want to leave?"

"Well, we might as well have dinner and spend the evening together. What's left of it. It'll be good for you to talk—you'll get all your feelings out and then you won't be mad at me. You can tell me what a rat I am. And then tomorrow morning I'll get my stuff out of here."

"Tomorrow morning?" she said.

"Well, it's late already. If you want, I can sleep on the couch."

"And then you'll leave, because it's more convenient in the morning. It always has to be what's convenient for you, doesn't it?"

"I'm a terrible, selfish person," Kerry said calmly.

"So am I. I want you to leave now."

"Now?"

"Right now." She stood up, her arms spread wide, thinking she probably looked like an avenging witch. "Get out!" she screamed at him. "Get your things now and get out!"

Don't leave me, she wanted to say. She was thinking it so strongly she couldn't understand why he didn't hear her. *Don't go, don't leave me, take it all back, you didn't say it.*

"Look, if you want I can just go, and then tomorrow I can come take my stuff while you're out. We'll set a time. I'll leave my key on the dresser."

Maybe he's changing his mind. She looked at him, trying to see behind those cool eyes. "Look," she said, "you're free now. You come and go as you please. You have a key. Let's talk about it a little bit."

"I should have gone a couple of weeks ago," Kerry said. "I wanted to tell you. If I had moved out when I wanted to then, I wouldn't have caused you all this pain by being late and forgetting things. It would have been better for both of us."

"Is there someone new?" She could have killed herself for asking it, it wasn't part of the game. He shook his head, no.

"I just can't be tied down, Margot. I have to be on my own." He went into the bedroom and began gathering the few things he had left in her apartment. She realized how few they actually were. The silk robe she had bought for him, a pair of jeans, some shirts and sweaters. He didn't even wear underwear. He went into the bathroom and took his toothbrush. He had always used her comb and brush, a habit she had deplored, but now she would do anything to have him back using them again. He dropped his razor into the wastebasket. It was one of those plastic razors that came free with a package of blades. She wondered if he had bought it on purpose to be temporary. The only reason he had bought it at all was that when *he* used *her* razor he complained she made the blade dull.

He tossed everything into a shopping bag he found in the kitchen. She watched him, pacing around after him, biting her nails until they hurt. When he had packed, he took his key—her key—off his key chain and put it on the dresser. Then he went up to her and put his hands on her shoulders, looking down into her face.

"I want you to know, Margot, that no woman has attracted me as much as you have. Ever."

She didn't say anything. He left. She listened until she heard the elevator door close after him, and then she locked and bolted her apartment door, went into the bedroom closet, shut the door, sat down on the floor, and screamed and screamed until she was completely hoarse.

JULY

July 1975

RACHEL FOWLER LIKED spending summer weekends at her house in East Hampton. It was casual, and everything smelled so good—the air, the ocean, her skin warm from the sun. She avoided getting sun on her face now, had for several years, because she was afraid of wrinkles, but she let her body in a string bikini get as tan as it could. She swam in her pool, never in the ocean, and she wore a bathing cap and kept her head out of the water. She wasn't going to negate those boring three hours she spent every month at the hairdresser's getting the proper amount of sun streaks put into her hair. Lawrence found sitting in the sun a total waste of time. He sat there, but he surrounded himself with books and papers. He did, however, turn from time to time to get an even tan. It delighted Rachel to see that he was just as vain as anybody else, it made him more vulnerable and lovable.

Kerry came for the weekend sometimes. He had a new girl. It surprised Rachel that he had gone on to one girl so quickly after breaking up with Margot. He always wanted what he couldn't have. Perhaps he couldn't quite win this new girl over yet, and that was why he lavished so much attention on her. She was a black model—beige, really—only twenty, and beautiful. She was so tall and thin that Rachel thought she was probably part Watusi. She made a hundred dollars an hour. Her name was Haviland.

"Haviland!" Kerry had said the first time he met her. "What kind of a name is that?"

"My mother read it off the bottom of a plate she was washing," she said calmly, and then she laughed at him.

Poor Margot. Rachel and Lawrence were giving a big party over the July Fourth weekend, and they were inviting Kerry (with his girl) and Margot. Rachel hoped it wouldn't be horrible for Margot. She couldn't leave out either of them, and Kerry had said he wouldn't come without Haviland.

Nikki and Robert were coming to stay at Rachel's house for the entire weekend. Rachel wanted Lawrence and Robert to become good friends so the four of them could go out together. It was so nice to have her best friend there for the whole long weekend, she could hardly wait. It made her feel warm and happy to think of Nikki. It was like having a sister but without the sibling rivalry. In preparation for college that fall Rachel had started reading psychology books, thinking she might take psych as another course. There were so many things she'd never even known she was interested in. She had been accepted by NYU, and so that was where she was going.

Sometimes Rachel wondered if there was more to her feelings about Nikki than just sisterly love. It was almost as if she had a crush on Nikki. She was a twelve-year-old in love with the camp counselor, except that she'd never gone to camp, and now it was a little late for these feelings, wasn't it? That was the main reason Rachel had suddenly become so interested in psychology. She wanted to know more about herself. She hoped she wasn't a lesbian. If she was, would it get worse as she got older? There was one case history she'd read about a married woman with two children who ran off with another woman at the age of forty and completely changed from liking men to liking women. Could that happen to her? She couldn't imagine ever not loving her husband, but on the other hand, could she love both Nikki and Lawrence at the same time, and what was that called?

She also couldn't understand the way Nikki behaved sometimes. She was sure Nikki was straight, and yet Nikki flirted with her just as if one of them was a man. Rachel wasn't sure which one. Nikki acted like a woman flirting with a man, but at the same time she took the active role and was so much more sophisticated that Rachel sometimes thought that Nikki was the man. Did one of them have to be the man, after all? Did Nikki just flirt with her because that was the way Nikki was conditioned? Did Nikki *want* her to have a crush on her? And if so, why? Rachel didn't dare discuss any of this with Nikki for fear of being rejected, so she just kept buying psychology books, hoping to find herself in one of them.

Nikki's daughter Dorothy worked in the mental hospital where Ellen Rennie had sent her anorexic daughter. Poor Ellen. Rachel had invited Ellen and Hank to the party too. It must be so awful for Ellen to have her daughter in a mental hospital, even though it was only for a month. Rachel thought Ellen was probably blaming herself. You always did, even when it wasn't your fault. Ellen had sent her younger daughter off for the annual visit to Grandma. Rachel wondered if the little kid felt rejected. And poor Hank's business was still doing so badly. Everyone had thought summer would be a better time for people to buy cars, but almost nobody bought Hank's big cars. Rachel thought even she, dumb as she was, could have told him that and warned him. But she never talked business with the men at parties, especially if she was going to have to tell one of them that he was doing something wrong.

Now, for the first time in so long, Rachel woke up every morning with the feeling that there was something to look forward to besides dinner. Knowing she was going to be working hard in the fall made the leisure of this summer suddenly precious. She had her books and her friends and all her new interests. Best of all, she had her thoughts. Sometimes something she read made her just sit and think for so long she lost track of time. Nobody had ever told her that was what education was for—to make you think. She'd had lousy teachers. Maybe after she'd gotten her college degree, if she wasn't too ancient, she would take some education courses and get a job teaching little kids. Delusions of grandeur! But why not? Lawrence was a self-made man. She would become a self-made woman.

THE PARTY WAS ON SATURDAY NIGHT. Margot and Ellen and Hank had taken rooms in a beach-front motel. Ellen had worried about the expense of the one night, but then she thought that having to drive all the way back to New York at four o'clock in the morning with a probably drunken husband was worse than the expense of the room. It would be good for Margot to get away too, although Margot was so odd lately that she didn't want to go at all until Ellen talked her into it. It was as if Margot had withdrawn from all of them. There was an icy shell around her now and she never had a kind word to say about anybody. It was ridiculous to let a man get to you that way. Ellen had told her so, and Margot had nodded grimly. Especially, Ellen had added, a man you knew in the first place was going to turn out to be temporary.

"It's not Kerry," Margot had said. "I hate him. I feel nothing for him."

"Then why are you so depressed?"

"Because when you've lived with someone for a while you get used to it, and then when he isn't there any more it's worse than you remembered it was."

"I'd be thrilled to be alone," Ellen said. "With the girls away, I keep thinking how nice it would be if Hank decided to take a little vacation by himself."

"So you could call your lover to come running over," Margot said. "Ellen, you have no idea what it's like to be alone. No idea at all."

146

MARGOT DID NOT LIKE THE HAMPTONS. She had grown to hate any place where youth and beauty were all-important. Any town near a beach, where people took their clothes off for all the world to look at their bodies and pass judgment, where lithe, tanned young girls had taken her place, depressed her. She liked her office, her work, the camera where she was queen if only for two minutes. She liked to sit in New York restaurants in clothes. She didn't want to be judged as merchandise. It wasn't that she couldn't go out on the beach in a string bikini with those kids, it was that she resented it. She knew her bustline was a little lower than it was ten years ago, and still lower than those girls' bee bites, but what made it difficult was that the men cared. Why should a woman be dismissed as a sexual partner just because she had a little cellulite on her upper thighs? What was so perfect about being perfect? When she was twenty, boys her age had resented her because she was bright and ambitious; now men her age rejected her because she was too old. What made them good enough to dare reject her at all?

Tennis bored her. She was bored with people who talked about tennis all day when they weren't playing it. Who wanted one big arm? Margot was a city person, and she swam basically as a means of getting cool when air conditioning was not available, not because she enjoyed the sport. In college she had played bridge, but she hadn't played for years and had forgotten how. In fact, she couldn't think of any pastime involving more than one person that she enjoyed except for talking and sex. Most talking smacked more of games than she liked. Her plans for the July Fourth weekend consisted of making a token appearance at Rachel's party, getting drunk, and hoping the whole weekend would be over with as quickly as possible. The only reason Margot was going at all was that the thought of being all alone in New York with no one to talk to frightened her more than the thought of being inspected and rejected by jerks.

She couldn't get it out of her mind that Kerry had left her because she was too old. If she had been of his generation she would have known how to keep him. But why, when she had never known how to keep any man of her own generation? Maybe she should have gotten married. Then she would have some man who was stuck with her, no matter how much they hated each other. Would that be better than loneliness? Was it better for Ellen? No, Margot thought, I'm honest and she's not. Ellen *likes* subterfuge, she thinks it's dramatic. I haven't got time, and it bores me to play games.

The Fowlers lived in a huge house on a dune, set far enough back from the sea so that beach erosion could never threaten them. They had a clear view and many glass walls with sliding panels. They had a heated pool. But best of all, they had a lawn covered with marble statues: fauns, cherubs, gargoyles, sundials, silver balls on cement pedestals, each different, so many that it was completely camp. It was a joke they enjoyed and shared with their friends. Among the statues were trees and bushes and flower beds, small tables with chairs set under gaily striped umbrellas, all with the sea breeze blowing gently. It was perfect for a party and a perfect place to get drunk.

The party started at six with cocktails. This year Rachel was being reverse chic and having a cookout—hot dogs and hamburgers and jug wine. She even had throwaway plastic glasses. The bartender was about nineteen and very attractive, Margot noted, and also not gay. Local talent making money on his summer vacation, or someone's son. But wasn't every man someone's son? She had to start thinking of them as people. If I don't stop this tendency, Margot thought, taking a glass of wine from the bartender and smiling at him, some day I can be a very old lady having a reunion of all my young men, like that movie about the governess, where they all show up with their wives and their baby pictures, and they tell her how they always remembered her. I must not get depressed. The bartender doesn't interest me. A smile does not a flirtation make.

Margot wandered around the lawn looking at the guests. Why did those beautiful young girls look at those ugly old men with

148

such admiration? Was it real or just charm? There were the divorced women, the ones who hadn't found lovers yet, sitting with each other and looking at the people who had someone with undisguised envy. I envy no one, Margot thought. I hate everybody.

She noticed that Ellen hadn't unloaded Hank yet. Ellen must be more in love with Reuben than she had been with her previous lovers, Margot thought. Staying by Hank's side was her way of being faithful to Reuben. Hank, on the other hand, seemed to have a straying eye. Margot wondered what he'd ever do if he found someone he liked. Stammer and spill a drink on her probably. Mr. Charm.

Lawrence and Nikki's husband, Robert, were in deep conversation. Rachel was wafting around being sweet to people. She had it timed so well—two minutes to each guest—that Margot thought Rachel could get a job in the control room. She wouldn't even have to look at the clock. Margot had a few more glasses of wine, nibbled on a carrot stick, and looked around to see if any of the men, even one, even a definite loser, seemed mildly interested in her. She might as well have been invisible. There were too many people and too much competition. Rachel loved having young, beautiful people at her parties along with the older ones she and Lawrence really liked; she arranged them the same way she arranged flowers: *this* would go well here. There was rock music coming out of the speakers outside the house, and the young, beautiful people were ignoring it because this year you didn't dance. This year you were cool. Margot counted the number of long skirts versus the number of pants on the women, and then counted the number of women who hadn't shaved under their arms for at least two weeks. That meant they had nobody. If they shaved, or if they'd never shaved and had long, virgin hair under their arms, it meant they liked it that way or someone else did. She listened in on conversations and drank, feeling like Invisible Scarlett O'Neill of her childhood comic-book days.

"Who are you staying with? Oh, I'm staying with them next weekend."

What jockeying for weekend beds there must be among the

homeless! What lust for a flow of weekend guests among the house owners and renters, with their lists and their plans! What would happen if it rained and one had asked no guests? Why did city people go crazy for two months every summer?

And then Margot saw Kerry. He was just coming out of the house, holding on to the tiny wrist of a very tall, very beautiful, very young black girl. They were both wearing faded jeans and tacky-looking T-shirts. The girl had her sandals attached to her belt loop, and no handbag. Margot had known he was going to be there, but seeing him for the first time since that awful night when he'd left her was like a physical blow. She felt personally insulted just looking at his radiant, handsome face. He didn't see her. He was too busy arguing with the girl. There were a lot of people on the terrace and Margot drifted along behind them, not too close but close enough to hear.

"*Why* can't you stay all weekend?" Kerry was saying.

"I have a date in the city tonight." The girl had the calmest voice Margot had ever heard. Not flat, just nonchalant.

"You came here with me for the party. We agreed."

"I'm *at* the party."

"Is he going to wait for you?"

The girl shrugged. "His show isn't over till eleven."

"It is still him. I thought you gave him up."

She just looked at him. That girl has cat eyes too, Margot thought. She and Kerry, two cats. He was trembling, with anger or frustration Margot couldn't be sure. She only knew she had never aroused such emotion in him.

"If you're living with me," Kerry said, "I don't want you going out with other guys."

"That's the way I am," the girl said calmly. "I have to be free."

She's living with *him*? Margot felt such pain she wasn't even sure where it came from; it was just an all-inclusive agony. *Kerry never asked me to live with him. He visited me. I chased him. He's chasing her. I made a fool of myself.*

Margot fled into the house. It was cool there and she wanted to die. She went into Rachel's bathroom and looked in the medicine

150

chest for sleeping pills. Nothing. Some tranquilizers that wouldn't work on a baby. A razor, she could cut her neck vein, the large one that stuck out when she lost her temper. She could lie in a warm bath and bleed until she was unconscious and then just slip into the water and drown. The epiglottis closes and they don't even find any water in the lungs. Wouldn't you know Rachel used an electric razor? God forbid she should nick her equipment. Margot walked slowly out of the house again and, passing the bar, picked up a glass and a nearly full jug of white wine. Swinging it nonchalantly from one finger by its loop handle she strolled down to the beach. It was getting dark. People were shapes, not the distinguishable person of the enemy. Just lumps making noise. She sat down at the edge of the sea, tucked her long skirt around her legs against the chill, and poured a glass of wine. She set the jug firmly in the sand just where the water lapped at it and kept it cool. Behind her, far up at the house, they were lighting the charcoal grills for the meat. She could smell the smoke and it reminded her of summers long ago when she was young and happy, when evenings like this were challenges instead of defeats. In those days she never knew what adventure would come next. Now she knew only that there would be no more adventure. She would always be alone. It was inevitable that she be alone and lonely, but not inevitable that it be always. She could kill herself if she wanted to. She could sit here and drink until it was completely dark and she was completely plastered, and then she could walk out into the ocean and let it take her. No one would even know. They would think she had gone for a swim to sober up. She would never have to bear the ultimate humiliation of having Kerry know she had nothing at all to live for.

RACHEL SET HER GLASS DOWN to greet a friend, and when she turned around again the glass was gone. It annoyed her because it was the third time that had happened this evening. She was sorry she had gotten plastic glasses in the first place. Whoever was grabbing them for the trash was overzealous, particularly

151

since hers hadn't been empty yet. When you were rich, people thought nothing of wasting your things. Now she'd have to go back to the bar and get another glass of wine or have someone get her one. If she could just catch whichever one of the help was carting things off so fast . . . She looked around. It was odd that other people didn't seem to be losing their glasses. On tables, all around, there were partly finished drinks, even full ashtrays. Rachel didn't approve of the full ashtrays. She went over to one of the boys she'd hired for the evening and asked him in her soft, sweet voice to clean up a little, particularly cigarette butts. Then she went to the bar, checked the ice and the wine, the sodas and fruit juices and diet drinks, to make sure enough was set out. The pleasant young bartender smiled at her.

"Lost your glass again, Mrs. Fowler?"

"You noticed."

"People must really be having a good time." He gave her a fresh glass and filled it with wine and ice.

Maybe it was a guest picking up the wrong drink, Rachel thought. But, then, why wasn't the guest's drink left instead? What's so special about mine?

She felt a strange, creepy feeling of warning, and she didn't know what it was. For the first time in her life she didn't feel comfortable in her own house. It was a lack of control, as if she'd been invaded by something or someone, as if she were only another guest here in this mob of people. She wondered why she had invited them all here anyway. Some of them she hardly knew, some she didn't really like. She just thought she was the hostess, but in truth the party itself had taken over, like a great monster with a life of its own.

You COULD ALMOST SEE Rachel's body through her dress, and he couldn't decide if he was glad or angry. He wondered what her husband felt about all the men at this party being able to look at Rachel's body and have fantasies. Or was he the only one who felt as if he were touching her just by looking at her? He wanted her.

152

It was painful being so close to her after all those frenzied hours of following her in the streets of the city. She had spoken to him tonight, she had touched his arm lightly in greeting and then had turned to his wife with the same warmth; they were all the same to Rachel, he was not really a man to her.

He watched her mouth moving as she spoke to guests too far away for him to hear the words, he imagined that soft mouth moving on his. Other guests even kissed her hello; why couldn't he? He was afraid to touch her because his dream of her was so close to the surface of his everyday life now that he didn't know how he could be able to control himself if once he touched her. He must not let himself be alone with her here, even though it would be easy. He who had followed her silently and unseen through miles of city streets could easily corner her in this house, tear off that indecent dress, and plunge into her flesh, fill her, bite and bruise her, and then tenderly kiss the ravaged goddess.

He was sane enough to know that witnesses were too close. He held himself in tight control, drinking a little to calm himself but not too much, thankful that all the people at this party were so busy trying to put forth a good impression that they had not the slightest interest in watching anyone else. After a while he felt free enough to wander about, speaking to a few people, moving on before he got trapped in a boring conversation, watching Rachel all the time. He was getting a pounding headache. She took little sips from her glass of wine, leaving the mark of her mouth on the plastic. Even a cheap bit of synthetic from the five-and-ten felt the intimate touch of her lips, but not he. She put her glass down on a table and held her hands out to two friends. He was behind her in a flash and took the glass, turning away quickly. Casually, as if he were just carrying two drinks to friends, he took Rachel's glass and his own to the end of the terrace. He left his on a table among the party debris. He held her glass to his lips, his mouth on the place her mouth had touched, tasting her lipstick, imagining he tasted the inside of her lips.

He had to step off the terrace then, into the safe darkness of the bushes. No one could see him. Perhaps the landscape architect had arranged these bushes so lovers could hide in their shadow and kiss. He kissed Rachel's lips on her plastic glass and opened his fly.

He came with such force that he shuddered. The sea breeze felt cold on his neck. He fantasized that from the place on her lawn where he had spilled his seed a phantasmagoric Rachel grew like a flower bush. He was a part of her life now, whether she knew it or not. He tossed away the glass. He had used it, so it was defiled. He zipped up his pants, wiped the perspiration off his face with his handkerchief, and went back to the party.

He didn't realize that his need to take these glasses she had kissed was so insatiable until he had taken another, and then a third. Three times in the bushes he shuddered with his lips on the echo of hers and his hand on his aching and hated cock. He felt completely drained. But oddly, he did not feel his usual guilt. It was as if at last the guilt had died. He felt instead the beginning of another emotion, one that he could not understand at all, because it was directed toward Rachel instead of toward himself.

It was anger.

On the beach, alone, Margot finished the jug of wine and lay numbly in the wash of the tide. The ocean had been rising. The water shot bubbling and stinging along her legs, above her waist into the wet sand, and then receded. Up and down, up and down, the tide was like ruffles all along the length of the beach in the moonlight. It took the empty jug and pulled it a little way toward the ocean, then gave up, playing with it, not strong enough yet to draw it away forever. She nudged the jug with her toe and it turned over. The water swirled around it, splashed over it, flashed along her body to her breasts, and went away again. The edges of her hair were all wet. She had to decide: get up and swim out to sea or give up the idea. If she just lay where she was, all she would get would be a nose full of sandy salt water.

She flopped over onto her stomach, her crossed arms holding her face up from the sand. She felt so heavy—wet, sand-covered, and drunk, not quite sure why she had wanted to kill herself but not entirely sure either that she didn't want to. It would be nice just to go to sleep for a long, long time, and wake up not remembering anything that had ever hurt. She opened her legs and let the surf pour up between them. It felt good, sensual. She would have loved to take off her underpants but she was too lazy.

A man was walking along the beach. She watched him coming closer and saw that he was tallish, with a nice body, young, and carrying something in his hand. When he came nearer she saw that he was the bartender, and he was carrying a can of beer. He was barefoot. He had seen her and was coming to investigate.

"Well, hi," he said.

"Hi."

"What are you doing in the water?"

"What are you doing away from the bar?"

"It's my break," he said.

"This is *my* break."

"Is it fun?" he asked. He was completely cool, noncommittal. Not making fun of her, not boyishly curious, nothing.

"The sea is my lover," Margot said. "But he runs out on me." She laughed.

He took off his clothes. He was wearing a tiny bikini thing underneath. It wasn't fair. He folded his pants and shirt neatly and laid them on top of a sand dune away from the water. He crumpled the empty beer can in his hand, the way he'd probably seen done on television, and tossed it away. Then he stood over her and looked her over curiously, as if she were something the ocean had tossed up. Which would he find her, mermaid or walrus?

"Do you want to go swimming?" he asked.

"No."

"You ought to get that sand off your dress. Why don't you take your clothes off and we'll wash them?"

That seemed sensible. "Unzip me," Margot said.

He helped her take off her long dress, which was heavy with sea water and sand, and then he dove neatly into a wave, carrying the fabric in his hand like a taper so she could still find him in the dark. His body was all tanned and disappeared in the deep water, but she could see his head bobbing as he swam back to her. He stood on the shore wringing out her dress, and then he shook it. It flapped with a snapping sound in the breeze. Then he laid her dress neatly on the stiff grass on top of the dune where he had put his clothes. Margot wondered why he was being so nice to her. She stood up and walked into the water. It was very cold. She waited until the sequence of big waves had paused and then ran out to shoulder high water and paddled around until her skin felt smooth again. She lay back and let the water fan out her sandy hair, cleansing it. Later it would be gummy and salty, but there was no later. A wave crashed down on her, knocking her under, spewing sea water into her mouth, and she threw up. Then she started to cry. She cried and cried at the same time she was trying to struggle back to shore in the knee-high surf, until she felt his arm around her, and then he picked her up and carried her back to the dune.

He had hidden a towel there. They lay on it and he showed her his supplies: two more cans of beer with pop tops, a package of breath mints, a half-empty pack of menthol cigarettes, a butane lighter, and a metal comb. He was just like a little kid running away from home for an hour with his treasures. Margot stopped sniffling and smiled at him. He smiled back, and then he offered her a cigarette, which she refused, and a can of beer, which she accepted. She decided he was adorable. When he kissed her she took off her bra and pants and tossed them away and then they made love.

NIKKI WAS ABSOLUTELY DELIGHTED with this party, with the whole weekend. When she saw Margot come straggling in, looking as if she'd gone swimming in her clothes, and like the cat that had swallowed the canary, she was very pleased. She looked around for an equally wet and scruffy man, but whoever he was obviously had entered the house more subtly. Maybe somebody's husband, Nikki thought. I hope not mine. She giggled at the thought of Robert cheating with anyone, especially her good friend, because it was so totally ludicrous. She was lucky he'd never cheated. He'd even sat next to her at dinner, which was thoughtful. She found him easily in the thinning crowd and put her head on his shoulder.

"Wanna get laid?" she said.

"Always," he said.

"I have an idea."

"What?"

"We'll leave early tomorrow and you drive me to New York. We'll go to my apartment and christen the bed."

He drew away from her. "I despise women who use sex to bargain," he said angrily.

"I'm not!"

"You are. You're just like the rest of them."

"Damn you, Robert!" Nikki felt tears in her eyes. "You always spoil everything."

"No, I don't," he said. "You do."

"I was having nice thoughts about you," she said. "Nice thoughts. Then you had to go and be horrible again."

"Don't do your little cry-baby trick. You go all little-girl when you want something. I'm tired of it."

"Good night, Robert," Nikki said, and went into the house, into their room, and shut the door. It was one o'clock in the morning and *that* was her bedtime. He didn't come looking for her, and she knew that he wouldn't. When finally he got into the king-sized bed that Rachel had considerately put in the best guest room, Nikki was nearly asleep from counting the sounds of departing cars instead of sheep. She looked at the clock on the night table on her side of the bed and saw that it was half past three.

"Where were you, washing the dishes?" she said.

"Good night," Robert said, and turned his back to her. He fell right asleep, and she didn't know if she was glad or sorry. She didn't know how she felt about him any more. But even though she was very angry at him, she was surprised at how easily she drifted into sleep just because he was in the bed with her. Habit was a curious thing.

The long Fourth of July weekend was over on Sunday. Ellen, Hank, and Margot left for New York just before noon, check-out time at their motel. Nobody spoke much in the car. Margot had a hangover, Hank didn't like to talk when he was driving, and Ellen got tired of chattering away to herself.

Nikki and Robert had a late brunch on the terrace with Rachel and Lawrence. The help had cleaned everything so well you wouldn't know there had been a party the night before. Robert was going to drive Nikki to Sayville and put her on the train to New York, the way they had planned. He would then go on to Wilton.

"But that's inhumane!" Rachel said. "And besides, it's the long way. You could drive her right into New York and then go up the East River Drive."

"I have a map—" Robert said.

"I'll make you a map with the shortcuts," Rachel said.

Nikki was pleased that Rachel, who was never assertive with men, was taking her side against Robert. He was so stubborn and childish. Now not only was her apartment off limits, but he had apparently decided New York was off limits too. This town ain't big enough for both of us, varmint. She stifled a giggle behind her cup of coffee.

Kerry was staying on in the house for a few days, alone except for the help. Haviland had insisted on going into New York with some people who had a car, to keep her date. He had told her to pack and be out of his apartment by the time he got back. He was gambling that she would still be there when he returned. After all, he was security against her other boyfriend, just as her boyfriend was security against him. He woke up early, had a

158

swim, and now was lying on the beach with the book review section of the *Times*.

The houseman put the Gellhorns' bags into their car. Nikki put her arms around Rachel and kissed her. "Thank you a million times. I'll call you tomorrow in the city." She was going to just shake hands with Lawrence, because he rather awed her, but he kissed her goodbye, which was a surprise. Robert did not kiss Rachel. Nikki thought he was probably annoyed that she had won what he considered a power play. Rachel and Lawrence were going to drive back after dinner to avoid the traffic. Nikki would really have liked to stay until they left, but she had to leave with her husband, it was only protocol. She realized that if she had liked Robert more today she would have felt free to tell him she would drive home with the Fowlers, but whenever she disliked him she was especially proper and nice.

Robert played the radio all the way into New York, and neither of them talked. What I really want to do when I get home, Nikki thought, is wash my hair and get into bed and watch television. I've been with so many people this weekend it'll be a relief to be alone. She supposed Robert would be secretly glad to get rid of her too.

He pulled up in front of her building, but left the motor running. "Got everything?"

"Don't you have to come up and pee or anything?"

"Nope."

"Thanks for the ride, then. I'll call you tomorrow, or you call me."

"You know I will."

"Bye." She took her suitcase and let herself into the building with her key. She took her mail from her mailbox in the tiny vestibule, and when she looked back through the iron-filigreed glass door Robert was gone. Bastard, she thought.

Nikki opened the door to her apartment, surprised she'd forgotten to double-lock it, and dropped the mail in horror. It slid across the bare floor. The place had been ransacked, torn apart, systematically robbed. She felt as if she were choking. She ran around looking at the carnage: her fur rug was gone, her color television, her cassette player, her clock radio, her blender, her toaster, her *bedspread*, goddamn them, her jewelry of course, and almost all her clothes. They had left the air conditioner because it was too heavy. That meant it was probably not a them but a he. Her burglar had come back.

Oh, how she would like to get her hands around his throat! She would kick him in the balls, she would kill him! She felt personally molested, this was *her* burglar, he had defiled *her* private life. It took her a few minutes for the realization to sink in that it was he who could have killed her.

How had he gotten in anyway? The lock on the front door was intact. The balcony, of course. The window was still open. He had come in the window, which she never locked—not that a window lock would have stopped him—and undisturbed during the long weekend exodus from this fancy neighborhood, had taken all her pawnable things out the front door. That was why it wasn't double-locked; she knew she'd double-locked it when she left.

Robert should have been here, the bastard. Then she thought about it and realized that Robert would have been so self-righteous, so smug, so hateful, insinuating that she had gotten what she deserved for leaving the nice safe country and him, that it would have been intolerable. She would never tell Robert. She wouldn't even collect the insurance—because if she did, the rates would go up, and he would find out about the robbery. She would just have to save and scrounge until she had replaced everything. Maybe she should call the cops. They might never find her things, but at least she could try. She felt so lost; there were a million things to do and she didn't want to do any of them, she just wanted to get into bed, pull the covers over her head, and cry. Why did he have to spoil her perfect apartment? She never let anyone in here unless it was a special friend. Who was this stranger who thought he owned her, who could just break in and help himself to anything he wanted? Now she would have to get an iron gate, bars, to put over her window, and then the burglars

160

would be locked out, but she would also be locked in. She might as well be in jail. Trapped. A baby in a playpen.

She called the police, and then she called the locksmith. She wasn't afraid the burglar would come back tonight. He knew she was home, that everyone who had gone away for the weekend was home or on the way. Besides, there wasn't anything else for him to take except her air conditioner and the furniture, and he would have to wait for another long weekend for those. She wasn't going anywhere. Not tonight, and not next weekend. She had rights too in this world. Nikki sat in her desecrated apartment and waited for the men in the uniforms and the man with the prison bars. She wanted a drink, but when she looked in the cabinet she saw with absolutely no surprise that the burglar had taken all her liquor too.

JILL RENNIE HAD NEVER quite gotten over her surprise that there were no bars on the windows at the mental hospital in the country and no locks on the bedroom doors. She had expected lunatics and attendants, straitjackets, all the stuff she'd seen in horror movies. But it was really a pleasant place. The kids were weird, but so were some of the "normal" kids at school. The patients here were separated according to age, sex, and degree of violence. Since she was neither violent nor suicidal she was allowed to spend her days as she pleased, provided she attended her daily session with the shrink, and let them feed her. She got regular meals, in small portions, and also a sort of milkshake they concocted with special things in it to build her up. One of the patients told her that the milkshake alone contained a thousand calories, and if you didn't drink it you went back on I.V. There had been another anorexic girl here last spring, and that's what had happened to her. The patient who told her this was a fourteen-year-old former junkie, and Jill didn't know whether to believe her or not about the calories. She damn well believed her about the I.V.

There were arts and crafts, painting, other hobbies, and sports. Jill had expected basket weaving, but there was none of that. She kept a notebook about the other patients because she thought it might make a good book some day. Most of them were upper middle class or rich. You had to be, at these prices. There were also a lot of legends, which she wrote down, about former patients. There was the girl who had swallowed ten pieces of silverware from the dining room in order to kill herself, then eaten a washcloth, and finally, when she had been very good and was declared cured, had gone to greet her happy parents in the hall, walked right past them, and jumped out the window. That window now had chicken wire in the glass.

The day after Jill arrived, an aide named Dorothy Gellhorn came to see her. Dorothy had looked her up because Jill's mother and Dorothy's mother—Nikki Gellhorn, an editor at a publishing company—were friends. Dorothy was nineteen and wanted to be a psychologist. Jill knew whenever Dorothy was trying to work on her, but she didn't mind because Dorothy was such an amateur. They became rather friendly. Dorothy always had interesting stories. Jill's favorite was the mystery murderer. The mystery murderer was a boy—or had been once—and he had killed both his parents. Since they were vastly rich and he was an only child, he had inherited their fortune, and instead of going to the state hospital for the criminally insane he was here, kept in seclusion, supported by his murdered parents' estate. He was in his forties now, supposedly. Dorothy had never seen him. No one was allowed to see him but his keeper. Jill thought he might as well be dead. But maybe he thought he was better off than when he had been living with his parents. Who was she to put down someone else's logic? She wondered if he'd planned it or if it had been done on the spur of the moment. Apparently he'd been fifteen at the time. The place where they kept him was way down at the other end of the campus, as Jill thought of it.

In return for her interesting stories Jill kept Dorothy up on what her shrink had said and what he had asked. Everyone here tried very hard to make Jill feel they really liked her and cared what happened to her, but Jill couldn't help thinking they considered her an interesting and unusual case. Junkies and pill-poppers and suicides they got here by the dozen. Twelve-year-old girls who screwed around and shocked their mothers—so what? That sort of thing went on all the time in the slums and the parents didn't go put their kids into a mental hospital. But rich people couldn't stand having such a reflection on them living in their very own home. Some of the concerned parents didn't even live in New York, a few didn't even live in America. They traveled around all summer and figured their weirdo kid was out of their hair.

As for the other patients, Jill didn't want to get too friendly with any of them. Her stay here was going to be so short that if she got to like someone she would miss her afterward. She liked Dorothy, but Dorothy was too old to be her friend on the outside. They had different interests. Dorothy liked men and sex, she had a boyfriend, she was planning her career. On her days off she went to parties with other aides and smoked pot. Jill had never even seen her in street clothes, just that uniform with *Miss Gellhorn* on the pocket. The patients were allowed to wear anything they wanted.

Jill's clothes didn't fit her any more, they were too tight. Her parents came to visit her and gave her new, prewashed jeans and some T-shirts. They also brought her some paperback books, even though there was a library here. Her parents tried to act like what their idea of perfect parents was, so the doctors wouldn't think they were responsible for Jill's bizarre behavior. They were so sweet to each other it turned Jill's stomach. She was tired and relieved when they finally left. She went into the bathroom, made sure it was empty, and threw up. It made her feel much better. She was glad she could still do it. Wouldn't do to lose her touch, when the doctors were giving her body back to her at the end of this month.

"Hello, Jill," Jill said to her reflection in the mirror. It didn't look like her and she had to keep reminding herself who it was. It looked like a puffy stranger. A pig with an apple in its mouth

163

for them to carve up and eat. "Don't worry, darling Jill," Jill said to this poor, piggy thing, ninety-five pounds this morning before breakfast, "I'll make you well again as soon as we get out of here."

AUGUST

August 1975

JILL CAME HOME from the mental hospital on the last day of July. Her family was delighted at the apparent change in her, and promptly stopped noticing her. It was not that they didn't care about her, but she seemed all right and they had their own problems. So as August went by none of them paid any attention to the "lunch dates" and "supper dates" with friends that kept her away from the apartment at mealtimes, or that she was losing weight, or noticed that on the few occasions when she shared a meal with the family she went promptly to her bathroom and threw up. She had her sixteenth birthday, and everyone assumed she had finally become interested in a social life. She replaced her new jeans and T-shirts with others in a much tinier size, and nobody even saw. All jeans looked alike.

Hank was worried about his business. The price of gas had gone up again, and summer motorists clogged the roads, but not in his big cars. It was impossible to switch franchises. He tried not to think of what might have been, but thinking about what would be was worse: bankruptcy. He had laid off employees, pared down his staff to the bone. There was ill will. Fear hung in his office like a poisonous vapor. He remained indecisive, helpless, afraid.

Stacey was relieved to be back from Grandma's. Her yearly stay among the geriatric set took quite a toll of her patience. She was happy to be back in the city she loved, where she could wander where she pleased, spend hours in the public library and museums, hang around with her school friends (the ones who were too poor to go away for the summer). Even the August heat wave didn't bother her very much. Inside most buildings it was cool.

Ellen's problem was Reuben Weinberg. Her affair with him was more a pleasure than a problem, because his wife was still away and Hank was so easy to fool. She and Reuben planned to go away together for a weekend at the end of August. He booked a room at a small old inn in Connecticut. He rented a car. Ellen told Hank that she was going to stay with Nikki in Wilton that weekend because Nikki's husband had to be away on business and Nikki didn't want to be alone.

"You know, we'll do boring girl things," Ellen told Hank. "Probably go antiquing. You can take care of the kids."

"All right," he said calmly. "Have a good time."

Ellen also told Nikki, to back her alibi. "But I haven't been to the country for a weekend since the robbery," Nikki said. "If Hank calls he'll get Robert, not me."

"Hank never calls," Ellen said.

"What if he asks?"

"You tell him we had fun. You certainly don't know anything about cheating. If Hank asks, he doesn't want to hear."

"I think it depends on the husband," Nikki said. "Mine thinks I'm here in New York having a big love affair. Which I'm not. Yours is just a different kind of person."

"You never told Robert about the robbery," Ellen said. "He never even suspected. When are you going to stop thinking your

168

husband has X-ray eyes and jumps over buildings in a single bound?"

"I stopped thinking that quite a while ago," Nikki said.

On the chosen weekend Ellen met Reuben at the garage. As soon as he drove out of the city limits and the ugly buildings were replaced with fresh, green, growing things, she felt as if all her problems had gone away. How wonderful to shed the past, to have another chance! She looked at Reuben, intent behind the wheel, but he noticed her watching him and turned to take her hand and smile at her.

"I love you," he said.

"I love you," Ellen replied.

Did she really love him? More than the others? He made her feel like her own woman, not the harried martyr she considered herself at home. She loved him, but she was aware now, and had been for a while, that she had deliberately chosen him, just as she had deliberately chosen all her lovers except Kerry, her one mistake. All her married life she had been making up for her greater mistake, that of choosing Hank—or letting him choose her—by being extra careful. Her love life was her sustenance. Without it she would dry up and die, or go crazy. But now, at forty, was that enough? This nice man, who loved her, might become available, as the others had. If he did, what would she do? Would she get rid of him as she always had with all the others, or would she consider him seriously? She was forty now, in young middle age, and she wouldn't be able to go on having affairs forever. How good it would be to settle down, to get rid of Hank, to have a new life, and to be faithful. How peaceful it would be, and yet fun, because Reuben was fun to be with. This weekend would be a test for them both. Ellen had never known a weekend that hadn't made a man see his moment of truth.

"I hear that Mary Logan is fed up with her publisher," Reuben said. "I'm having lunch with her agent next week and I'm going to see if I can sign her. Don't say anything."

"Oh, I won't," Ellen said. How nice to be privy to these little secrets, to be so close to the source of power!

169

The inn was on the outskirts of a tiny town nearly two hours away from the city. It was surrounded by trees and hills and had a lake with an old gristmill. The lake was stocked with trout and bass which were cooked and served up fresh for dinner in the inn's dining room. Ellen and Reuben went to their room, made love, showered together, and went downstairs to have drinks on the terrace and watch the sunset.

"Do you know," Reuben said, "that Herbert Ellis called me up at home last night at four o'clock in the morning, collect, to complain that there were none of his books in the Everflow, Idaho, train depot?"

"What a nerve."

"Well, he can't find me this weekend." He smiled and took her hand.

They had dinner at a table in the quietest corner of the inn's dining room, lit by candles, served by a waitress dressed in Revolutionary costume.

"What would you like to do tomorrow?" Reuben asked Ellen.

"Just poke around. What would you like to do?"

"That sounds great."

After dinner they had brandy on the terrace until the mosquitoes drove them indoors. They went to their room, made love again, and went to sleep, nestled together in the too-small double bed with the antique four-poster frame built for midgets of a former generation.

Saturday was sunny. After breakfast they got into the car and explored the countryside. They didn't talk much but they were very companionable. Ellen felt she had known him for a long time. There would be no unpleasant surprises. When she saw a barn with a sign *Antiques For Sale* she gave a shriek of joy.

"Oh, let's look!"

He parked and they went into the barn, looking at everything and pricing the things they liked. Ellen had hardly any money with her and didn't intend to do more than look. She didn't know the difference between real and fake anyway. They paused at a tray of old jewelry.

"Those wedding rings always make me feel sad," Reuben said.

"Why?"

"I wonder who they belonged to and why they ended up here."
He picked one up and showed it to her. "See inside? They put
their names. They must have loved one another. Maybe she died
and the ring ended at auction with all her things . . . maybe the
marriage didn't work and she sold it."

"People didn't get divorced in those days," Ellen said.

"I wonder if they were happy or unhappy," he said. "You wear
a ring and you're not happy. I wear a ring and I'm unhappy too.
I wonder if my wife is happy. We don't discuss it. Is your husband happy?"

"I suppose so," Ellen said. "I don't know."

"In those days it didn't really matter," Reuben said. "People
accepted their fates. Today it's the opposite; they can't wait to
change things that don't suit them. You and I are caught in the
middle. We're living with values that no longer apply, but we're
used to it. There ought to be something better, something
more."

"May I help you?" The owner, who had waited respectfully in
the background, came up to them.

"Where did you get these rings?" Reuben asked.

"Oh, all around. That's an old one, a hundred years old. See
the color? Eighteen karat."

"I wouldn't want someone else's ring," Ellen said. "It might be
jinxed."

"The kids like them a lot," the owner said. "Antiques are big
with them. It's the whole back-to-nature thing. An antique
doesn't count as jewelry, it's more like heritage, history. I sell a
lot of old wedding rings to kids."

"Kids are so romantic," Ellen said.

"We are too," Reuben said. "Except our wedding rings *are*
antiques." He smiled, and the owner smiled back and put the
case of jewelry away.

"Just look around till you find something you like," he said,
and left them to their browsing.

171

"I feel like having a drink," Reuben said.

They drove back to the inn. They sat on the cool porch over-looking the lake and Reuben ordered champagne. When it arrived at once, cold in a silver bucket, and Ellen saw that it was Dom Pérignon, she realized he had ordered it in advance. When? This morning after breakfast? Last night? In the city?

"You didn't mind when I said our rings were antiques?" he asked her.

"I was a little insulted," she said with a smile, "but as long as you don't think the same thing about the wearers . . ."

"No, we're younger than we ever were. It's our marriages that are old." He refilled their glasses. Ellen felt a little high. She hardly ever drank before lunch. "I want you to think about something," Reuben said.

"Okay."

"Are we going to have just another romantic, self-deceptive love affair or is this going to be important to us?"

"It happens I have been thinking about it," she said.

"And . . . ?"

"I think it's something one has to think about. I haven't found any answers yet, have you?"

"Yes. I know it's important. To me anyway. I wanted to tell you this so you wouldn't be afraid to start thinking it might be very important to you too."

Ellen sighed. "I'm afraid it is important to me already."

He beamed at her. "Then maybe we'll be among the few lucky ones."

"Who are they?"

"The ones who change their lives just when they've given up hope that they ever could."

For the first time in one of her affairs Ellen didn't ask what would happen to her children or his children. She just drank her champagne and looked into his eyes. He was the same as the others. He wasn't special, he had just come along at the right time. Timing. That was the whole secret of love. She realized she hadn't loved any of the others at all. It was just that love was part of her peculiar morality. But she could love this one, she could adore him, because he would save her. No, because she would *let* him save her.

"Do you believe me?" he asked.

"Yes."

"Will you let yourself trust me?"

"Should I?"

"Yes," Reuben said. "Because I won't hurt you. I never could."

And I won't hurt you either, Ellen thought. She didn't say it, because she knew it would scare him too much to think that she was perfectly able to do so.

NIKKI WAS AWARE that she was changing, and she liked it. For one thing, she noticed the world around her in a less romantic way, and instead of being disappointing or making her bitter, it made her feel more secure. All her life she had lived in a pack, and now she only had to take care of herself. She talked to Robert every day on the phone, but when he asked her which train she was taking up to the house on Friday she always had some excuse—special meetings at the office, extra work. The August heat wave gave her a good excuse because they'd never had their house air-conditioned. One weekend she invented an ovarian cyst. Gynecological problems always repulsed Robert, and he asked if she would be all right and then dropped the subject. He never offered to come into the city. He had never given in to her on anything without a great deal of subterfuge on her part, and she didn't intend to trick him now. She regretted that she still didn't have the courage to tell him that she found weekends in the country with him unpleasant, that they made her uncomfortable. The secret excuse she had given herself, fear of another robbery, was no longer valid. Her windows had bars, her door its super lock, and she was not afraid. Saturdays she went to the stores, which were all having sales, and replaced her ward-

173

robe. Luckily all she'd had in the apartment was her summer clothes. The winter ones were in Wilton in garment bags with mothballs, a dread habit she'd inherited from her mother.

The clock radio, the little color TV, the cassette player, all were replaced too, by Nikki, not the police. The police never did find any of her things. She realized that she had never really expected them to. She registered with an organization that fed your Social Security number into a computer at the police station, and she stenciled her number on everything of value with a special marker they lent her. The point seemed to be that a burglar wouldn't steal something that was registered, because he wouldn't be able to fence it. She was quite proud of herself for never having told Robert about the robbery.

The last thing she replaced was the rug, but instead of fur she got a Rya on sale. Fur was *nouveau riche* anyway, she decided. She didn't get a new bedspread either. A bedspread was something a suburban matron had. She bought a blanket cover, so she could lie on the bed and read, and found it cut her morning bed-making time too. She was less neat than she used to be. She did things in order of their importance to herself, not to other people. Perhaps it was the hot weather, or the fact that it stayed light so much longer in the evenings during the summer, but Nikki discovered she wasn't as frantic as she used to be about having a dinner date every night. She was getting used to her own company, and she found she liked it.

At the office she automatically asked for a raise, as she did every August. To her great surprise she was not only given the money she asked for but was promoted too. She was now managing editor. Everybody in executive positions had been stepped up one notch. She had new stationery with her name and title on it. All her spring books had done well, and she had brought in two good new authors, but she suspected that the main reason she had been promoted was the change in her attitude and behavior in the office. She still flirted and acted cuddly, but she was stronger, more sure of herself, and occasionally she dropped the pretense altogether and let them know she was aware of how bright she was. This did not seem to offend anyone—in fact they respected her for it. I am probably the last of the emancipated ladies, Nikki thought ruefully. Look at all I missed!

She had decided not to take her vacation this summer. Robert had not said anything about it. When she suggested casually that they might take their vacations together in the fall and go somewhere instead of just puttering around the house in the country, he replied vaguely that it might be a good idea if he could clear up his work load. She realized he wasn't looking forward to going away with her any more than she was looking forward to going away with him. Fall was such an exciting time in New York, and Nikki decided to get tickets to a lot of plays. If Robert didn't want to go she could take Rachel or Margot or Ellen.

There was a rumor going around among all the female employees of Heller & Strauss, from typists to editors, that they were going to snare John Griffin. Movie stars writing their autobiographies was in this year, and Nikki wasn't surprised that John Griffin would join the group; if every taxi driver thought he could write his life story, why shouldn't every actor? But what surprised her was that John Griffin's book was going to be a serious novel and that she was assigned to be his editor. She doubted that John Griffin, from the image she'd gotten of him, would have enough respect for a woman to let her mess around with his words. He couldn't even walk in the street without women clutching at him, his two marriages (and divorces) had been stormy and well publicized, his love affairs equally so. He was known to relax in the company of men and had no women friends or business associates. Women were to marry and have children with, or to take to Europe on location as part of the entertainment. She hoped his manuscript wasn't bad and that they would get along. It would be a rotten trick if they had assigned him to her just because she was known to be a devious flirt.

He came in alone, without his agent. That was nice. He was taller and even more handsome than he seemed in the movies, or perhaps movie stars just seemed larger than life. His skin was

175

tanned, his teeth were perfect (real?), and his eyes a deep blue. He was wearing a suit and tie, even carrying an attaché case, and he shook Nikki's hand. So far she liked his act. What she didn't like was that he had obviously asked to meet her before he entrusted his manuscript to her, and she resented being auditioned just as much as he did, although she was more used to it by upbringing.

"I hope you like it at Heller & Strauss," Nikki said pleasantly. "We'll all do everything we can to help you, and we're all on your side. I can't wait to read the book."

"The hundred pages," he said. "The rest is in outline."

"That's great. A hundred pages is fine."

"I know I'm going to need help," he said easily. "I've never written a book before and sometimes my ideas run ahead of my words."

"That's what I'm here for."

He looked toward the open door of her office. In the hall there was nearly every woman in the place, from nineteen to ninety, gaping at him.

"God, I'm sorry," Nikki said. She went to the door and closed it. "That won't happen again."

He shrugged. "I'm used to it, but when it comes to my baby— my book—I feel a little vulnerable."

"They certainly won't read it," Nikki said, "—until it's published, of course. I will read it, and our editor in chief, Pete, whom you've met, and that's it. Your work will always be sacred. As for your person, once you're out in the hall, I can't make any guarantees." She smiled but did not giggle. The new Nikki. She was proud of herself.

He opened his attaché case, took out an agent's folder with a thin manuscript in it, and handed it to her. "This is it," he said. He then took it back and wrote something on the folder. "This is my private home number. Please call me when you've read it, even if it's in the middle of the night. You can talk about business with my agent, but please talk about rewrites with me."

"Of course," Nikki said.

"Where can I reach you when you're not at the office?" She wrote down her apartment number and gave it to him. He glanced at it and put it into his pocket.

"That's unlisted," Nikki said. "Don't send it to the cleaner's with the suit."

"You'd be surprised how well I can take care of myself."

"I'm sure."

He stood up. "When will I hear from you?"

"I'll call you first thing tomorrow morning. Is ten too early?"

"I'll be waiting." He shook her hand again, and she walked with him down the hall to the elevator. Even the men were gaping at him. While she and John Griffin were waiting for the elevator Nikki allowed herself to give him a guarded once-over. Almost too handsome, but apparently nice and sincere, at least about his book. Perhaps later he would show fangs and claws. Well, lots of writers did, even when they weren't movie stars. He seemed to trust her. She was glad she had decided not to play her usual role with him.

She realized she didn't expect his hundred pages to be very good. But that was unfair. He was prettier than she was, and although they were the same age he would still look a lot better than she did when they were sixty, but that didn't make him dumb. The poor man was probably sick and tired of being a sex symbol. After all, he'd never had to work to be one as she had. Maybe they could be friends.

When she walked back to her office Nikki was conscious of the envious looks she was getting from everybody. Reuben winked at her as if she were half in bed with John Griffin already. The office world was so different from the world outside. Here she was their sex symbol, back in Wilton she was just another suburban housewife. Here her brains and push meant a great deal, she was respected, she felt sure of herself. If John Griffin had made an appearance in Wilton for some reason, he would never even have noticed her, nor would she expect him to. Here he needed her assurance, comfort, and talent, and was waiting for her verdict. *This* was her world, not Wilton. For the first time

177

Nikki realized how many times Robert had knocked down her ego when she went home and how often she'd had to build it up from scratch.

She read the first hundred pages and the outline of the Griffin novel that night. He had been wrong about his ideas running ahead of his words: his words ran ahead of his ideas. On and on. There was promise of an excellent plot, and she could see how with a lot of work it could be a best seller, but it badly needed tightening, and the story really started on page 75. How could you tell an author to throw away the first seventy-five pages of his first, dearly beloved novel? She knew how, she had done it before. Get him on the right track, build up his confidence and enthusiasm, and then when he had written enough to make him feel he wasn't a failure, gently explain how much better the story would be if it began where it really did begin. Sometimes she even managed to make an author think the cut was his own idea. This sort of editorial leading was something Nikki did very well.

She telephoned John Griffin promptly at ten o'clock the next morning from her office. He answered on the first ring.

"Good morning. It's Nikki Gellhorn. I think your book is going to be tremendously exciting."

"Yes, but did you like it?"

"Very much. I'll be happy to work with you on it and give you as much time and help as you want. It has a wonderful story. It's so unusual. Could you come into the office this afternoon and we'll talk about it more?"

"Three o'clock?"

"Perfect."

In their meeting they discussed the plot and character development, how soon things would happen, and he took avid notes in a tiny illegible handwriting. By six o'clock Nikki was exhausted, but he was excited and eager to begin writing the rest of his book. He was now thinking in terms of the forward flow.

"A lot of the things I wrote," he said, "I was scared, fishing. Some of it doesn't seem to make too much sense to me now. I mean, it's not getting on with it. Do you know what I mean?"

"Absolutely," Nikki said.

"I want to go on now, but maybe later we can go back and get some of the fat out. I didn't realize that all I had to do was tell the story. For some reason I thought I had to embellish everything or no one would take me seriously."

"You tell it your way and it'll be terrific," Nikki said.

He gathered up his notes and put them into the attaché case. "How soon do you want to see more?"

"Whenever you want me to."

"How about twenty-five pages? Would that be all right?"

"I'm here every day. Give them to me and I'll read them right away."

"You know," he said, "you're a very easy person to work with."

"But so are you," Nikki said. When he left he kissed her lightly on the cheek. She was glad everyone but Pete had gone home. Her little kiss of appreciation would have gotten her a lot of office teasing.

For the next two weeks John worked like a machine. He brought in pages and she read them and encouraged him, sometimes asked him questions about his intentions to keep him on the right track. She knew she would have to do an allover cutting job when he had finished the whole novel, but it wasn't going to be as difficult as she had feared. It wasn't a major plot overhaul. Nikki always dreaded those, and authors hated them, rightly so.

One Friday he asked her if she would have dinner with him. She did, going straight from the office because that was the way he wanted it. Everywhere everyone looked at them; at him because he was a movie star, at her because they didn't know who she was or why she was with him. He took her to "21," where the management didn't allow table hopping or autograph hunting, but they couldn't prevent staring. Nikki enjoyed it.

They were seated downstairs, where people could stare at them to their heart's content. The restaurant looked like a speakeasy, which it once was, with a long bar and red-checked tablecloths. Hanging from the ceiling were all sorts of miniature toys: trucks, planes, cars, sports equipment, each of which had been put there by the person who owned the company it represented. On second thought, Nikki decided, it didn't look like a speakeasy, it looked like a little boy's room. And all the little boys, grown up and rich now, were lining the bar.

They talked about the book for a little while, and then they talked about music and politics, two subjects that he knew much more about than she did. Then he told her funny stories about things that had happened when he was making some of his movies. She was glad she had seen almost all of them. Out here in the restaurant they were more in his world than in hers, she was not as safe as in her office, but she reminded herself she was still his editor and he needed her. It would be too easy to be impressed just because he was a celebrity, and she couldn't let that happen.

"You're married?" he said. "Or divorced?"

"No, I'm married," Nikki said. "We're . . . semiseparated."

"How separated is that?"

"He lives in the country and I live here. We haven't seen each other for a while, but neither of us has admitted it yet. It's odd, I guess. I haven't quite gotten used to it myself. I don't know what will happen. And you?"

"I have an apartment in New York and a house at Malibu. People think I live in California, but I don't if I can help it. I like New York."

"So do I!"

"How do you find being alone? If you *are* alone, I mean."

"Oh, I'm alone," Nikki said. "I like it."

"Both my ex-wives remarried almost immediately. They hated being alone. But it's more difficult for a woman in Hollywood. It's such a married-people's town. And there's a lot of nineteen-year-old competition—every beauty contest winner from East Gnat's Ass wants to be a movie star. I don't like young girls. When I do, I'll know I'm getting old."

"Hurray," Nikki said. "A grown-up."

"You better believe it. I'm fifty."

"I thought you were forty-two!"

"That's my publicity age. How old are you?"

"Forty-two."

"You said it so fast I believe you. But I would never believe it from looking at you. You look thirty."

"I feel thirty."

"So do I," he said. "That's why I'm trying to be a writer at my age and I'm *not* writing my memoirs."

"You wouldn't give up films!"

"Oh, no, I like the money too much. I don't think this book is going to make me a fortune, although naturally I'd like that."

"I'll tell you a secret," Nikki said. "If it won't make you so conceited you're impossible to work with. I think this book of yours is going to be a big, big best seller."

"You really do?"

"Yes, I do. One never knows these things for sure, and we all make mistakes, but I have a strong feeling about this book."

He leaned over and gave her a light, happy kiss on the mouth. "Thank you."

"Thank *you,*" Nikki said. "You just made me a celebrity. I think that woman over there just fainted. Unless it was from the weight of her earrings."

He took her home in a cab after dinner, and she didn't ask him to come up for a drink although she knew he would have. She wasn't sure it was a good idea. She'd never invited a man upstairs, and since she was separated from her husband, it might look too much like an invitation into her bed. She couldn't imagine any woman ever inviting John Griffin upstairs to her apartment without intending that invitation. He told the cab to wait, walked her to the outside door, waited until she had opened it, and then she shook hands with him.

"Thank you, I had a marvelous time," she said.

"So did I."

It was only when she was safely upstairs, alone in her bed in front of the television set, that she realized it had never occurred to her to offer to take *him* to dinner. After all, she was his editor,

181

the company would pay for it, and that was customary. But from the outset he had made it clear that *he* was taking *her* out. What does he know about author's rights, she thought, he's a movie star. And kind of an old-fashioned man. I think I just had my first date.

John asked her to have dinner again with him the following Wednesday. "I'd love to," Nikki said, "but this time let me take you." He looked annoyed. "It's on the company," she said quickly. "I'm *supposed* to take you to dinner. It makes them happy. I just want to reciprocate."

"I want to have dinner with you, not the damn company," he said. "I can afford it."

"I know that."

"Don't be so insecure. You don't owe me anything. I'm not going to jump on you. Why are you laughing?"

"Because any woman would give her eye teeth to have you jump on her, and you're promising not to molest me."

"My sex life is mostly myth," he said. "I don't do it with groupies, I can't stand the vapid girls-around-town, the scalp hunters, and any type of moron. It's hard to find an intelligent, human woman who isn't already in love with someone. I happen to like you as a friend. You're pretty, and you're a good person, and you're very smart. You're not looking for something. I like to be with you, that's all. If you're free tonight let's have dinner."

"I'd love it."

In a way she was a little disappointed that he so obviously wasn't after her. She supposed that no matter what he said, she couldn't possibly compete with the beautiful women he met all the time. On one hand it was a compliment to be considered a friend, on the other hand she had been brought up to think there had to be something wrong with a girl who was considered just one of the guys. She reminded herself sternly that she was the new Nikki.

He took her to Romeo Salta, and the captain recognized John with delight. She liked being made a fuss over. The front room seemed cozy and warm, with paintings on the walls and an open view of the Italian kitchen in the far back, but it was actually a large room with uninterrupted sight lines. They were seated side by side on a leather banquette against the wall. For the first time Nikki realized how much a part of the entertainment a restaurant's patrons were, and tonight she was the entertainment. But she quickly forgot it. She felt comfortable with John. When dinner was over she didn't want to end the evening because she was really having a good time. She'd ask him up for a drink. Why not? He was safe.

She asked him casually in the cab, and he looked pleased. He seemed very large in her small apartment. She put on the air conditioner and picked out a cassette that she knew he would approve of and put it in the player while he looked around.

"This place is like a fortress," he said. "Why do you need all those locks and bars?"

"I had a robbery."

"You should live in an apartment house with a doorman."

"I suppose so. But I like this place."

"You should come to California."

"Sure. Brandy?"

"Fine."

She poured brandy for both of them and they sat on the couch. "What's your apartment like?" she asked.

"Messy compared to this. I love your place. It's very open and to the point, like you." And then he put down his glass and kissed her.

She didn't know what to do. She was supposed to be honest and not play games, but how could she be that way when she didn't even know what she wanted? She couldn't believe John Griffin actually wanted to go to bed with her, but he was in her apartment at night kissing her, she had invited him here, and grown-ups didn't just sit and neck. She wished she'd had an affair so she would know what to do. Then he stood up, took her by the hand, and led her to the bedroom. Obviously there was nothing to do now but go through with it. It was what she wanted, she might as well admit it. She'd sensed it was going to

183

be somebody eventually; how lucky that it was this man who was so attractive and sexy and seemed to like her.

He made love to her all night, in all sorts of athletic positions she had never even heard of. It all seemed unreal. She enjoyed it thoroughly, but at the same time she seemed to be outside herself, observing. I am in bed with John Griffin, she told herself. Is he this good because he thinks he has to be, or do all men act like this the first time they go to bed with a new woman? How would I know? I've never been to bed with anyone but my husband, and he doesn't do all these things. Maybe men learn things from their wives and girl friends. God knows, Robert never learned anything from me!

Finally, at dawn, he slept. He snored, and that amused her, because she could imagine how horrified his fans would be. She poked him and he rolled over and stopped snoring, and then she set the alarm to give herself two hours' sleep, and slept, exhausted, but exhilarated too. She felt very close to him. He was a nice, nice man.

In the morning she made coffee. He didn't seem tired. She was not really tired either. She hoped that she could handle this professionally. She still had to edit his book and tell him what was wrong with it. She didn't even know if sleeping with someone changed the way you worked together! What a nuisance to be so innocent.

She went to the office and he went home to work. Alone for the first time, she was overwhelmed by guilt toward Robert. How could she have done such a thing to him? Cheating on your husband was so castrating, it meant you had excluded him from something that used to be just his province. It was keeping secrets. It was lying. It was making him second choice. It was making fun of him; even though you weren't, he would think you were. It was hurting him. It was cruel. She hadn't called him last night, and ordinarily she would have called him this morning from the office, but she was afraid he would sense the guilt in her voice, and so she couldn't call. She hoped he wouldn't call her. No, Robert was so busy in his office, he would wait till tonight to call. Maybe by tonight she would have collected herself enough to deceive him. *Deceive.* What an ugly word. Oh, poor Robert, suspecting her and blaming her—and now she had done it, so caught up in the moment that she had thought about him only in the abstract, like a past lover.

She tried not to think about John Griffin, but even while she was feeling guilty toward Robert she was wondering if John would call, hoping he would. If he didn't call her they could both pretend it hadn't happened. But it wasn't something you just ignored as if it happened all the time and was nothing. It was something to her. She would never tell him how important it was to her because she had too much pride, but if he didn't call she knew it would cause her great pain.

When she came back to the office after lunch her phone was ringing. Be John. Please be John and don't be Robert. I'll be good.

It was John. "Are you free for dinner tonight?" he asked.

"Yes," Nikki said.

"I'll pick you up at seven at your apartment."

On the way home from the office she bought some wine and vodka. She ought to call Robert, otherwise he would call when John was there, and she didn't know how she would be able to handle that. She put the wine into the refrigerator, the vodka in the liquor cabinet, and sat down next to the phone. She picked up the receiver and then put it down. Let Robert call her. If she sounded odd she could say she had just jumped out of the bathtub.

Bathing and dressing, putting on fresh makeup, she felt as excited as she had been over twenty years ago dressing up to go out on a date. It wasn't as if all the years in between hadn't happened, but they were pushed into the background. Everything was new again. When she opened the door for John she was surprised at how handsome he looked, as if her prince would have turned into a frog just because he spent the night with her.

They had a few drinks and then they went to Orsini's for dinner. He didn't seem worried about what her husband would

185

think, and Nikki wasn't either as long as they were out in public. She had to get a good book out of him, everyone knew movie stars needed a lot of personal attention, so it was not abnormal for them to be seen together so frequently. She asked him what he'd written that day, he told her, he seemed enthusiastic, and she felt vindicated. Then they talked about other things. They never talked about the fact that they had gone to bed together the night before. Maybe people didn't discuss it—how would she know?

The restaurant was very dark and romantic, with little lamps on the tables. They did not hold hands, although they could have for all anyone would have cared. After dinner he took her home and came upstairs without even a questioning look. She turned off the bell on the phone.

It was the same as the night before. She thought they would probably both die if they didn't get a good night's sleep, but at the moment she wasn't tired. It just seemed so unreal. Was this what Ellen did with her lovers, what Margot did? But not every night? She wondered if John found her irresistibly sexy, or if he was oversexed, or if this sort of thing just went on when an affair was doomed to end. She didn't for one moment imagine that she could ever be the wife of a movie star. She couldn't stand the strain, and besides, why would be pick her?

The next day was Friday. John had asked her for dinner. Nikki knew she had to call Robert to tell him she wasn't coming home, but she couldn't face it. She wished she could be the sort of woman who could just tell him: "I have to have dinner with an author tonight, there are problems with his book." How easy it would be if she didn't feel that Robert knew her too well. All this time she had been angry because she felt that Robert didn't understand her; now she was suddenly thinking of him as perceptive, a mind reader. What powers her guilt was giving to the same husband she'd known for all these years! She left the office early, washed her hair, and when John came to pick her up she rushed him out of the house after only one drink, saying she was starving.

186

He said he was glad she was starving because he had made reservations at the Côte Basque.

Nikki had never been there, the only thing she knew was that it was the formidable restaurant that didn't allow women in if they were wearing pants suits. She was glad she had gotten very dressed up. The front room had a bar, banquettes, and a display trolley of incredible desserts. The main room had charming murals of the Basque country and fresh flowers on the tables. They were seated in the front, which was apparently the place to be seen. If you were going to cheat on your husband in secret you should really try not to do it with a movie star.

After they had dinner he took her back to her apartment and kept her up all night. Saturday they slept all day. Nikki was relieved to find he was human after all. When they woke up she turned on the phone bell, and then they went out to buy some food for supper and for Sunday brunch.

The people in her supermarket did double takes when they saw him, and as soon as one woman asked for his autograph it seemed as if everyone in the store wanted one. He signed good-naturedly. When they escaped to her apartment he said he had to get a few things and would be back.

She was cooking cheerfully when he appeared with a flight bag in his hand. He had brought toilet articles and a robe, underwear, socks, jeans, and some shirts. It was certainly more than he would need for Sunday.

"Which drawer can I have?" he asked, just like a roommate.

"Take the bottom one."

"You get a drawer in my apartment in exchange," he said.

"Good. I believe in equality. Do you wash dishes too?"

"I do if you cook. If I cook, you wash. And I'm a great cook."

My friends would never believe this, she thought. I don't even believe it. She was opening the wine when the phone rang. She jumped.

It was Robert. He sounded annoyed. "I take it you're not coming up?"

187

Robert's dry voice seemed even more unreal than this man neatly putting his underwear into her dresser drawer. She willed Robert to be a total stranger, it was the only way she could handle it.

"No—oh, no, I'm sorry. I tried to call and you were out," she lied.

"It was *I* who called and *you* who were out," Robert said.

"I've been working."

"They take advantage of you," Robert said.

"I know."

"You're coming next weekend?"

"Of course," Nikki said, guilty despite her best efforts.

"It's Labor Day weekend," he said.

"Already?"

"The first of September. It's early this year. We got a postcard from Lynn. She'll be back with her boyfriend and they're giving us the pleasure of their company. Dorothy is coming unless she has to work, but even if she does, she gets one night off to be with us. We'll have a family reunion. I thought we could have a cookout one night, and another maybe pick out a nice restaurant."

"I'll take Friday off and come up early," Nikki said.

"You could come up Thursday after work."

"That's what I'll do. I'll take my bag to the office and catch the six o'clock."

"What are you doing tonight?" Robert asked.

"Just having a bite at home and cutting a manuscript. I have to work with the author all day tomorrow. She's from out of town."

"She picked some time to come to New York," Robert said.

"I know."

"I'm having a quiet evening too. I brought some work from the office, and I'll get a good night's sleep."

"I'll see you in a few days," Nikki said. "I'll call you tomorrow night."

"Good night," he said.

"Good night." She hung up and turned around slowly to face

188

John. He didn't seem to have heard a word. "I have to go home to see my kids next weekend," she said, knowing he had heard, no matter how bland his look. He was, after all, an actor.

"Of course," he said. "How old are they?"

"They'll be twenty in October. They're twins. Girls. They were born three days after my birthday, so we always celebrate together and make a big thing of it. We're good friends. I really *like* them as well as love them."

"That means you were a good mother."

"I hope so. Do you have children?"

"Three. Two boys and a girl. They're old enough so that we can be friends too. They all want to be directors. I guess that says what they think of their old man."

"It's hard to be the same thing your parents were," Nikki said. "My daughters don't want to go into publishing. I don't want to be just a housewife like my mother was. Do you want to do what your father did?"

"Be a miner? I should say the hell not!" He laughed.

"A coal miner?"

"What other kind is there?"

"I just never read about it in any of your publicity," Nikki said.

"I don't like to use it. I'm me, not my past. He was killed when I was sixteen. I lied about my age and enlisted in the Navy. I had to get a friend of mine to take my physical for me. I had rheumatic fever as a kid and I have a bum heart. That would have kept me out of the service but not out of the mines. The Navy never found out until my ship was torpedoed and they were examining me in the hospital. They tossed me out—honorably of course. Then I went to acting school on the GI Bill, and the rest is, as they say, history."

She went back to opening the wine, thinking about the little boy with the bad heart whose father had died in the mines, and she realized how easily he had led her away from the embarrassment of a phone call from her husband and having to lie in front of her lover. Obviously John was an old hand at this sort of thing.

"I'm very fond of you," she said, handing him a glass of wine.

189

"I'm fond of you too. You're a good lady."

"Shall we eat at seven?"

"Whenever it's ready."

Is this right, she wondered, or should we have said we were in love? But we're not in love. I have a mad crush on him, and I dearly like him, but it's not love. Love is when you really know somebody. But I wish he'd said he loved me. I wouldn't have believed it, but I wish he'd said it anyway.

ON THURSDAY EVENING when Nikki left for the country she was very depressed. She told John her husband was listed in the phone directory but not to call unless it was a problem with his book, because lying made her uncomfortable. She had never been so straightforward before with any man, but he didn't seem offended. She thought afterward that she should have said nothing at all. She wondered if John would have second thoughts about their conflict of interest and try to get rid of her as a lover or as an editor. She knew it would matter more—if she had to make the choice—to keep him as a writer. She was learning things about herself every day. It was as if, having determined to change her life, she had opened herself to all sorts of realizations and insights. They had always been there waiting for her, but she had kept them at bay.

Robert picked her up at the station. When she saw that he had Lynn in the car Nikki was overwhelmed with relief. She kissed them both.

"Where's the love of your life?" she asked Lynn.

"He's back at the house making a gigantic pot of chili for supper. It's his specialty. We had a great time, but I'm glad to be home. I've got too used to comfort, not to mention a bathtub I didn't have to scrub three times before I would dare get into it."

Between listening to stories about Europe and then Dorothy's surprise appearance at midnight, it was easy to act natural. They were all so warm and cozy together, a family who loved one another, and Nikki could tell that Robert was trying. She was certainly trying harder than she ever had before. John seemed very far away, a dream she'd had, or perhaps a nightmare; nothing that was part of this family reunion. Yet when she got into bed with Robert, Nikki stiffened with fear. Would he be able to sense anything different about her? But that was silly, that was like her mother's horror stories when she was young about boys knowing everything bad you'd done before you met them.

Robert moved toward her and put his arms around her. "It's been a long time," he said.

"Yes," she whispered. She tried not to be too different when he made love to her, not to do anything she'd learned or to act peculiar. To her amazement she didn't have to fake an orgasm, it just happened. He didn't seem to find her changed, and she knew her mother had fooled her. The worst was over. Nothing bad could happen to her now.

Sunday night one of John Griffin's old movies was on television. Lynn and Dorothy had never seen it and they insisted. Nikki watched him on the screen, younger, and he seemed like a stranger. It was hard to believe he had ever happened to her. Yet she was going to see him again on Tuesday, and keep on seeing him. She hoped nothing in her face would betray her to Robert. She wanted to tell the girls he was one of her authors, that she actually knew him, because she knew they would be so thrilled, but she didn't dare. Not in front of Robert. Her sense of unreality could only carry her so far in this charade. She said she had seen the movie and fled into the kitchen, where she baked a cake from a mix. They ate it afterward.

"This is like old times," Robert said happily. "I missed your cakes."

On Monday night Robert drove her to the station. It was his way of compromising, not making her stay over until Tuesday morning. They hadn't had an argument the entire four days she'd been home.

"Tell you what, Nikki," he said, "next weekend when you

191

come, why don't you bring me a key to your apartment? Then maybe we'll make a date the next week and I'll take you to a play in New York and stay over."

She looked at his profile in the dark car. She couldn't read his expression. This must have been very difficult for him. But he wanted her back, he wanted to try. Robert had always had a lousy sense of timing.

"What a great idea!" Nikki said.

"That is," he said, "if you still want me. If you haven't found someone else."

Nikki put her hand lightly on Robert's knee. "You'll love my apartment," she said.

"*Our* apartment."

"I love you."

Safely on the train, speeding through the dark, she began to shake all over. She put her cupped hands on the back of the seat in front of her and rested her face in her hands. She didn't want any of the passengers to see her cry. She wasn't crying from relief, or disappointment, but simply from weariness and inability to cope. She *wanted* her marriage to work. She couldn't turn Robert down when he'd offered her his pride. That meant he loved her. And she loved him too, if only because he had become so much a part of her life during all these years that he was more than just a husband; he was family, her twin. But she couldn't give up John just yet. She knew she would always regret it if she didn't see this love affair through to its natural conclusion. She would always remember it as something wonderful she could have had that she had thrown away. John had offered her equal drawer space in his apartment. All right, if that was how it had to be, so be it. She would have both of them if it killed her.

SEPTEMBER

September 1975

EVER SINCE THAT NIGHT on the beach at East Hampton Margot had been living a triple life. The first part was her work life, where she was an efficient robot. No one on the news show, no one in the studio, no one in the office knew what she did with her private life. She was more unassailable than ever, almost cold. She had an unhappy look in her eyes that was at the same time too threatening for anyone to come close. The second was her secret sex life, which took her prowling to every decent place a man with similar intentions might be found. It was the lunch restaurants where a hamburger on a roll cost $3.50 and the customers were all slim and young and dressed in outfits that burlesqued poverty. It was Bloomingdale's on Saturday mornings. It was to a few carefully selected bars in the Village, or midtown where newspapermen and advertising men hung out. She accepted every invitation to a party that crossed anyone's desk at the office. The others didn't bother to go, but if they did, she operated at the

195

party so swiftly they had no idea what she was up to. She wanted to sleep with as many young men as possible. They had to be attractive, employed, and not maniacs. None of these qualifications was actually provable except for the first, which was subjective. She never saw them more than once, even though several called. They all left her with a deep sense of guilt and dissatisfaction that sent her out to find another to wipe away the presence of the one before. She had never seen the East Hampton bartender again.

The third part was her secret depression. Sometimes it took the form of a journey into the past. She suddenly seemed to have total recall. Every unkind, unthinking word that had ever been spoken to her by her mother, an aunt, a teacher came back with the pain it had inflicted the first time. She seethed with anger. She thought of all the insults she had been intimidated by or had believed. She remembered the many times she had been accused of not being feminine by men who wanted something of her or women who felt threatened by her success, and how she had backed down and tried to please them. She regretted lost chances to fight back, words she had left unspoken, old, long-gone bonds she should have cut before she had. She felt the waste of her life. None of the good things she had now—her job, her friends, her health, her money, her looks—made any difference. The best years had been stolen from her by enemies.

On nights when she didn't go out to find a man Margot stayed at home drinking vodka and diet tonic and listening to old records that brought memories back even more vividly. She could not concentrate on new music. It irritated her. With the eagerness of a masochist she crawled to the past that had battered her. She should never have trusted anyone. She should have handled all of it differently. In her mind she had angry conversations with these shadow enemies of the past and told them how much she despised them. She brought these scenes up to the present and imagined police coming to her door to tell her that Kerry had been killed violently and that they had to question everyone in his address book even though she herself was not a suspect.

196

"What did you expect?" she would say to these cops. "He had such weird friends I'm just surprised he wasn't killed ages ago."

With characteristic self-absorption, Ellen never noticed that Margot was different. She telephoned with her endless seismographic records of her orgasms with Reuben, her mental turmoil because the affair was getting so serious, her gloating because it was. Now Margot could retaliate. She told Ellen about the best of her pickups, glamorizing the occasion as much as she could; she told Nikki, she told Rachel. They all seemed pleased that she had gotten over Kerry so well and was so popular. The only one who had a discouraging comment was, of course, Ellen. "Why do you want them so young?" Ellen asked. "There's no future in that."

"You're a fine one to talk about future."

"All right. Next time I'll know better."

"Are you planning on a next time?"

"Maybe . . ."

More of Ellen's bragging that Margot couldn't take seriously. She would never leave Hank, she was a coward.

Margot's fortieth birthday was approaching. Ellen decided that this year instead of taking her to lunch she would give her a surprise evening birthday party at Maxwell's Plum, inviting just their closest women friends, Nikki and Rachel. It couldn't really be a surprise though, because if she didn't tell Margot in advance, Margot might break their date, having met some young man somewhere. Margot was rather pleased about the party. She imagined herself on the deck of the *Titanic*, drinking gaily as the rest of the world went off in lifeboats. The image quickly turned to herself doomed and hysterical on the *Titanic*, while her parents, every man she had loved, all her friends, were being saved. Then she saw herself in a lifeboat crowded with strangers, being rowed to safety, and those she loved doomed on the ship above her, pressed to the railing, acting brave. The image made her cry. She didn't want to have to make the choice of which fantasy she preferred—they were all horrible. Why did she torture herself

197

this way? She seemed to have so little control over her thoughts lately.

She asked her doctor to give her another prescription for sleeping pills. They were barbiturates and had been reclassified, so you could only have a month's supply and couldn't renew them. She took them infrequently, never when a man was there, and saved them. You never knew. Drinking lulled the images, and if it didn't, at least it gave her the courage to go out and look for male company. Margot doubted if she could pick up a man without first having a few drinks. It was so contrary to everything she had been brought up to believe about aggressiveness. She never drank during the day when she was preparing her spot, and never before the show. She was very careful now. Previously she'd had a glass or two of wine at lunch with a friend; now she was only a night drinker. Alcohol had suddenly begun to bring out the worst in her. She never knew which she would become: the adventure seeker or the recluse.

On her birthday Margot, Ellen, Nikki, and Rachel met at Maxwell's Plum at half past eight. It was already crowded. In the center of the restaurant was a huge, raised bar filled with young people who had come to pick up strangers and find love of one kind or another. All had dressed and groomed themselves carefully for the night's adventures. Around the edges of the room was a sidewalk café, where blue-jeaned couples could linger over a hamburger and watch the action. The whole place was done in extravagant Art Deco, with ceramic and stuffed animals hanging from the ceiling. But the best part was the open back room, raised for a good view of the bar, with a glittering Tiffany glass ceiling of many colors, Art Deco light fixtures, bouquets of flowers on the tables, and a lengthy menu. Ellen had reserved a table in this expensive back room and all of them had dressed up. They were going to show Margot how nice it was to be a sophisticated, financially secure grown-up, so her birthday wouldn't bother her.

They had two bottles of wine. It went fast with four people. They ordered a third bottle halfway through the meal. Margot idly thought of putting the whole bill on her credit card so Ellen wouldn't have to dig up her share, and realized she was high. They were all in good spirits. Nikki and Rachel had chipped in to buy her a Rykiel sweater she had coveted, and Ellen had bought her an Elsa Peretti necklace.

"It's worth being forty to get all this loot," Margot said gratefully, not really meaning it.

They were jolly, they laughed and shrieked like schoolgirls. "Let me tell you about the graffiti I just saw in the ladies' room," Nikki said. "It said, 'Sex without love is even worse.'" They all shrieked with laughter. "Worse than what?" Nikki said. They laughed harder.

"I have to go pee anyway, so I'll write an addition," Margot said, rising. She had to pass the length of the back room to get to the stairs, and looked down at the crowded bar. There were a few rather passable men standing there hoping to pick up girls. When she came down the stairs she had a better look and saw one who appealed to her. He was tall and tanned, with dark hair and light-looking eyes, a nice body in the inevitable body shirt, with a suede jacket slung over one shoulder. He held what looked like a spritzer. Definitely cruising. She walked over to him and gave him a fey half smile.

"I know you," he said.

"Oh?"

"You're on television. Margot King! Right?"

"Right."

"Buy you a drink?"

She nodded in the direction of the table of women. "I'm doing an interview right now. Later?"

He looked at the table and his glance stopped at Rachel. He almost licked his lips. "Coincidence, I'm in market research myself."

"Lesbians," Margot said. "Very dull. I'll be through at—" She looked at her watch. "Why don't you come over to my apartment at eleven."

"Will you be there?"

"Of course." She wrote her address on his napkin and went back to her table.

"Who was that?" Ellen asked.

"A guy I know."

"What's his name?"

"I haven't got the faintest idea," Margot said, and smiled down at the handsome young man who was looking at her now instead of at anyone else in the room. He held up two fingers to her in a sign that was meant to mean eleven. Margot nodded.

"What did that mean?" Nikki asked.

"V for victory," Margot said.

"Did you pick up that strange man?" Rachel, horrified.

"Sure," Margot said. "Didn't you ever in the dim, evil past?"

"Lots," Rachel said.

"Well, I'm still living my dim, evil past," Margot said.

"It's incredible," Nikki said. "You walk through the room and they fall at your feet."

They all nodded and smiled admiringly, but Margot couldn't be sure if they meant it or if they thought she was crazy and were just being nice because it was her birthday.

She was home at a quarter to eleven, put her birthday presents away, brushed her teeth, combed her hair, had a drink, and waited. He appeared at ten past. Too insecure to wait in the street in case I wasn't home yet, she thought. He saw me leave, but he still wasn't sure. That means he'll try harder. Insecure ones always do. It never does them any good; I like the idea more than the act, but I'll send him away happy.

Early in the morning he had to leave for his office. He took a carefully folded tie out of his jacket pocket. "Stopped off home to get this last night," he said, as if he were enormously clever. Margot gave him a new, wrapped toothbrush so he wouldn't use hers. (She'd bought a dozen of them at the five-and-ten after the first young man she'd picked up had.) She pretended to be too sleepy to offer him breakfast. When he left she was relieved. She threw the razor blade he'd used into the garbage and changed the sheets.

RACHEL HAD STARTED as a freshman at NYU. She was taking American History, Government, Economics (as a prelude to learning banking), and Psychology. She always got to lectures early so she could get a good seat, fourth row center; she thought of them as house seats. In her shirt and jeans, her books on her lap, she would sit and watch all the other students come into the lecture hall. There were so many of them! She'd never seen that many young people all together at one time in her life. There weren't so many kids when she was young, even in her high school, which everyone in town considered big. The lines here to register for courses had been endless. The mobs at the local bookstores, the lines at the library, the lines to eat, the lines for everything. The professor used a microphone. These waves of young people, how did they feel? Anonymous, competitive, scared? She was glad she knew what the future held for her and didn't have to worry about competing with all those other people for a job after graduation. Rachel was so fascinated by the ideas her professors bombarded her with, and so busy with the homework and papers they demanded of her, that she hadn't bothered to make any friends yet. But she didn't feel odd or left out because she was older than the other students. They didn't seem to feel any generation gap. No one seemed to wonder why she was here, and girls and boys smiled at her as they passed in the hall as if she were another one of them.

One boy always seemed to seek the seat next to hers in Psych I, and he had introduced himself to her as Andy. He was her height and skinny, with long red hair to his shoulders, a moustache and a little beard. His moustache and beard were brown. He had fresh, clear skin like a child's and guileless brown eyes. She thought that without all that hair he'd grown on his face he would look about sixteen years old. It was funny how young these kids looked to her. Andy was really the only person here who made an appreciable effort to be friends with her, and Rachel was grateful for his efforts. He always talked to her before and after the class, but never bothered her by whispering during the lecture. He took notes seriously, and so did she.

She realized after a while that he had a crush on her, and the thought was delightful. She told Lawrence about him. Lawrence only said he was surprised more boys didn't have crushes on her. He had been so supportive of her schoolwork, cutting down their social life, arranging things so she would have time to study. He even discussed his work with her at home, explaining what he did and how the things she learned in her economics course did and didn't have relevance to what he did every day. Lawrence seemed proud of her, and Rachel was proud of herself. The other students were all just as frightened of failing as she was, and therefore it wasn't so frightening any more. They were all new together.

One beautiful fall day after class Andy asked Rachel if she wanted to sit in Washington Square Park in the sun for a while. She had a free hour between classes, and she felt so young today that she decided a few minutes in the dreaded sunshine wouldn't turn her into an instant prune, so she said sure. On the way he bought a hot dog with sauerkraut from a man with a cart and offered to buy her one, but she declined.

"My breakfast," he said. He also bought a Coke.

She wondered if he had any money or not; you couldn't tell with these kids, they all looked poor.

The little park was full of kids from school and older people on their lunch hours or with nothing to do. Two girls were playing violin duets, a straw hat at their feet, and passersby tossed coins into the hat and sometimes even a dollar bill. Old men sat under the trees playing chess. In the playground children ran in the sun, watched by their mothers.

Rachel and Andy found some space on a bench and sat down. "Where are you from?" she asked.

"Iowa. Where are you from?"

"New York."

"I mean before that."

"Oh," Rachel said. "Kansas City. Do I still have an accent?"

"Well, to me those other kids have an accent. I think a New York accent is really weird. They don't pronounce their r's."

Rachel laughed. "How did you end up here?"

"That's quite a story. When I graduated from high school I decided to drive to California. I had this Duster with a special engine I put in and racing tires. It was a couple of years old and had twenty-six thousand miles on it, but I thought I'd get there without any trouble. Well, I got to Los Angeles and then the thing broke down on me and I needed five hundred dollars to get it fixed. There was no *way* I could get five hundred dollars—I didn't even have a place to sleep. So, anyhow, I met some other kids and moved in with them, and then one of them had the idea that I should go on a TV game show and try to win a new car. At least some money. Her father knew somebody who knew somebody, so I applied to a lot of shows and I waited around a couple of months, and then I got on this game show, 'Wheel of Fortune'—did you ever hear of it?"

Rachel shook her head, no.

"Anyhow," Andy said, "you spin a wheel and get money for guessing the letters, and if you guess the puzzle you spend the money on prizes. You don't get to keep the money, you have to spend it. I kept hoping I'd get the car, right? So what I won was a trip to New York. That's how I came here. I really liked it here. It was funny, because everybody I knew told me I would hate it. But I think New York is great. So I called my parents and told them I wanted to go to college here. They were delighted because they'd given me up for a bum. My father really wanted me to go to college. He's a doctor. So they sent me money and I applied to NYU and got accepted, and here I am. That's why I'm older than the other kids, because I lost a year."

"How old are you?" Rachel asked.

"Nineteen."

"No wonder you like me, because we're both so old," Rachel said, smiling at him.

"What made you decide to go to college now?"

"I wasn't ready before," she said.

203

"My father would really have given *you* up," he said and laughed.

"Well, in between I got married," Rachel said.

"Are you still married?"

"Sure."

"How does your husband feel about this?"

"He's very supportive."

"Doesn't feel threatened?"

"No. Which is quite mature of him. He's very sure of himself. He doesn't have to prove himself at my expense."

"Yeah," Andy said thoughtfully. "You know, things aren't that much different with kids my age. A lot of the guys feel threatened by the girls, even though they won't admit it. A lot of them are really male chauvinists even if they're eighteen years old. It's the way they were brought up. I'm not. But it's funny, they don't think of girls as people at all. Their fathers never treated their mothers as people, so they just accepted that as the way things were. A lot of kids are from much more protective environments than they realize—or if they realize it, they won't admit it."

"What do you think you'll major in?" Rachel asked.

"Maybe psych. How about you?"

"Well, I was going to try banking, but psych is really my favorite course. I think I might major in psych."

"And then what? Graduate school?"

"I hadn't thought about that yet," Rachel said.

"But if you don't go to grad school you'll never get a decent job," he said. "Even if you want to be a social worker . . ."

We're sitting here discussing my future as if I was a kid like him, Rachel thought, amused and flattered. He doesn't think I'm somebody's mother dabbling in education. He really knows that I care. It never occurred to him that I could go right on being my husband's wife and social director.

"I thought I might take an education course and teach little kids," Rachel said. "I'd like to make them care more about learning than I did when I was young."

"Do you like kids?"

"I never really thought about it."

"Well," Andy said, "you'd better like them if you're going to teach them."

"You're right."

"Do you have kids?" he asked.

"No."

"Other people's kids aren't the same anyway," he said. "You don't feel guilty about their problems and you don't get so mad at them."

"I bet I would get mad at them," Rachel said.

"That's normal."

"You know, Andy, you're very smart and mature for your age."

"Come on," he said, annoyed. "I don't talk about your age, so don't make fun of mine."

"I wasn't making fun of it. I'd adore to be nineteen."

"So you could do it all over again better. My father says that."

"Okay," she said, "you got your revenge." They both laughed.

"Listen," he said, "they're having a revival of *Freaks* at the Village Cinema. Did you ever see it?"

"No."

"Neither did I. But it's something we ought to see if we're interested in psychology. Do you want to go with me later?"

"I have two more classes," Rachel said.

"I meant after classes."

"I have to go home then."

"Oh."

She realized she had hurt him. He seemed so casual and she felt so totally outside of his world that she had forgotten he really did seem to have a crush on her. "I have a better idea," she said. "My husband and I are giving a party Friday night at our apartment. Why don't you come?"

"Do I have to wear a suit?"

"No. Just not jeans."

"Okay. I'd like to come. Do you want me to bring anything?"

"A date if you'd like to. Not if you don't feel like it."

"Do you *want* me to bring a date?"

"Only if you want to. It really doesn't matter. Not all my friends are as ancient as I am. I think you'll have a good time."

"I'll think about the date," he said. "Actually, what I meant was, did you want me to bring some wine or anything?"

I hope he doesn't faint when he sees the apartment, Rachel thought. A bottle of sangría in a paper bag in his hand, and the maid takes his coat. "No, thanks anyway," she said. "That was sweet of you to offer. But just bring yourself."

He looked delighted. He wrote down her last name and her address in his notebook. "What time?"

"Eight. And there'll be food."

"Oh, good, I love a free meal!"

She looked at her watch. "I have another class."

"I'll walk you."

They strolled out of the park and toward the building where Rachel had her next class. Andy reminded her of the little boy who had carried her books in the sixth grade who had been red-haired too. Actually, he hadn't carried her books, he had punched her on the ear, but she had known then that he had a crush on her. Even at that age she had attracted funny little boys.

THE ENORMOUS SIZE of the student body had made it easy for him to follow Rachel ever since school began. No one paid attention to his obvious difference in age; they thought he was a professor or possibly a part-time student. He lost himself in the crowds and let them sweep him along, keeping her always in sight. He noticed that she came out of one class with the same red-haired boy every time, and he saw them go to Washington Square Park. When he saw them sit down on a bench, side by side, engrossed in conversation, his insides lurched and he felt nauseated. A wave of hatred toward this boy came over him, and then transferred itself toward her. Of course the boy liked her, who would not adore her? But why was she leading him on? He knew what the boy wanted. They all wanted that. But did she want it? Here downtown, away from everyone who knew her, far from her rec-

206

ognized and exemplary life, was she indeed someone else? Why would she waste her time on that young hippie if she didn't want to rut like all the other bitches? His goddess, dressed in those hideous teen-aged clothes—faded jeans, Snoopy sweatshirt—sitting next to a filthy boy who reeked of sauerkraut, her length of leg touching his, her soft mouth smiling at him. He closed and opened his hands and wanted to choke her.

As soon as he imagined her dead his eyes filled with tears. He couldn't kill her, he loved her. But he wanted to tear her away from that hairy-faced boy and restore her to her rightful place. It wasn't right for her to be here with these people. She didn't belong here. She was giving away pieces of herself to people who didn't deserve her, demeaning herself. She had to be punished. He didn't know yet how he would punish her, but he would think of a way.

NIKKI KNEW she would have to confide in someone. The strain of juggling her husband and her lover was more than she could handle without being able to talk to somebody about it and be reassured that she wasn't losing her mind. She had resolved never to tell anyone, because she had always rather looked down on women who had to boast of their sexual conquests, but this was more than just a conquest; it was a real problem of how to hold her life together. Robert had his key to her apartment now, and had gotten into the habit of coming in twice a week and sleeping over. He always referred to it as "our" apartment, although he never offered to share the rent. She wouldn't have let him take it over even if he'd wanted to. This apartment was her safety. Robert was really trying to be different, but if he had control of the apartment she would have no refuge that was truly her own, and then he could behave any way he wanted to. They were both aware of this. He felt the apartment was her weapon, and Nikki was not sure he wasn't partly right. If having a place to hide was a weapon, then it was.

When she knew Robert was not coming into New York she

207

spent the night with John at his apartment. She would meet him there at seven thirty carrying a change of clothes in her tote bag for the next day at the office. She left a few toilet articles and other things at his place. She didn't want to leave too much. She didn't want to belong to him any more than she did to Robert. She wanted to belong only to herself. John seemed to understand that much better than Robert did, but he was her lover, not her husband, and so it was easier for him to understand.

She really did want to make her marriage work. That was why she stayed at John's apartment when Robert was in the country, just in case Robert decided to surprise her by driving in and using his key. She would make sure that Robert never knew anything about John. He would leave her if he knew, whether he wanted to leave her or not, because that was the way he was.

She decided she would tell Rachel. Of all her friends Rachel was not the wisest, but she was the most discreet. Besides, Rachel had had more of a past than Nikki ever had, so perhaps she knew and understood more about the feelings Nikki couldn't figure out in herself. They made a date for lunch on a day when Rachel had no classes after twelve.

Nikki arrived at the restaurant first and was having a drink when Rachel came in. Rachel looked radiant. She was wearing wool slacks, a cashmere sweater, and a suede coat. Her face glowed with happiness. Nikki glanced at herself in the mirror beside the banquette where they were seated and thought she looked pinched and tired. What good was sex and love if they made you look like that?

"You look so marvelous I think I'm going to enroll in college," Nikki said.

Rachel smiled. "I just love it. I'm so glad to see you! How are you, are you all right?"

"Have a drink first," Nikki said. "Then we'll talk."

"Perrier, please," Rachel told the waiter. "With ice and lime. I have to study this afternoon," she said to Nikki. "Each one of my professors thinks his class is the only one anybody takes."

"Robert has started staying over in my apartment," Nikki said.

"Well, that's wonderful! I knew he'd come around. Did he say it was beautiful?"

"Yes. He's trying hard to be nice."

"But you seem worried."

"Do I look awful?" Nikki asked.

"No, you don't look awful. You just look as if you've been under a strain. Nobody would notice it who didn't know you as well as I do."

"I'm going to tell you something in the strictest confidence."

"Of course," Rachel said.

"I'm having an affair with John Griffin. Robert doesn't know."

Rachel beamed. "That's fantastic! I've always had a crush on John Griffin, he's my favorite actor. You ought to be happy. He can have any woman in the world and he picked you. Is he nice?"

"Yes, he's nice."

"Is he good? Oh, I shouldn't ask that, I take it back."

Nikki thought it was interesting that Rachel didn't ask her if she was in love with him or he with her. Obviously Rachel was wiser than she appeared. Ellen would have assumed wild love, and Margot would at least have asked. "Yes, he's good," she said.

"It's difficult for you, isn't it," Rachel said sympathetically. "Some women thrive on affairs, but not you. I couldn't handle it, I know."

"It's not the juggling that's hard," Nikki said. "I've always been very efficient and calm. It's not even the guilt. I faced the guilt when I decided to keep on with John even though Robert had come back. What's so difficult is . . . I want it to work with Robert, I really do, but I have this feeling that what's making it work is . . . well, John. I mean, he's a crutch for me in a way. He makes me feel sure of myself. And Robert senses that security and it makes him afraid he'll lose me. So he tries to be nicer."

"What are you going to do?"

"I don't know. It will all take care of itself eventually."

"That's what's making you so exhausted," Rachel said thoughtfully.

"What is?"

"Letting 'it' take care of itself. You're not the kind of person who can let other people run your life for you, Nikki. Maybe once you were, but not now. You have to feel in control of your life. We all do."

"I can't control either of them, but I don't want to," Nikki said. "I could send John away—that's control. But I can't make him fall madly in love with me and ask me to leave my husband, and I wouldn't want to. Robert is being wonderful, but I don't ever feel it's permanent. I think he's just trying to get me back. If he could convince me that he really takes me seriously—my worth, I mean—then I'd feel safe again. I just haven't felt safe for such a long time."

"What exactly do you want Robert to do?"

"I don't know. He'll have to do it, and then I'll know."

"Do you love him?"

"Robert?" Nikki said.

"Yes. Do you love him?"

Nikki thought for a few moments. "I don't know," she said. "I'm so tired. Sometimes I wish both of them would go away and leave me alone."

ELLEN HAD FACED the early Labor Day weekend with foreboding, knowing it meant the end of summer and that Reuben's wife and two children would be coming back to the city. All over New York the summer bachelors were getting their winter divorces from their girl friends, relegating them back to the five-thirty quickies, the after-dinner "walks," the endless waiting for phone calls. Ellen expected more from Reuben, but it was important to leave the arrangements to him. Now she was testing him. He did not fail her.

He had a bachelor friend who lent him an apartment. Ellen and Reuben met there for lunch or after work every weekday, and on Fridays they took the afternoon off and met there right after lunch. Ellen made sure that the bachelor friend of Reuben's did not know whom he was taking there, had never heard of her in fact. It was a pleasant little apartment—a bedroom, a living room, and a kitchen—but it had a temporary look. The man who lived there had been through a divorce that stripped him of most of his material possessions; he had heavy alimony and child-support payments, and his apartment was furnished with castoffs. Ellen felt this was an unwholesome atmosphere for her romance with Reuben.

She bought some hardy green plants and set them in straw baskets in the living room and bedroom. They made a tremendous difference. At least the place didn't look as if whoever lived there had given up. She said the plants were a thank-you gift for their host. Reuben bought a set of nice wine glasses and a Lucite cooler.

"I don't know how anybody can live like that," Ellen said. "He ought to get a girl friend. Bachelors have the shortest life expectancy of anybody, and I can see why. Did you look in his refrigerator?"

"You've made a difference just being around," Reuben said. "You always make any place you're in come to life."

"Why, thank you."

"This isn't the best arrangement," he said, "but I thought it would be safer than a hotel. And nicer."

"I just want to be with you," Ellen said.

"And I with you."

The switchboard at Heller & Strauss was turned off at five o'clock and Ellen didn't bother to give Hank or the girls her night line, so when she said she was working late they had to believe her. Some evenings she didn't get home in time to fix dinner, but they went right along without her, scrounging for themselves. She was glad Jill and Stacey were old enough to take care of themselves. Reuben's wife was used to his working late. The only difference in his life was that now he left the office early; he came home at the same time as usual.

Ellen became aware of what a sacrifice Reuben was making for their affair in terms of time he had ordinarily spent working. In the afternoons when they met at their borrowed apartment he always had manuscripts with him, to take home to edit. He groaned over one that was a thousand pages long, saying he had hoped the paper shortage would have ended books like that. But he loved his work, even when he complained. He was excited by the business dealings as well as the creative part. "Look at this, the perfect disaster novel—I signed it for very little money, it needs a lot of work, but I can sell it for a good six figures to paperback." Ellen wished she had something as interesting in her life to keep her busy. Part of Reuben's mind was always on his responsibilities, but she was an adult now and she realized she wouldn't want a man who ignored his career for her. She never wanted to be anywhere near another failure.

What was painful was the weekends. Reuben immersed himself in manuscripts from the office, and tried to be particularly attentive to his two sons. He neglected his wife to the point where she worried about his health, never imagining it was because he was thinking about another woman. Ellen, who had no weekend work, took long walks, cleaned the apartment, and yelled at her daughters. She thought about Reuben. They had discussed accidental meetings at various believable places, such as a museum or a department store, but had then rejected the idea because it would be too painful to pretend. They longed for another whole weekend away together, even an entire night, but they couldn't figure out how to arrange it.

"This is much worse than I anticipated," Reuben told her.

"In what way?"

"In every way. I'm obsessed with you. I can't keep up this charade at home. I want to leave my wife and live with you all the time."

"Oh, wouldn't that be lovely . . ."

"No, I'm not kidding. I mean it, Ellen. Would you leave your husband?"

"I . . . hadn't really thought about it except as a daydream. What would we do then?"

"I'd marry you of course. I'm a man who has to be married. I want only one woman. There's no reason not to be married if one doesn't want to run around. I want you and me to have a real home, a life. We could sleep in the same bed together every night, take our vacations together, have all those weekends to ourselves. You'd love my kids, Ellen. And I know I'd love yours. We'd have a normal life instead of hiding like criminals."

All right, Ellen told herself, now you have to decide. You do what you've always done and break it off, or you play for time, or you make the move. This is it.

"You look so miserable," he told her tenderly. "Why do you look so sad?"

"I'm thinking."

"Does my idea sound so horrible? If it does, I'll take it back."

"No, don't take it back. I like it. Would you really do it?"

"I will if you will."

"All right," Ellen said.

She had no intention of telling Hank anything until she was totally sure of Reuben; in fact, she wasn't really going to face the enormity of the whole idea until Reuben proved he meant what he had said. It was not that she didn't believe him, he was the same as the others, but this time something more was required of her and she had to protect herself.

On the last Monday of September Ellen and Reuben met at the borrowed apartment at lunchtime. They made love, as they always did, and then they lay in bed eating sandwiches and drinking wine.

"I told her over the weekend," Reuben said. He sounded almost too casual, but there was a catch in his voice that made Ellen sure he was telling the truth and was only trying to control his overwhelming emotion.

"And what did she say?"

"She said goodbye. She's a proud woman."

"What did you tell her?"

"I said I wanted to live apart from her and think things out. And that I feel our marriage is over. I didn't tell her about you because she knows who you are and I didn't want to make it any harder for you when you tell Hank."

213

"Did she ask if there was someone else?"

"Yes," Reuben said. "I guess that's natural. I said there was, but I wouldn't tell her who."

"Thank you."

"It's your turn now."

"I know," Ellen said. "I will. But where will you live?"

"I'm moving out this weekend to the Salisbury. It's a residential hotel on Fifty-seventh Street. I'll have a living room and a bedroom and bathroom and a real kitchen. We can live like human beings. You can move in with me this weekend."

"I can't move in with you till we're both divorced," Ellen said, horrified. "That's adultery. Your wife will name me corespondent, my husband will kill me!"

"I guess you're right," Reuben said sadly. "I was moving too fast. But it all seems like a fantasy come true. I feel so free. I feel guilty of course, but I feel reborn too. You're going to tell Hank tonight."

"It's Stacey's birthday this weekend," Ellen said, remembering. "She's going to be fourteen. We got her tickets to a rock concert, it's her first big grown-up night out with her friends. We're going to have a family celebration dinner before. I can't tell Hank till after this weekend."

"Then when will I see you?"

"I'll spend the day with you Saturday and help you get your new apartment all fixed up. And I'll come over Sunday morning and spend the whole day."

"And then we'll have our own place," Reuben said.

"It *is* like a dream come true," Ellen said.

"Do you trust me now?"

"Of course."

They kissed. "I want you to trust me," he said against her mouth. "Trust me."

"I do."

"There's nothing to be afraid of."

"I know."

"I'll take care of you now."

They made love again. Sex was explosive. She thought of this man, a real man, finally taking care of her after all these years of being the strong one, and she felt herself melting into his soul with relief and gratitude.

But afterward she thought that there were so many things Reuben couldn't do for her even though he wanted to. He couldn't leave Hank and the girls for her. She had to do that for herself. She was glad it was Stacey's birthday on Saturday. It put things off a little. She would live for the moment.

Reuben moved into the Salisbury Hotel on Friday afternoon. Ellen bought hardy green plants in straw baskets and put them in every room—the living room, the bedroom, the kitchen, even the bathroom. Dampness was good for plants. On Saturday she helped him arrange his things. There wasn't much to arrange; he had put his clothes in the closets and dresser, his books and papers were scattered around on tables the way he said he liked it, and he had ordered in a supply of food from a nearby market. There were six photographs of his two boys on the dresser, all in thin silver frames. He had lined them up like a reproachful shooting gallery, directly opposite the bed. They christened the bed that afternoon. Ellen was glad he was facing in the opposite direction from the photos.

What kind of man, she wondered, put pictures of his kids right opposite the bed, so he would have to face them first thing in the morning and last thing at night, and after having sex? How could he stand it? Maybe his wife had made him take the pictures with him. Or maybe he had taken them to give the appearance of a doting father. Or maybe the pictures didn't bother him the way they did her. Men had different sexual makeups from women, different systems of morality, she thought. She didn't know how Reuben could get an erection looking at a baleful photo of his sons. It didn't seem to hinder him.

There was a bottle of Dom Pérignon waiting for them in the refrigerator. They drank a toast.

"To our new life," Reuben said.

"To our new life."

215

She saw that he had even bought her a toothbrush. It sat on the ledge of the bathroom sink in its box, like a party favor. He had put a little card on it with her name and he had tied a silly bow around the box. Ellen was so touched that she wanted to cry.

OCTOBER

October 1975

THE DAY AFTER her sister's fourteenth birthday party Jill got her first period. She scrounged around her sister's messy closet until she found the tampons. It was ironic, she thought, that she was sixteen and taking her baby sister's tampons, because she had thought she would never need any of her own. Having a period horrified her. She tried to get the tampon in, but she got too tense and couldn't. She didn't want anything invading her body, especially down there. She threw the thing down the toilet and flushed it, put on her raincoat, and walked down Broadway until she found the drugstore that was open on Sundays. She was getting terrible cramps, so she bought an assortment of pills for that, some aspirin, and some pads that were supposed to stick to your underpants. She just helped herself to the things she needed and slammed them down on the counter as if she was used to such purchases, and the man who added her bill didn't pay any attention to her at all. She had joined the rest of the female world. He had no idea what a trauma this was for her.

Luckily her mother was away all day. Jill was relieved about the new guy, because he kept her mother out of her life when she most needed privacy. She took her pills and curled up on her bed, her knees to her stomach, wondering why cramps burned so badly when they were supposed to just cramp. Tears rolled down her face. She supposed now she would grow and change in every way. She wanted to die.

Stacey was out doing homework at a friend's house and her father was watching some sports thing on TV. Jill locked her bedroom door and waited on the bed until the pains got milder. She felt a little groggy. She got up and inspected herself in the mirror on the closet door, and then she stripped off all her clothes and inspected herself again, front, back, and side. She didn't look any different. Her buds of breasts felt sore but they didn't look bigger. There was a reassuring hollow between her hip bones, and her ribs went right up to her collarbone, it seemed. When she put her knees together she could get her fist between the insides of her thighs. Her backside was absolutely flat. She could count every little button on the back of her spine, and her shoulder blades stuck out like the tail fins on an old car. There was no place on her body where she could pinch the skin and find even a morsel of fat. She went into the closet and stepped on the scale. Eighty-nine. She'd lost all the blubber they'd forced on her in the hospital.

Jill danced in front of the mirror, admiring her thin naked body, praying to whatever power there was up there that nothing would change. She wasn't really having a deluge, just the beginning of a period. Maybe she wouldn't have them every month. Stacey didn't in the beginning. She wasn't built like Stacey anyway, so maybe her body wouldn't change much. God, she hoped not. She didn't want men looking at her. She was scared.

She got dressed again, put some records on the stereo, and went to bed. Those pills really knocked you out. She'd never taken any pill before except vitamins. She slept, and when she woke up it was seven o'clock. The last record had clicked off and the apart-

220

ment was awfully quiet. She wondered where everybody was. Then she remembered her horrible condition and raced to the bathroom to inspect the pad. She wished everything was still normal like it was yesterday. She felt cold.

They were all in the kitchen, her parents and Stacey. They were having cold cuts again. "We were just going to wake you up," her mother said.

"I'm just going to heat some soup," Jill said. "I have cramps."

"Again?" her mother said. "Poor thing."

Jill thought it was funny that after all the months of faking, this time she had real cramps. She took the soup to her room and held the mug against her stomach for warmth. When it cooled she went into the bathroom and flushed the soup down the toilet. She inspected her face in the mirror. The same face, a little thinner than it used to be; she was getting older. The childish roundness was gone. She was getting to look more like her mother than ever. Those cheekbones, that horseface. She sucked in her cheeks. Oh, God, in a few years nobody would be able to tell them apart!

When she got back to her bedroom her mother was sitting on the bed. "Feeling better?"

Who said you could come in my room without my permission, Jill thought furiously. "Yes," she said, "some."

"I used to have cramps too," her mother said, "until after I was married. Once you have a sex life they go away."

"Do we have to talk about that?" Jill said.

"I just thought it's been so long since we had a real mother-daughter talk. I really don't know very much about you lately, Jill. I don't know how you feel about things; you won't tell me. I don't know who your friends are, if there's a boy you like. We ought to be able to share more."

"Why?"

"Because I want to be your friend." Her mother took a pack of cigarettes out of her sweater pocket and lit one. She looked around for an ashtray, but there was none. Jill coughed pointedly and waved the smoke away.

"I thought you gave up smoking," Jill said.

"I just bought this pack yesterday. See, it's more than half full."

"I wish you wouldn't smoke in my room."

"All right," her mother said pleasantly. She dropped the lit cigarette into the empty soup mug. It sizzled as it went out in the bit of liquid that was left in the bottom. Jill wanted to throw up.

"How's school?" Ellen said.

"Fine."

"You must have different teachers this year. Do you like them?"

"They're okay."

"What's your favorite subject?"

"English," Jill said. She felt humiliated at having to answer these childish questions, especially since she knew her mother didn't give a damn about any of it. She wondered what her mother would say if she started giving *her* the third degree, starting with "Where were you today, I know you weren't with Margot like you said."

"Maybe you'll be a writer."

"I doubt it," Jill said.

"You ought to start thinking about college."

"All right."

"Do you have any idea where you want to go?"

"No."

"Would you like to go to my old alma mater?"

Jill shrugged. I'd die first, she thought.

"They have co-ed dorms now," her mother went on. "It seems so strange. How would you feel about living in a co-ed dorm?"

Jill shrugged.

"They say it's just like brothers and sisters," her mother went on. "Incest taboo. You date boys from other dorms. Still, I wouldn't like to have to share a bathroom with boys, would you?"

"No."

"It's a funny thing to say to one's own daughter, Jill, but I hope when you go to college you'll have a few affairs. I wouldn't want you to do it now, you're too young, but later, when you're older, I hope you do. I hope you're not a virgin when you get married."

Jill stared at her mother. I'm dreaming this, she thought.

"We were all so innocent and so scared," her mother went on. "We were full of guilt about nothing. Your generation is luckier. You can be friends with boys, share things with them. You can talk to them. When you get married, you won't marry a stranger."

"Why are you lecturing me?" Jill said.

"Oh, Jill, I'm not lecturing you. I just want to be your friend. I want you to be *my* friend. I want you to understand life, and I think I can help you. I used to have wonderful talks with my mother when I was your age."

"That's when she told you to marry a stranger," Jill said.

"We couldn't be frank about those things," Ellen said. "But I can be frank with you, and you with me. You're lucky to have an understanding mother. If you don't use me, you're going to be sorry."

Jill felt the guilt her mother always tried to arouse in her, and then she felt rage radiating through her body right down to her fingertips. It crackled like electricity through the wires of her arms and legs and pressed in on her heart. She struggled for breath, and sighed deeply.

"I have a headache, Mom. Could we talk another time?"

"*Will* we talk another time? Will you talk to me?"

"Yes, sure. But not now."

"All right," Ellen said. She picked up the mug she had defiled and kissed Jill on top of the head. "Get in bed and watch TV. You'll feel better tomorrow."

"Good night, Mom."

Jill locked her door and opened the window wide to get the smell of smoke and her mother's perfume out of the room. She felt as if she were strangling. The air rushed in, and she leaned out, gulping it. She drew back after a moment. Heights frightened her. She was always afraid she might fall or get carried away by some madness and jump. She shivered and shut the window except for a crack. Didn't her mother realize that when she was talking about when she was young and ignorant and had married a stranger, she was talking about Jill's father? Her mother's past was like another person in the room. She tried to imagine her mother as an eighteen-year-old girl at college going out with boys. In the olden days they had dates, and they kissed goodnight and necked, and they wanted to save their virginity for their husbands. Jill knew all about that from her friends. They sat around and talked about their parents' high school and college days, and they were amazed and amused. Jill and her friends adored old movies about the fifties. She liked that television show about teen-agers in her mother's day. She supposed her mother had been brought up to believe you had to be married *before* you ran around. It was really weird what those old people thought. But I could have tolerated all that, Jill thought, if she only didn't try to *manipulate* me all the time. She has to manipulate everyone. It's like she doesn't feel safe and satisfied until she has us all following her rules. She does that to make sure we're all in our places, like toys in a box. If she knew I never went out alone with a boy in my life she would have a fit. I know what it's like to have a brother-sister relationship with a boy. It's all I have. I never want any other kind. I think my mother is crazy. I think she's really a certified lunatic. But nobody puts *her* away, because she's the boss around here. God, it's terrible to be a kid and have no power at all! I wish she was dead.

THAT MONTH, October, two things happened that Margot thought were quite incredible. One was that Kerry finished the novel he had been writing, handed it in to his publisher, and the word swept the publishing business that it would be the hit of the following fall. Margot heard it first from Nikki. Even though Kerry had a different publisher, Nikki had heard. It annoyed Margot that he was not a failure. All this time she had been consoling herself that Kerry was just a rich dilettante, that he would never finish his book, that it just gave him something interesting to talk about to impress people. Now he had managed to fool her again.

That black model was still living with him. Apparently she knew how to handle him. It further annoyed Margot that a twenty-year-old girl knew more about how to handle a man than she did at forty. She felt that everything she had ever learned about men and life no longer applied. She was as ignorant as a new-born baby. What defenses did she have any more when the world had changed so?

The other incredible thing that happened was that Margot broke her rule about keeping her private life separate from her work life and went to bed with someone from the show. He was a new young cameraman who went out with her one day when she was taping with the mobile unit. She had never seen him before. He was tall and rough-looking and sexy, and she figured him to be about fifteen years younger than she was. They had a drink together when they finished working, and she let it drift on until she ended up in his mangy little apartment on the lower East Side. By now she was used to mangy little apartments. That was where young boys lived. The double bed completely filled the small bedroom, and he hadn't changed the sheets for months. There were bars on the windows because he lived on the ground floor. He had a motorcycle which he kept right in the apartment so no one would steal it. It filled half the tiny living room. The worst part was that he lived with his brother, and in the middle of copulating, the brother appeared and looked right at them, then calmly went into the living room, where he spent the rest of the night on the couch.

No, that was not the worst part. The worst part was that Margot knew the brother was looking at them and she didn't care. She felt perversely proud of herself that the young man *knew* she was sexy and desirable.

In the morning she had breakfast with the two of them. The brother was an unemployed actor and he was two years older. She loved that she had gone to bed with the younger one. The older one was as attractive as his brother, and he looked at her as if he would have liked to have a chance with her if she wasn't already taken. She wanted to tell him she wasn't taken, that she'd forgotten his brother's name. She was beginning to feel hostile as her customary guilt took over. As soon as they finished breakfast she left and took a taxi home. It cost her a fortune.

The young cameraman didn't call her. She realized he was used to casual sex. She hoped he would never mention what had happened, not to her and especially not to anyone at work. She arranged her schedule so she could avoid him. Why hadn't she picked someone respectable she had interviewed? There were plenty of them; lawyers, scientists, businessmen, even employed actors. Published writers, movie stars, congressmen. Why did she pick the dregs? Why couldn't she control her insatiable ego? Or lack of ego . . .

She kept seeing that tiny room again in her mind, the filthy sheets, and the black iron bars against the grimy windowpane. The little curtains that had so touched her because he cared about his place now seemed as tacky as they actually were. The glamorous motorcyle (that meant youth!) now struck her as offensive. The older brother's uncurious eyes burned into her mind. Had he thought she was pathetic, a joke?

Her boundaries were melting. She could no longer count on the rules she had set for herself to control her instincts of the moment. She was increasingly depressed and couldn't sleep at night. She got more sleeping pills and began taking them regularly, with a drink to speed them along. She poked a hole in each end of the small capsule with a pin so they would act faster. Sometimes she crashed into a dreamless sleep, but some nights the pills didn't work at all. She would lie in bed, perspiring, reliving moments she would have given anything to make not have happened. She redid the dialogue in her mind, making the scenes come out the way they should have instead of as they had. Finally she would get up and take another sleeping pill, sometimes even another. She was afraid they would be gone, and what would she do then?

226

She got another prescription. The doctor didn't seem to notice their frequency. She still had her little hoard. Every night when she took her pills she felt sorry for herself because she was alone. Weekends were unbearable. Everyone she knew had someone to spend weekends with. Saturdays were all right because the streets were full of people, the stores were open, she could shop or pretend to shop. But Sundays were endless. She read the entire *New York Times* and watched television. After a while she found she couldn't even read the *Times*, she could only look at the ads and the headlines. She was too nervous to concentrate. It was impossible to read a book. She was too depressed to go to a movie alone and too depressed to call someone to go with her. She napped a lot on Sundays during the day. Then at night she wasn't sleepy at all and had to take an extra pill, sometimes two extra. She drank all evening. At times she wondered if she wouldn't be better off the way she had been before, making a fool of herself with anonymous young men. Other people did it.

Her depression was like a physical pain. Although it was only October, already she was thinking of Christmas and New Year's Eve. Nobody her age paid any attention to New Year's Eve any more, but you couldn't avoid Christmas. Should she go home to her family? She hated her family, what was left of them, and they acted as if they hated her. Besides, traveling during the holiday was intolerable, and she would probably have to work. Whom did she have to give presents to? A lot of people in the office she didn't even like. She would have to brave crowds and spend a lot of money, for what? Maybe she wouldn't give anybody anything, start a new trend. Let them hate her too. Business gifts were hypocritical anyway. She knew the minute she heard those carols on the radio and in the street she would go into her usual bad mood. Rachel would give a party; that was nice. Kerry would be there in his glory as the future famous author; that was not nice. He would be with Haviland. That was not nice either. Margot would have no date she wasn't ashamed to be seen with, so she would be alone. That was the worst. She would have loved to bring someone they all would recognize from the show, but they were all married. Christmas they would be with their wives and kids. Ugh.

At work Margot continued to be the good robot. It was difficult to concentrate, but she forced herself through each day. It was the nights that were so bad. She didn't want a blind date, she was too old and tired to spend an evening making forced conversation with a stranger. She didn't want to inherit the problems of a lonely man her age. The only alternative was prowling.

She prowled again. Sometimes she was rejected. She realized that what she had finally brought herself to offer to a stranger was no longer appreciated as a prize. It was all too available. She went to singles bars and saw the girls in the ladies' room primping and comparing notes on the men. The girls were all sloppy and interchangeable. The men were unappealing and interchangeable too. All these unappetizing people performed various sexual acts with one another for the price of a drink, and it made the entire idea repugnant. She wanted to offer herself to a man and have him be glad, thrilled, enchanted. She was fifteen years too late. Unless, of course, he loved her. Where was she going to find a man to fall in love with her? She didn't have the faintest idea how to begin.

ELLEN WAS SO RECKLESSLY spending all her free time with Reuben that she realized she could have lied to him and said she had told Hank, and he would have believed her. But she couldn't lie to Reuben too. Not if she intended to marry him eventually. Her second marriage would be based on truth, not lies.

"I want everything out in the open now," Reuben said. "Why can't you tell him? Do you want me to?"

"No, not you! That would be horrible. I *will* tell Hank, darling. Just let me pick the right time."

"Are you afraid of him?" Reuben asked.

"Hank? Oh, no. I do feel sorry for him though."

"Ah, yes, pity. That's their ultimate weapon."

"We have all the freedom we need now," Ellen said. "What more could we have? We see each other every day at the office, I'm here with you almost all the time. Do you want to call me at home? You wouldn't have the poor taste to do that even if Hank did know—no, especially if Hank knew. Not until either he or I had moved out."

"What are you going to do about that?" Reuben asked.

"Moving out?"

"One of you has to."

"I'm not so sure," Ellen said. "We could sleep in separate rooms. I could put Stacey in with Jill and take Stacey's room. The problem is, Hank has no money, and it's taking all my salary just to make ends meet. I took a loan out from the bank to pay for the girls' school. Hank had to cosign it. It was so humiliating. I'm the wage earner in this family, but I don't make enough, and besides, I'm a wife, which is just like being an underage child in this country. A single woman could take out a loan. Margot could take out a loan in a minute. But I had to bring my husband in to cosign it with me. How could one of us move out? We're both too poor."

"You could move in with me," Reuben said.

"How would that look?"

"What do you *mean* 'How would that look?' " He laughed. "You have the most bizarre system of values, Ellen. People move in with other people every day. Married people. It is not a federal offense."

"Your wife would take all your money. She'd have a right."

"I don't care. I can make more."

"How would we live?"

"We'd live the same way we're living now," Reuben said. "Except you wouldn't be nervous and frantic any more. I'd take care of you. You'd still have your job. Believe me, I can take care of your children and my children where school is concerned. You said Stacey's so bright; we'll get her a scholarship. Those things happen. When you and I live together—"

"When we're married we can get an apartment," Ellen said,

229

"and the girls will live with us. But if I just walk out, then they'll have to stay with Hank, and they need me. I think we should both get our divorces and then get married and then live in an apartment."

"It's all right with me," Reuben said. "But we can't get our divorces until we tell our spouses, can we?"

Ellen smiled weakly. "I know."

"You don't even have to leave him. I'll be fair and self-sacrificing about that. Just tell him. You can't get a divorce until you tell him, Ellen."

"I will. I'll tell him."

"When?"

"It's almost November. I'll tell him right after Christmas. I can't ruin Christmas for the girls."

"You'll tell him after Christmas."

"Yes. I will. It's the perfect time. We'll start off the new year with a new leaf."

"Christmas."

"Reuben, Christmas is important to Hank!"

"I forgot, it's the goyim's major holiday," Reuben said.

"Well, you wouldn't tell your wife and kids on Chanukah, would you?"

"Ellen, my darling, my wife doesn't even know when Chanukah is."

"Well, what I meant was that Christmas is a hell of a time to be alone."

"I'll be alone."

"You won't. You'll have to go visit your kids."

Reuben sighed. "That I will. With sacks of presents."

"So you see? It's a family holiday, no matter whether you're religious about it or not. We aren't religious. I haven't set foot in a church since my wedding except to go to someone else's wedding. I'll tell Hank after Christmas. Then if he wants to move into the Y or live with a friend, he can. Or he can stay on in the apartment. But at least we won't have to spend Christmas pretending to the girls that we're happy."

"I bet you haven't fooled them a bit," Reuben said.

"Oh, I'm sure we have."

"Whew. You're a tough lady."

"What do you mean?"

"You're stubborn."

"I just want to be fair," Ellen said. "Let's set a target date. January first, 1976. Everything fresh and new. We'll have clear consciences and start our new life out in the open."

"I hired a divorce lawyer," Reuben said.

"You *did?*" she said, amazed.

"Well, I don't know how to do it myself."

"When did you hire him?"

"Last week. Just to set up a preliminary division of property. I don't even have any idea what I own or what I want to take, and my wife doesn't either. We aren't terribly materialistic people. The biggest fight is going to be over the books and records."

"Oh, Reuben. You're such a wonderful person and I'm sorry I've made things so difficult for you."

"You certainly have," he said. "But nothing is worth having that isn't hard to get."

"Oh, sweetheart."

He produced a sheet of paper on which he had typed a paragraph: *I, Ellen Rennie, the undersigned, swear to tell my husband Hank on ——— that I am in love with Reuben Weinberg and want a divorce. Signed ———.* "Sign this," he said.

She took it and read it. "Oh, Reuben, what are you going to do with that?"

"Put it on the bathroom mirror so you have to look at it every day."

"Also the maid," she said. "I'll sign it if you put it in the drawer."

"I'll put it on my cock. Just sign it."

"Okay." She took the pen he offered her and filled in the date January 1, 1976, and signed her name at the bottom.

"January first!" he said. "I thought you were going to tell him after Christmas."

"That's an outside date. Contracts give an outside date."

"Not this contract," Reuben said. He tore it up. Ellen felt a surge of panic.

"Oh, Reuben don't leave me! I'm sorry! I'll sign anything you want. I promise. Please—"

He smiled and took a Xerox copy out of his briefcase. "I knew I might have trouble with you so I made a copy. Write 'December 26, 1975.'"

Ellen took the copy and filled in the date he wanted and signed her name. Her hand was trembling. Reuben took the contract and looked at it with satisfaction, then he tucked it neatly into the corner of the desk blotter.

"I would die if you left me," Ellen said.

"I won't leave you."

"Promise."

"I promise I won't leave you. I'm going to marry you." He put his arms around her and she finally felt her heart stop pounding so hard. He kissed her face. "Poor, scared Ellen," he said.

"I love you," she said.

"I love you," he said. "I've proved it, haven't I?"

"Yes."

"And you're going to prove it too, aren't you?"

"I'll start proving it now," Ellen said and led him into the bedroom. It wasn't what he had meant, but it would suffice for the moment.

NOVEMBER

November 1975

RACHEL REALIZED that in the past two months she had been so busy with college and her new, full life that she had stopped thinking about Nikki in the mooning adolescent way she had before, and now thought of her as a good friend and an equal. Her crush had evaporated, replaced by the genuine concern one has for a dear friend. All her frantic scurrying through those psychology books to find out the ramifications of her "aberration" had produced only one thing—a love for psychology, which had made her decide to major in it. But it was her own instinct and not anything she had read that convinced Rachel now that she had never really been in love with Nikki, she had been in love with the free life Nikki seemed to represent. She hadn't been a lesbian at all, she had been lonely.

She was happy for Nikki because of her affair with John Griffin, but in her heart she hoped Nikki would eventually get back together with Robert. Rachel knew it was hard for her to see Robert the way his wife saw him. He seemed pleasant, bright, and attractive. When he was in a good mood he was warm, a man you could feel at home with. But Nikki saw him in all his other moods, and he had invested a good deal of his masculine identity in her as his Wife—capital W. Rachel knew that Nikki was far better able to cope with loneliness than she had ever been. But she wondered if that was because she had been lonely at the beginning of her adult life, when she was a new, single girl in New York, before she had met Lawrence, while Nikki had chosen loneliness much later, when she was a grown woman, with an established career, two grown children, and knowledge of the limitations of the accepted alternative.

School had opened many doors in Rachel's mind. Now she tried to analyze people's motivations and feelings. She no longer felt like just an ornament, even at her own parties. She still performed her chores by rote, but there was something added: she saw her guests as people. She could zero in on who was lonely, who was shy, and link that person with someone friendly. She realized that many people at parties were even more uncomfortable than she had been, and that the most gregarious of them might be so only because of prefortification by alcohol or a pill. She wished she could think of a man for Margot, who was the loneliest person she knew. The change in Margot during the last several months was apparent. Nothing seemed to please her. Her mouth was clamped firmly shut in an expression that might seem to the onlooker to be disapproval, but Rachel knew it was pain.

She invited Margot to every party she gave. Her entertaining was much more limited lately because of schoolwork, and she wanted to introduce Margot to as many people as she could, but in all honesty Rachel had to admit the pickings were lousy. She could never be the sort of happily married woman who assumed any single or divorced man was "going to waste" if he wasn't immediately grafted onto one of her single or divorced friends. Some people were blatantly incompatible. Margot was almost impossible to please. Where someone else might just tell a man she would prefer him to change a habit she didn't like, Margot would use it as an excuse to get rid of him right away. Those newly di-

236

vorced men were like kids. They had been out of the mainstream for so long they thought nothing had changed since the fifties. They had to be taught. But Margot insisted that any man her age or older was "already ruined." Rachel was glad Margot wasn't a schoolteacher.

Margot had even flirted with Andy, but she seemed to frighten him off. He was aware that she wasn't interested in him as a human being but just as a conquest. He was thrilled to be included in the Fowlers' social life, and he fitted in very well, but he didn't carry fitting in so far as to sleep with Rachel's friends—not that Rachel would have minded at all if he did. He had been so sweet at the first party Rachel invited him to that Lawrence had liked him very much, and he had become a sort of son to them. When Rachel knew that one of Lawrence's friends had a daughter more or less the right age for Andy she would invite her, and he either took to the girl or not, depending on what kind of person he thought she was. Apparently trying to suit people to each other didn't really work no matter what their ages; they had to suit themselves.

Rachel invited Ellen and Hank more often than she used to because Ellen and Margot were so close she didn't want Ellen to feel hurt knowing that Margot was always there and she seldom was. Lawrence didn't like Ellen. He said she was full of hostility. But as long as she was included in a large enough group of people so he could avoid her, he was perfectly willing to let Rachel invite her. The first time Ellen saw Andy she rushed over to Rachel, fairly licking her chops.

"Well! Who does *he* belong to?"

"To himself," Rachel said, smiling.

"He's not gay?"

"No."

"How old is he?"

"Nineteen."

"Where did you find him?"

"At school. He's in my psych class."

"Freshman or sophomore?"

237

"Freshman," Rachel said. "He lost a year traveling. Ellen, you aren't tired of Reuben already, are you?"

"Oh, no," Ellen said. "I want him for Jill."

Hank came over. "Want who for Jill?" he asked.

"That red-haired boy," Ellen said. "Isn't he cute?"

"He's too old for Jill," Hank said.

"Why? He's nineteen, she's sixteen. When I was sixteen I would have been thrilled to go out with a nineteen-year-old boy."

"She's too young," Hank said angrily.

"Oh, fathers and their precious daughters," Ellen said, amused.

"Well, I do think she's a little young for him," Rachel said. "There's such an enormous difference at their ages."

"You're supposed to be on my side," Ellen said.

"You're perfectly free to ask both of them," Rachel said mildly. "Excuse me." She went to the door to greet Nikki and Robert. She hoped Andy didn't think he *had* to ask Jill out just because Ellen was her friend. He was so polite he'd probably agree to anything to pay her back for her hospitality. Well, she wasn't going to worry about it; he was old enough to take care of himself. Maybe they'd even like each other—although she doubted it. When she had been sixteen she couldn't think of a single thing to say to a nineteen-year-old college boy.

In November it was Rachel's birthday. She was thirty-six. For the first time since she had been twenty-one a birthday didn't bother her. Thirty-five was such a banal number, thirty-six had to be better. In the morning Lawrence waited to have breakfast with her. She had a nine o'clock class. Every year on her birthday he had left a fresh white carnation on her breakfast tray for her to find when she woke up, but today he handed the flower to her. She decided to wear it to class.

"You don't get your present till tonight," he said.

They had decided to have dinner together, just the two of them, at Lutèce. He had offered to invite any other people she would like to have, but Rachel wanted him all to herself. He seemed flattered and pleased. She realized for the first time that Lawrence had always been much more acutely aware of the dif-

238

ference in their ages than she would have imagined, and that her life as an undergraduate had worried him. He was afraid she would grow so much intellectually that she would want someone who would spend more time with her. Instead, as it turned out, it was he who was spending more time with her. Now at night when he was working in his den she sat there too and studied. It was not that he had been locking her out but that he thought she would prefer to watch television.

At psych class Andy slid into the seat beside her. She had been putting her books on the seat to save it for him, but he always got there so early that there was seldom a problem. "What's the flower for?" he asked.

"It's my birthday. Lawrence always gives me a white carnation. I don't even know why."

"Oh, why didn't you tell me it was your birthday? I would have gotten you something."

"I don't want you to spend your money on me," Rachel said.

"Well, let's do something special," Andy said. "Please? Come on, let's cut classes the rest of the afternoon and I'll take you to the Aquarium."

"The Aquarium?"

"It's *great!* Have you ever been there?"

"I don't even know where it is," Rachel said.

"It's in Coney Island."

"You want to go to Coney Island in November?"

"The Aquarium is open. You'll love it. It's one of my favorite places. I used to go there a lot when I first came to New York. I haven't been there for a long time. It doesn't take long on the subway."

"The subway?" she said in horror.

He grinned. "You said you don't want me to spend my money on you, and I can't afford a cab."

"All right, silly." She grinned back at him. "I never cut a class before. I hope it isn't habit-forming."

"It isn't. I do it all the time."

They both laughed. She had never imagined she would go on

239

the subway, but it was a nice day and she felt safe with him. Evidently people had to go to the Aquarium on the subway, and they probably went a lot of other places on it too, so she would risk it. Andy would be too offended if she paid for a cab.

Rachel hadn't been on the subway for almost fifteen years. She was astonished at the change. The outsides of the silver cars were covered with brightly colored graffiti done in acrylic paints: names, numbers, and even the most beautiful and innovative drawings she had ever seen outside an art gallery. She had read in the newspapers about kids doing that, and how angry the authorities were, but she thought it was marvelous. It was pop. The world was pop. Who could believe some of the things that went on? Was it worse for kids to write their names on the outside of a subway car? They even wrote inside the cars. She hadn't read about that in the papers. Maybe it was new. She longed to write her own name, but all she had with her was the felt-tipped pen she used to take notes in class, and that wouldn't even be noticeable. Besides, there were other adults in the cars, and they probably wouldn't approve at all.

The train racketed and shrieked through the tunnel, rocking, on its way to Coney Island. She and Andy had to shout to each other in order to be heard.

"It's not so bad, is it?" he yelled.

"One thing you have to say for it," Rachel yelled back, "it's fast."

"It's the silver bullet. Biggest bargain in town, except for the Aquarium."

Bitch! He had followed her when she cut her classes with that repulsive little Andy, and when they got on the train he got on the car behind them, standing near the glass so he could watch them. She didn't belong on the subway and she didn't belong with a hippie kid either. He saw their mouths moving but he couldn't tell what they were saying. What was he telling her that made her laugh so? Her face lit up when she was with the kid and

240

she looked like a teen-ager herself. He wanted to grab them both and smash their heads together.

He still loved her, but his love had turned to pain and an incredible rage since she had become friendly with the boy. If someone so unlikely as that Andy could have her, why couldn't he? She knew him, she could have picked him if she wanted him. Women did that all the time. They were aggressive. They saw a man they wanted and chose him as if they were simply buying a new dress, took him away with them, used him, and gave him away or forgot him when they were bored. Rachel was saving the seat for Andy now in class; nothing escaped his watchful eye. Twice he had sneaked into the lecture hall, and he had seen her put her books on the chair next to hers until Andy came. He bet she didn't tell her husband *that*.

That flower she was wearing—who had given it to her? Her husband or the kid? She'd worn it to class, so it must have been from Lawrence. What kind of gesture was that toward a princess on her birthday? He would have given her masses of flowers, smothered her in them, overwhelmed her with the generosity of his love. Yes, he knew everything about her, even that it was her birthday.

He never ceased to be amazed at the facility with which he slipped from one life into another: his life at home and then this. He even fooled himself. When he was away from her he was always drawn to her, even though he now felt this almost constant anger that made him ill.

The train stopped at Coney Island and the two of them got off. He got off too. For a moment he had the wild idea that he could push the boy off the platform onto the tracks of an oncoming train, but he realized she would see who had done it. He would have to push her off too, and that was not the plan he had for her. His plan, which was carefully forming in his mind, was not to destroy her but to have her. He would punish her, and she would be sorry, and he would own her. It was a plan with many risks. He could not go too far, only far enough. But he had to be sure nobody knew who had done it, in case of an accident. He could never be absolutely sure he could control the violence within him. That sort of thing was so hard to gauge. He had to protect himself. It reassured him to know now that he wasn't crazy. A madman wouldn't make such careful plans, he would just go ahead and do it.

He followed them at a distance until they went into the Aquarium. After a decent interval he went across the street, paid his entrance fee, and entered the darkness. He could hear them before he saw them. In a while his eyes grew accustomed to the darkness and he could see them too. There were plenty of columns to hide behind. The floors and walls were covered with black carpet. Set into the walls were large illuminated fish tanks, almost like stage sets, containing all sorts of sea life. Everything else was black, to further enhance the dramatic effect of these living tableaux. There were sharks, piranhas, barracudas—the carnivores of the sea. He felt very much akin to them as he slipped silently from column to column, his footsteps so quiet on the black carpet that he might be swimming, his eyes seeking her out in the dark. His tongue tasted her blood, and he sighed, very softly, no more than a breath, the sound mingling with the artificial air in this windowless and timeless place.

RACHEL DIDN'T LIKE it here. She didn't want to hurt Andy's feelings by making him leave, but this dark, sinister place made her feel creepy, and she longed to hurry out. Besides, she'd never even liked fish. She'd never had a fish tank at home, she didn't think they were very pretty, and a lot of the fish in those huge tanks set into the walls were killers. She wondered if the glass ever broke.

"Isn't this great?" Andy said.

"It scares me a little," she said.

"It is kind of scary, but it's so dramatic. That's what I like about it."

"To scare me?"

"No, Rachel! I mean it's what the ocean is really like. It's pitch dark way down. It's like this. You and I would never see any of these things."

"I think I'd rather see them on a plate," Rachel said.

He grinned at her. "You really are a city girl."

"I have the feeling I'm being watched."

"So do they."

"I hate their eyes. I feel as if I'm being watched from all over. I have just decided I'm never going to be a scuba diver."

The ocean wasn't lit up like those fish tanks, Rachel thought. In the real ocean it was dark, and strange shapes brushed by you, soundlessly, and they could sink their teeth into you if they wanted to. She shuddered. It wasn't the fish that frightened her, with their lethal teeth, it was this place itself. The fish were sealed into their watertight compartments. But this black and silent place seemed sealed off too, so far away from the real world that it might even be underground. She kept having the feeling that there was someone or some *thing* in these halls themselves, not inside the tanks, but here with her and Andy, something dangerous. It almost seemed to breathe. A few times she looked back, glanced around, but there was no one there but the two of them. She wasn't a superstitious person, but she was conscious of an evil force and she didn't know what it was.

Andy took her hand. "You look so pale," he said sympathetically. "There's nothing to be afraid of."

"I'm not pale, it's the light."

"I wanted you to have a good time on your birthday," he said. "We should have gone to the Planetarium, I guess."

"No, this is interesting. But can we go now?"

"Okay. But the best thing is—"

"Now!" She surprised herself with the sharpness of her tone. She was frightened. "Let's run, I'll race you," she said, to make a joke of it, and turned in the direction of the exit. She should have known not to make a race of it, for of course Andy was far ahead of her in a minute. She heard her breath rasping as she ran, and then she knew it wasn't her own breath—there was someone else behind her. Her heart pounded with panic, and her legs ached as she fled, too breathless to call.

She burst out into the sunlight. The reassuring world was still there, so ordinary, so wonderful. She looked back, and there was no one there.

They returned to the city on the subway, and Andy insisted on riding with her all the way to the stop near her apartment building, even though he lived in the Village. She kept assuring him that she could get off with him and then take a cab, as she always did from school.

"I don't want you to be alone on your birthday," he said. "I can at least deliver you to Lawrence."

He really was sweet. She knew there were a lot of things he liked that she couldn't enjoy any more, but she could always enjoy his enthusiasm. She hoped he wouldn't outgrow it or have it eroded away in this harsh city.

When she got to her apartment Lawrence still wasn't home, so she had a steaming hot bubble bath, listening to records and drinking a glass of wine. She usually didn't drink in the tub, but she had been through a lot this afternoon and she felt she deserved it.

When she was dressed and made up, Lawrence came home. He took a shower, shaved, and dressed, and then they had some champagne in the living room. "Come in the den," he said, "and I'll give you your presents."

There was a great pile of boxes on the floor in the den, reaching almost up to Rachel's head. Each was carefully wrapped. On the very top was a tiny box.

"Which first?" she asked.

"The little one."

It was a pair of small diamond earrings, rather old-fashioned-looking, edged in gold. "I love them!" she cried.

"Now the big ones," he said, pointing at the boxes.

She rushed to him and gave him a hug and a kiss. "Thank you for my earrings." She put them right on.

They weren't boxes at all, they were books. It was an entire encyclopedia, the biggest set she had ever seen. Lawrence had had each volume wrapped separately. She wondered where she could ever keep them, until she noticed that he had emptied out the whole bottom shelf of one of the bookcases that lined the wall.

"Oh, they're wonderful!" she said, delighted.

"I just wanted you to know that I appreciate *all* of you," he said.

The two of them put the books into the shelf in alphabetical order, had another glass of champagne, and left the masses of torn gift paper and ribbons for the maid to take away. Lawrence had his chauffeured limousine downstairs and they went to the restaurant.

Rachel loved Lutèce. The lovely town house, the fireplace in the dining room, the fresh flowers on the tables, the big crystal wineglasses, and most of all the food. She always ate whatever she wanted to on her birthday, even though she starved herself for a week afterward to do penance. She and Lawrence had a long, leisurely dinner, comfortable in each other's company and in their love. She was glad she had insisted they invite no one else. She hadn't seen Lawrence so relaxed in a long time. Between courses he held her hand under the table.

After the enormous dinner they had coffee and brandy, and then they went home in the limousine, which had waited for them.

"This was the most perfect evening," Rachel said. "Thank you."

"You're welcome."

Their apartment looked like a funeral home, filled with white roses. White roses in vases all over the living room, in the den, even in their bedroom. There must have been ten dozen of them, over a hundred roses. Rachel sneezed. She looked at Lawrence, about to tell him he was crazy to have done it, when she realized he was as surprised as she was.

"Who sent those roses?" he said.

"I don't know, where's the card?" She was rushing around looking for a card, but there was none. "Minnie!"

245

The maid came in. "Yes, Mrs. Fowler?"

"Where's the card that came with these?"

"There wasn't any card."

"Well, who sent them?"

"A delivery boy brought them just after you and Mr. Fowler left. I put them in water."

"Where are the boxes?"

"In the trash. You want me to get them?"

"I'll go with you," Rachel said. "There'll be the florist's name on the boxes at least," she told Lawrence. "Maybe the card is somewhere too."

"I looked for a card," Minnie said. "I thought if someone spent that much money there'd be a card."

Rachel went to the service entrance, where Minnie had neatly piled up the empty florist's boxes. She didn't know why the white roses made her feel so uncomfortable. They were vulgar, but they shouldn't seem ominous. They were probably from some business person who wanted a favor from Lawrence and thought he'd make a good impression by overwhelming her. But Rachel couldn't imagine anyone with such bad taste, unless it was some oil sheik, and even they had better taste if they did business with normal people like Lawrence. The roses were like an intrusion. The air of the entire apartment seemed heavy with their sweetness. She rummaged through all the boxes, but there was no card. She phoned the florist.

"This is Mrs. Fowler. You sent me about ten dozen white roses, but there's no card. Who sent them?"

"I don't know, Mrs. Fowler. My assistant took the order. I'll ask him." She waited. "He says the man didn't write a card."

"Put your assistant on, please."

"Hello." A younger voice, also a man.

"Who bought all those white roses?" Rachel asked.

"I don't know. It was a man. He paid cash and he didn't want to write a card."

"What did he look like?" Rachel demanded.

"I don't remember. Just a man. I don't know—forties maybe. He had a hat on."

"Didn't you ask him for his name?"

"We don't if they pay cash. But it was such a big order, well, I asked, and I gave him our card because I'd never seen him before."

"Would you look up his name, please?" She didn't know why her voice was so sharp with nervousness. She felt as if someone had inflicted these roses on her, not given her a present.

"Oh, I don't have to look it up," the young man said, "I remember it."

"What was it?"

"Mr. Smith."

LAWRENCE INSISTED on throwing out the roses because they were making her unhappy. She kept pacing up and down the bedroom saying, "Oh, shit." It was like some enormous practical joke that had backfired—but why? What was the point? Was she supposed to be pleased or upset? Who was "Mr. Smith"?

"Well, whoever he is," Lawrence said comfortingly, "when he comes to visit and there aren't any roses, he'll wonder why."

"But nobody's coming to visit."

"Maybe it's somebody we dropped from our list," Lawrence said.

"If I was thrilled, which I'm obviously not, what good was it going to do him if he was so sneaky about it?"

"Maybe he'll call."

"Things like that are so *mean*," Rachel said.

"Forget about it," Lawrence said. "Come to bed. He's just out a lot of money."

"Maybe it's somebody I don't even know," Rachel said. "He might have seen my picture in 'W' after the party at East Hampton. He's trying to buy his way into our affections, like Gatsby."

"Don't worry about it," Lawrence said. "Let's go to sleep."

Rachel got into bed next to his comforting warmth. She felt as if somehow their evening had been ruined by an intruder, and she held on tightly to her husband, wishing that their lives were different, that they didn't know all those people, that the two of them could just spend their lives alone, from time to time seeing only the few friends they really liked and trusted.

In November John Griffin's book was finished, and edited by Nikki. He wrote the way he had sex, tirelessly. She'd never had an author who worked so fast. As to being edited, although he was careful and thoughtful about every change she wanted to make, he was reasonable too, and he finally let her make most of them. She thought part of the reason he was so amenable was that he had a deadline: he had to go away on location to make another movie. His novel was planned for publication the following September. She could see his attention already wandering away from the small but important final changes she was making in his book to the script he had at home that he was reading, re-reading, and becoming involved in.

When his manuscript was all finished she took him to lunch to celebrate. He let her sign the check. He was leaving for Yugoslavia the next morning.

"You're a lovely lady," he said.

"Thank you. You're a lovely man."

"I wish I could do something for you."

"You have."

"I mean, I want to give you something."

"You've already given me a wonderful book."

He smiled, pleased. "But I mean I want to give you a present. Or do something for you."

"Authors don't have to give editors presents," she said, laughing. "Even rich authors."

"I don't mean as an author to an editor," he said. "I mean from me to you."

Nikki looked at him. His face was calm and she couldn't read

248

his eyes. What am I supposed to ask for, she thought, a piece of jewelry? A hundred dollars? A screen test? Does every woman he goes to bed with want something?

"I don't want anything," she said.

"Are you sure?"

"Absolutely."

"Would you like to stop at my apartment before you go back to the office?" he asked.

"All right," she said, pretending to be as casual as he was pretending to be.

At his apartment he made love to her for the last time. They both already knew that Robert had decided to come into the city for the evening. Knowing this was the last time with John for a long time, maybe forever, made her want to let herself go more than ever before, so naturally she couldn't let go at all. She hated goodbyes. He was as enthusiastic as always, and she had to call her secretary to say she wouldn't be in that afternoon.

When she had to leave he didn't seem to want to detain her. She saw the partly packed suitcases on the chairs, the already packed ones lined up, the script on his dresser. She was already out of his life, and he was entering the next adventure. Going down in the elevator she consoled herself with the knowledge that she was going to meet her husband for dinner, and so she was just as cold as John Griffin. Or was he cold? If you played a certain game you had to keep to the rules.

Robert was trying hard to be charming. He told her at length about a new case he was working on, and Nikki found herself drifting away. John Griffin . . . if anyone ever knew! She missed him, and she felt sad.

She lied to Robert when they went back to her apartment and told him she had her period, so he would keep away from her. She couldn't face the idea of two men in one day. She took a sleeping pill before they went to bed, because even though she was tired, she was nervous, and when she went to sleep she dreamed that she and John Griffin were riding away on a horse together, up into the sky, like in a Chagall painting.

She didn't have anything to write to him about, but she kept hoping in the office that he might at least send her a postcard. He never did. Well, maybe it took a long time for mail to arrive from Yugoslavia. Besides, he was very busy. But she knew he wouldn't ever write. One day, at the end of November, she read in the *Post* and the *Daily News* that John Griffin was involved in a new, torrid romance with a starlet in the film he was making.

For some reason it hurt her, although it really didn't surprise her very much. Why wouldn't he have an affair? He was a very sexual man. Besides, actors were always in love with whoever was playing a part in their lives at the moment. For a while she had been his costar, and he had been playing his serious-author role. Now he was in another fantasy, across the world. She felt as if she had never really known him, and yet she felt that she knew him as well as anybody. She knew all there was to know about John Griffin. What was she expecting, secrets?

She went home to Wilton for the weekend as she always did. "Look, Nikki," Robert said. "I want you back."

"I know," she said. "I think we're both close to it, don't you?"

"No. I've changed, but you haven't. I've been making concessions. But you have everything your way."

"I do?" Nikki said, surprised.

"I drag myself in to that tiny little apartment after a long, hard day at the office, I take you out, I sleep over and have to get up early and take the damn train to Stamford, and what do you do?"

"What do you want me to do?" she asked.

"Do you want to come back? Do you want us to be the way we used to be?"

"You mean happy?"

"Yes. Happy."

"You know I do, Robert. I'm trying. I want everything to be the same. Maybe after a long time marriage just changes."

"Bullshit! Our marriage never had a chance," he said.

"What do you mean?"

"I mean that there are jobs *here*. You could work in Stamford. You could work on the local newspaper—they'd be glad to have you. You think that company you work for is the greatest thing in the world. It's nothing. It's just a second-rate company. Why don't you wise up, Nikki? You're throwing away your life for false gods."

"Thou shalt have no other god before me," she murmured.

"You think those people you work with are intellectuals. They're just second-rate failures. They're living in a tight little world where everyone lies to everyone else and people tell each other they're powerful and important. Do you think anybody outside of publishing even heard of you? Do you think if you left that the world would fall apart?"

"I am the lord thy God and thou shalt have no other . . ."

"What are you mumbling about?" Robert said.

"What do you *want*, Robert. What do you really want?"

"I want you to quit that job and get rid of that apartment and come home. I want us to share our life together. The girls are grown and on their own and we only have each other, Nikki. I want you to be with me."

"But you don't even know me."

"I know you better than anyone else in the world does."

"No," Nikki said. She felt as if she were going to cry. "You just know me longer, Robert."

"Doesn't that count for anything?"

"It counts for a lot. It makes it very hard to leave you."

"You know we can't leave each other," he said.

"Robert, didn't you even wonder why I didn't get mad when you said what you just did about my job and my friends and my life and my self-respect?"

"Because you know I'm right. Look, maybe I was a little harsh, but I just don't want you to waste our lives, Nikki."

"I didn't get mad because, Robert, I don't care what you think about me any more."

"You're just saying that to get back at me," he said.

She shook her head, no.

"Go ahead," he said, "get mad." He sounded a little frightened.

"I'm not mad, Robert. I'm very hurt, but I'm not angry. You

don't want *me* back. You just want someone to fit in with all your ideas of what your wife should be."

"You *are* what my wife should be."

"Obviously not. The way you described me, I wouldn't want *that* person back."

"I want to change that person," Robert said.

"I know," Nikki said. And she smiled, a cold, deadly smile without any flirtatiousness or humor. It was more a grimace of resignation. "Dinner is at seven." And she went upstairs to pack her clothes.

The easiest thing to do, she decided, would be to have a lawyer serve Robert with papers. She had nothing else to say to him. She felt bloodless. A year ago, even six months ago, if he had said to her what he had just said she would have argued with him and cried. It would have seemed a betrayal of the grossest kind. But now it just seemed like a nasty little boy kicking and screaming at his nurse. She didn't want to be kicked and she didn't want to be his nurse either. She wondered if he really meant what he had said about her. It didn't matter. He had been able to say it. She could no longer live with a man who had such a deep contempt for the best she was able to do.

THEY ALL KNEW Nikki had left her husband. Nikki told Rachel, Rachel told Margot, Margot told Ellen. Poor Nikki, Rachel said, knowing only her own happy marriage. Poor Nikki, Margot agreed, knowing only the loneliness that kept coming closer and closer, threatening to choke her. Lucky Nikki, Ellen said, and I'm next.

Nikki refused to take alimony, although her lawyer urged her to. He mentioned the many years she had been married to Robert, the sacrifices she had made, the two children she had borne and brought up so well. He talked about inflation, the cost of living in New York, the fears she should have of being fired, or of retirement. Nikki didn't want anything from Robert, except that he continue to support their daughters until they no longer needed him, even if they didn't live at home. She knew he would,

252

of course. As for herself, she wasn't sure if Robert would be willing to support her or not, but she felt that if she was leaving him over his protests the only thing she wanted from him was her freedom.

Ellen was trying to decide what to give Reuben for Christmas. She didn't have much money, and what little she had was for Jill and Stacey, who both needed new winter coats. She didn't plan to give Hank anything. It would be too hypocritical, since she was going to tell him the very next day that she wanted a divorce. She finally got an idea for Reuben from a needlecraft book she was promoting. She would make him a needlepoint pillow for what would be their new apartment. At least she would make the front part. Maybe she'd better do it in crewelwork. She hated handicrafts, and crewel was a lot faster than other needlepoint. It wouldn't cost much if she made her own design and just bought the canvas and wool. She had already decided what to embroider on it: the day of her liberation and the joining of her destiny with Reuben's, December 26. She bought the materials and started working on the pillow in the office during her lunch hours whenever he had a business lunch. She felt that she had made her first real commitment, and she smiled as she worked on it. Wouldn't Reuben be surprised and delighted!

Ellen was being remarkably pleasant lately to everyone. Even Thanksgiving dinner went smoothly in her household. The girls helped her cook, Hank washed the dishes, and they all watched those dopey parades on television together. She wanted them to remember her well when she disrupted their lives, so that they would have faith in her and know she would continue to make them happy even though she was exchanging one husband for another. All except Hank, of course. She knew he would be devastated. But he'd had enough years of her life. It was time she thought of herself. If Nikki could make the break when she didn't have anybody to go to, how cowardly it would be for her to continue to hide here in this pretense of a marriage when a man who adored her was waiting.

Ellen had just finished the *Dece* in her crewelwork when Reuben came into her office. She shoved the thing under some papers on her desk. "What a surprise," she said. "I thought you had a lunch date."

"I broke it."

"To be with me?"

"Yes."

"Oh, lovely. Let's go."

She put on her coat, and they walked to the elevators together, pretending to be casual, even though everyone in the office knew.

"I thought I wouldn't be able to see you until this afternoon," Ellen whispered. "This must be my lucky day."

"I couldn't wait," he whispered back.

They carefully avoided looking at each other in the crowded elevator. When they reached the street he asked, "Are you hungry?"

"There's something to eat in the apartment, isn't there?"

"I didn't notice. Let's pick something up."

They took a cab and stopped at the deli near his building to buy sandwiches. Then he insisted on stopping at the liquor store to buy a bottle of wine and a bottle of vodka.

"I suspect we're planning to take the afternoon off," Ellen said, smiling.

"We might," Reuben said, but his answering smile was tight. She wondered what was the matter. Mad at his wife, probably. Certainly not mad at *her*, she hadn't done anything.

"You seem upset," Ellen said.

"Let's get upstairs."

They went into his apartment in the hotel. Ellen thought it seemed different, but she couldn't figure out at first what it was. Then she noticed it was neat. All the papers and books that had littered the living room were gone. She took off her coat, and while Reuben was messing around in the kitchen she went into the bedroom and looked around. It seemed too clean and colorless too. The photos of his two sons were gone. She ran to the closet and looked inside. There were no clothes hanging there,

254

but instead there were two large suitcases standing on the closet floor. She lifted one and it was heavy. She rushed to the dresser, opened all the drawers, and saw that they were empty, except for one, in which the few little things she had left in his apartment were neatly folded. They would all fit into a shopping bag, and indeed he had put a clean shopping bag next to them, folded too.

"Reuben!" Ellen went into the living room just as he was coming out of the kitchen with two large glasses of vodka and ice in his hands. "What happened, are you moving? What's going on?"

"Take this," he said. He handed her the drink and she saw that his hand was very steady. He didn't seem upset, but he wasn't himself either. He took a long drink from his glass. "Sit down, Ellen."

She sat on the couch. "Will you tell me why you're all packed?"

"Ellen, I'm going home."

"You're *what?*"

"I went to the lawyer with my wife— Look, don't interrupt me, okay? This is hard enough as it is. I sat there and discussed dividing up our things, and the money she wanted, and all of a sudden the whole thing became terribly real. I mean, before it was a dream, a wish, a fantasy. But in the lawyer's office, with papers to sign, it wasn't make-believe any more. And my kids. I . . . . I just couldn't stand to look at their faces. They were scared, Ellen. They're just little boys. They need their father. I felt so guilty. I missed them. I can't go off with you, Ellen. We can't get married. I can't leave my kids."

"*Your* kids?" At first, while he was talking, the enormity of what he was about to do to her had left her numb, but now she saw it all, and she was filled with anger. "*Your* kids? You can't leave *your* kids? What about what I was going to do for you? What about *my* kids?"

"And my wife."

His words hung there between them as if they were visible. They looked black, Ellen thought, like burned paper. *And my wife.*

"That's it," she said. "Coward."

"I'm so sorry. You don't know how badly I feel, Ellen."

"Liar."

"I never lied to you, I swear it."

"You were going to leave them."

"I was."

"But you took one look at how much it was going to cost you . . ."

"Do you think that's unimportant?"

"I'm sure it's essential."

He shook his head. "It's the guilt, Ellen. I just can't leave them. I'm going home tonight." He finished off his glass of vodka in one long series of gulps and looked very relieved. "Drink your drink, Ellen, you'll feel better."

She threw the vodka in his face, glass and all. He ducked the glass, and it bounced against the rug and lay there. Some of the liquid had splashed on his shirt and tie. He took out his handkerchief and carefully mopped it off. "I don't blame you if you hate me," he said.

"I despise you. I despise cowards."

"You have every right to despise me. And I'm sorry."

Ellen looked at him, and suddenly she realized that she was doing all the wrong things. No man had ever left her before. Instead of throwing a tantrum she should be acting weak, crying, begging him not to leave her. Why would he want to come back to a woman who behaved the way she was doing? She let her eyes fill with tears, and then she was genuinely unhappy and she began to cry. "Oh, Reuben, don't leave me."

"Please don't cry," he said sadly. "You make me feel worse. Ellen, please believe that I didn't ruin your life. Nothing has changed for you. Thank God we didn't do anything rash. You can go on just as before. You'll find someone a lot better than me. You can have any man you want. You don't need me."

"I do need you," she said. She blew her nose. "This is a terrible thing to do to me. How can you do it?"

"Guilt," he said. "It's my most prominent characteristic." Surprisingly, he was smiling. He looked as if the confession had been a catharsis for him. He went into the kitchen and made them each another drink. Then he sat in the chair, still not next to her on the couch. Ellen had the horrible feeling that Reuben was never going to touch her again. She wondered if she should try to get him into bed. Would that work? If it did, for how long?

She wiped her eyes and drank a little of her drink, looking at him, and then she lit a cigarette. He let her look at him, sitting there silently under her gaze like a prisoner in the dock, waiting for sentencing. She looked at the old acne pits, the crooked teeth, the face she had found so irresistibly sexy, and she remembered all the reasons she had first chosen him. She had wanted him for his guilt. She had always chosen well, and she had never been wrong. Reuben Weinberg, she had thought when she picked him, is a man with the proper amount of guilt. He'll never leave his wife.

She had been right. She had chosen him too well.

SHE LET HIM LEAVE the apartment first, with his suitcases, just to be sure he really meant to leave. She watched from the window and saw him drive away in a taxi. She threw her things into the shopping bag, and then she put it down next to her purse on the floor and made herself a fresh drink. She was in no condition to go back to the office this afternoon and she couldn't go home yet. Methodically she smoked the rest of the pack of cigarettes even though they made her throat hurt, and drank two more glasses of vodka and ice although she disliked the taste. She felt numb and was probably drunk. She looked in the bathroom for her toothbrush, but it was gone. Then she remembered the piece of paper he had made her sign promising to join him on December 26. What a liar! He had even lied to himself, which made him weak besides. She hated him. How dare he ditch her? He had been

257

lucky to have her. What had he done with that piece of paper? She looked into the wastebasket and saw some empty envelopes, some crumpled pieces of paper with scrawls on them, which, on inspection, seemed to be work from the office. And underneath all of that were some tiny pieces of paper that he had torn up as if a detective were going to come after him and investigate his tracks. Ellen put a few of the little pieces together. They were the infamous contract. "I, Ellen Rennie . . ."

She gathered them up and methodically flushed them down the toilet. Did Reuben think he was the only one who had to protect himself? Weak, castrated bastard! She had to get out of this place before it stifled her.

She fled to the street. It was dark already, and Sixth Avenue and the cross street were clogged with traffic, bumper to bumper. Everyone was going home. She had a home too. She would go to it. She only hoped that Reuben was as miserable as she was, and that he always would be, forever and ever.

DECEMBER

December 1975

THE CHRISTMAS HOLIDAY season brings out the worst as well as the best in everybody in New York. Christmas was truly meant for children. For adults it is a time of remembering, of depression, of loneliness. Every year there seem to be fewer celebrations. Perhaps it is a backlash against consumerism, or inflation, or simply the lack of money. When we were children Christmas was the time of anticipation, of decorating trees and waiting for Santa Claus with his gifts; as adults, it is we who have to buy the gifts, or make them, decorate the trees, pay the bills, and there is never enough time.

"Let's not give each other presents this year," Margot said to Ellen.

"But we always give each other presents."

"It's so expensive," Margot said. "I'm not even giving those horrible office gifts."

"I want to have a really bang-up Christmas and forget my troubles," Ellen said. She had been nervous and irritable ever since

Reuben had left her, and she avoided him in the office. Luckily she had no business to do with him anyway that couldn't be passed on to someone else in the publicity department. "Nikki says we should have a party."

"I hate parties," Margot said.

"How about lunch! Someplace corny and terrific, like the Rainbow Room."

"With presents?"

"We'll just have the four of us," Ellen said. "You, me, Nikki, and Rachel. That's just four presents."

"Well, you do the calling," Margot said. "I'm too busy."

What a grouch Margot was lately, Ellen thought. You'd think a nice Christmas lunch with three friends was a big effort for her. "All right," she said pleasantly. "What day? Let's see, Christmas comes on a Thursday this year, so Wednesday they'll shut the office early. It's a short week and everybody always has to shop at the last minute, and there are all those office parties, so what about Friday the nineteenth?"

"It suits me," Margot said. "I have nothing to do for the rest of my life."

Nikki said the nineteenth was fine, and so did Rachel. Lawrence had to be away Thursday and Friday on business that week, so lunch with her friends would cheer her up. Rachel said she would make the reservation in her name at the Rainbow Room, which they all agreed was an inspired choice. So high in the sky, with the magical view that made the city look wonderful instead of the way they saw it every day, the aerie beloved of tourists and lovers.

"Would you believe," said Rachel, "I've never been there?"

"Neither have I," said Nikki. "Let's make it early, twelve thirty, so we can get good and drunk."

Each of them marked down December 19 in her appointment book. A festive pre-Christmas lunch, one decent thing to look forward to. And so, each was now going toward her destiny.

IT HAD NOT OCCURRED to Margot that anyone would find her recent behavior different, for the reason that she didn't care what anyone else thought. It was hard for her to concentrate on people at all. She was in a deep state of what she could only describe as grief. At night she drank her vodka and took her sleeping pills, feeling as heavy and invisible as a black star in the galaxy, burned out, dead. In the mornings when her alarm rang she lay in bed for a long time wondering where she would find the courage to get up and face another day. Pain held her heart in a vise. It made her head ache and her breathing labored. Often she sighed deeply. She thought she must be the loneliest person in the world.

How could she ever go on? This year was coming to an end, another would start, and what would be different for her? She could hardly imagine struggling through the rest of this week in her pain, much less another whole year. She couldn't remember when she had taken a vacation. Year after year she let the opportunities slip away, taking her vacation as vacation days, wasting time, because she never had any place to go or anyone to go with. She thought now of all the places she had wanted to see and never had because she had been working so hard. Kerry was taking Haviland to Paris for Christmas. He was rich now. His novel had been sold to paperback for two hundred and thirty thousand dollars. Margot had money saved, she could have gone to Paris, but who wanted to spend Christmas in Paris alone? Or Christmas anywhere alone? She didn't miss Kerry at all any more, but she would always miss the happiness of those months when she really thought she would at last have someone to go somewhere wonderful with.

So long ago, when she was in college, she had spent two weeks with another girl on Cape Cod. After college she was too busy working and too poor to go anywhere. For a few years she had spent vacations with her family, until she found the difference between their idea of fun and hers insurmountable. She had been young then, she had wanted to be out, to dance, to laugh, to flirt. Now she felt like a robot. The smile, when it came, was automatic, forced. Two days she called in sick and didn't go to work, but lying in bed immersed in this black grief was worse than facing people, so she returned. Always she carried within her this pain, irremediable. What could stop the anguish—a drug, an adventure, a love, death? She knew that if love came now she would be unable to accept it. How would she be able to see love or even kindness when everyone seemed at such a distance? She was apart from them even while they were face to face, speaking. The pain made her move slowly as if deep in thought. But her thoughts were empty, and sometimes she did not even think at all. Sometimes hours went by without her noticing, and other times she thought she had been sitting in the same place for an hour and it was only minutes.

She was never hungry any more, but she was very thirsty. It was from the sleeping pills and the liquor. She had two doctors now, and neither of them knew about the other. One gave her Seconal, the other Dalmane. Dalmane gave her a bitter taste the next day. They always made you pay, one way or the other.

She had not sent Christmas cards this year. Last year's cards, enough left for this year, lay dusty on a shelf. She received cards and didn't bother to open them. She merely glanced at the return address. She wasn't even curious enough to open the ones with no return address on them. A voice inside her said that some of them might be invitations to parties where perhaps she might find someone who would change her life. But Margot knew that was no longer possible. She could not go to a party, and if she did she would find no one who could possibly want her the way she felt now. She longed only to die.

She never telephoned her friends any more. They assumed she was very busy. Ellen called sometimes to complain. Reuben still was with his wife, there was no one interesting in the office, and Jill was looking skinny again. On and on, blah blah. Margot let Ellen talk until she was spent, wondering what it must be like

264

to be so self-absorbed that you didn't even care if the person at the other end grunted or not.

Rachel called at the office inviting Margot to a small dinner, and Margot lied and said she was busy. It was all she could do to get home from work and crawl into her apartment, her hole. She hadn't had the window washer for months, and the grime kept out the world. She kept her shutters closed, where before they had been open to the sun. Her plants, untended, unwatered, died. She let them lie there, stinking in their pots. Dust accumulated on everything. The cleaning woman had left, and Margot had not bothered to hire another. Every day she thought, Today I must find someone to clean up that mess. But, then, perhaps tomorrow she wouldn't be here any more, she would have done it, taken the pills, finished this meaningless life.

She told herself her life had all been wasted. Nothing had worked out the way she had dreamed when she was young. But she knew it didn't matter. What mattered was the loneliness. There was nothing worse than being all alone.

On Thursday night Margot counted out her pills. The phone rang and she let the service pick it up, as she usually did. Often she forgot to call her service for days, and they assumed she was away and picked up her phone on the first ring. She hadn't paid them either. A pile of unpaid bills lay tossed on the cluttered dresser along with unopened mail and part of whatever she had worn and taken off recently. Her clothes were on the floor, on chairs, in the bathroom. For a while, in a better mood, she had briefly wondered what would happen when she ran out of things to wear, but now it wouldn't matter any more. The landlord could stop sending her letters about the back rent and take his apartment. She had ten Seconals and twenty-five Dalmanes. The drugstore's was the only bill Margot still paid; she was afraid they would cut her off. Now she was cutting them off, all of them.

For a moment she felt happy, if happiness was an absence of pain. She walked through the quiet apartment to the kitchen with the pills in her hand. Somewhere she had read that it was impossible to take so many pills, so you had to empty the capsules into

265

some taste-disguising liquid like orange juice. She tried it with one Dalmane in a spoonful of juice. Not too bad.

She carefully opened the other Dalmane capsules and dumped them into a tall glass of orange juice, mixing them up carefully with a spoon so there wouldn't be a useless lump at the bottom. She would take the Seconal in the normal way, to reassure herself that she really was doing this. She would get into bed first in case it worked too fast. She wanted to drift off to sleep, not fall on the floor.

She put on a clean nightgown. For a minute she thought she ought to write a note, but she couldn't think of anything to say. What was the point of writing that she was so lonely she couldn't go on any more? Who would care? Nobody wanted to be bothered with lonely people, they added nothing to life but guilt and gloom. Whoever found her would see the empty pill bottles and figure out soon enough what had happened. People killed themselves every day around Christmas. It was the disease of the season of joy.

In bed Margot drank down her ten Seconals with the glass of orange juice containing the twenty-four Dalmane capsules. Almost immediately she felt relaxed. Her door was carefully bolted, her phone was in the closet with the bell turned down, and she was safe. She could die in peace. She, who had never lived in peace, would at least have that.

It drifted through her mind that tomorrow was the Christmas lunch with Ellen and Rachel and Nikki. Tomorrow had seemed so far away that it didn't exist. Now it wouldn't, for her. Sleep came in a strange way, numbing, as if something had seized her. Her body felt so heavy that she couldn't move. The pills took over, with their power, and Margot gave in to them, grateful that at last something was taking over the life she could no longer bear or control.

JILL AND STACEY were making Christmas candles in milk cartons. You poured in the wax around the wick, and when it hardened you cut away the paper container. You could dye the melted wax and even scent it. They had decided to make some red ones, some green, and scent the red ones with cinnamon and the green ones with pine. The advantage of these candles, besides their being inexpensive and fun to make, was that you could give them to everyone indiscriminately, so no one felt favored or short-changed. They were giving them to their parents and all their friends. Jill liked the idea of giving the candles to her mother, because it meant she would be able to keep them herself.

Ellen came into the kitchen to observe them. Jill didn't like her mother breathing down her neck. "Oh, would you girls make three more for me to give as gifts?" she said.

"Oh, Mom," Jill said, "this isn't a store."

"You don't have to be so selfish," her mother said.

"Sure, Mom," Stacey said cheerfully. She would do anything to buy her mother's love—a lot of good it ever did her.

"Thank you, Stacey. Jill, use a potholder."

"I intend to."

"If there's a mess, I want you to clean it up. We have to eat on that table."

"Who are you giving them to?" Jill asked.

"Margot, Nikki, and Rachel," her mother said. "We're having a pre-Christmas lunch tomorrow."

"What were you going to give them if we hadn't made the candles?"

"I bought them pomander balls at Bendel's, but they cost too much, and now I can return them."

"I bet we could go into business and sell these things," Stacey said.

"Mom, why can't we eat in the dining room tonight?" Jill said, annoyed. "Then we wouldn't have to clean up anything until we're done."

"Because your father isn't going to be home for dinner and it's too much trouble for me to carry everything back and forth."

"We'd help you," Stacey said.

"Just do as I say," her mother snapped.

267

"Ooh, she's in some mood tonight," Stacey said when Ellen had left the room. "What do you think's bothering her?"

"Her boyfriend dumped her," Jill said.

"You're kidding! How do you know?"

"The good old telephone, how else?" Jill grinned. "She told Margot all about it. Also, he never calls, and the others used to after *she* ditched *them*."

"She's going to catch you some day," Stacey said.

"Never. The telephone is like dope to her. She's a phone junkie. When she gets attached to that thing an earthquake wouldn't blow her off. She doesn't know I'm on."

"I don't know why we can't eat in the dining room," Stacey said. "After all, we're making three of these for her."

"Parents have to be unreasonable to prove their power. Don't you know that? If we gave in to reasonable requests they'd never be sure, would they?"

"You're right," Stacey said thoughtfully. "I never thought of that before, but you're absolutely right."

They cleaned up the kitchen in time for dinner, deciding to finish the rest of the candles another time. Their mother had picked up two barbecued chickens on the way from the office. The smell of them made Jill gag. Stacey ate with her customary enthusiasm, and Jill didn't eat anything. She wondered why her mother wasn't nagging her. This was indeed a most unusual event. Maybe her mother was so upset over the lost boyfriend that she didn't notice, but Jill doubted it. She must have some other devious plan. Her mother was full of them.

After Stacey washed the dinner dishes she went into her room to do homework. Jill had no homework she couldn't put off until another day, which was her usual attitude until the last minute, when she was stirred into a frantic burst of activity. She set up the ironing board and started ironing her jeans for school tomorrow. There was one thing she had to say for herself: she wasn't sloppy. She washed her hair at least three times a week and she always wore neatly pressed clothes. Such rituals comforted her.

268

She spent a great deal of time attending to her skin. When she'd started having periods she had been worried that she would start to have zits too, but her complexion was as clear as ever. Jill attributed this in part to the fact that she didn't eat.

She was pleasantly lost in her own thoughts when her mother appeared in the kitchen. "Jill," she said, "I have an idea."

Jill knew that tone. It meant I have an idea you'll hate.

"Rachel knows a lovely young boy I think you ought to meet," her mother said. "His name is Andy. He's nineteen, and he goes to college with her. He's a freshman because he lost a year traveling. He seems like a very interesting person."

"I don't want to meet a boy," Jill said.

"He's very good-looking," her mother went on. "He has long red hair and a moustache and a little beard. He's thin, you ought to like that. I think you'd make an adorable couple."

"I don't want to be an adorable couple," Jill said. She dug the iron into her jeans. Why didn't her mother leave her alone? The thought of the boy was like a threat hanging over her. He was probably some young guy who wasn't interested in her mother, so her mother wanted to keep him in the family. It wasn't *her* job to keep young studs in the family. Boys made her nervous, especially any boy her mother might pick out. That was just too incestuous for words.

"I don't see any harm if you just meet him," her mother went on. "I'll have Rachel give him your phone number. You just go out with him once and see what happens."

"Kids my age don't go out on dates," Jill said. "We go in groups or we go steady. I don't want a boyfriend."

"You're sixteen. It's time. Do you want to be alone while all your friends are having fun?"

"I have friends and we *have* fun," Jill said. She was getting sick to her stomach. Her mother seemed enormous, ballooning until she filled the whole kitchen with her presence. *Go away. Oh, please, go away.*

"Jill, why don't you grow up?" Her mother's voice was sharp

269

and angry. "You can't be an infant forever. You can't deny that men are half of the human race. You have to go out. You might like him."

Jill tried to shut out her mother's persistent voice. She made noises in her head to drive the voice away, she thought of the words of songs, she imagined a train screaming through a long tunnel. She bent over her ironing, not looking at her mother, willing her to disappear.

"If you'd get interested in a nice boy instead of thinking about yourself all the time . . . perfectly nice boy . . . well recommended . . . what's so horrible about going out with a nice boy?" The voice kept intruding on her inner defenses, poking at her, trying to tear into her. Nineteen was too old. Any boy her mother would force on her was the wrong boy. Her mother wanted her to go to bed with a boy. What did her mother know about the way boys grabbed at you? Her mother didn't have to go out alone with some horny stud, she didn't know how boys behaved on dates. Her friends knew. You had to go to bed with a boy unless you were just friends. Why didn't her mother shut up and leave her alone?

"Jill, you could answer me! You could look at me! Why are you so stubborn? All right, if you won't decide, then I'll decide for you. I'll call Rachel right now."

She wants me to be just like her, Jill thought. Terror and rage filled her. She had never known such rage, it was overwhelming. She took the first thing at hand, which was the iron she was holding, and threw it at her mother as hard as she could.

The hot iron hit her mother squarely on the side of the head. She fell instantly. On her cheek there was a triangular mark just beginning to redden, and from the corner of her mouth came a small trickle of blood. She was very still. Jill suddenly realized she was dead.

I've killed her, she thought. *I killed her.* She didn't feel anything—not grief, not fear. The only thing Jill felt, unaccountably, for the first time, was hungry. She opened the refrigerator and took out a chicken leg and ate it.

HE STOOD OUTSIDE Rachel's apartment building in the cold December darkness and waited. His patience was endless. He knew her husband was away tonight and she would be alone. The only problem left to overcome was how to get into her building without being seen by the doorman and thus perhaps later recognized. But he had figured that out too. It was the holiday season and there would be parties. If not tonight then surely tomorrow night, Friday. He had two chances. He would wait. His overcoat collar was turned up and his hands were in his pockets, but he was not cold. He simply wanted to be as inconspicuous as possible. He stood away from the bright street lights, near the bench next to the low stone wall that kept people from going into the park. If anyone noticed him they would think he was a bum or a mugger and would walk by him as quickly as possible, eyes averted. He watched the cabs and cars going by, and he had seen her come home earlier, swathed in fur, carrying gift-wrapped packages in a shopping bag. She had not left. She was there, upstairs.

A taxi stopped at her building and disgorged four people. As soon as they went inside, another cab pulled up and a couple went in. They were dressed for a party and carried small packages. He moved forward, light on his feet, poised to spring. The next to arrive was a taxi with four again, and while one of the men was paying the driver he crossed the street just in time to melt into her building along with the group.

The doorman was calling upstairs on the house phone and had his back to him. He went up in the elevator with the four people, two men and two women, all looking carefully into the air in the manner of people in elevators, not sure if he was going to the same party, not going to speak to him until they saw him there. They got off two floors above Rachel's apartment. He got off with them. They went to the right, so he went to the right. There was a long metal coatrack in the hall outside an apartment that had a Christmas wreath on the door. People were hanging up their own coats, and his group joined them, politely waiting their turn, still not speaking to anyone until they would be introduced later inside. He noticed the fire exit and just disappeared through it. Nobody saw him go, nobody cared.

He ran down the two flights of stairs to her floor. Out the fire exit, down the hall to her apartment. He paused for a moment to turn down his coat collar, smooth his hair, look as normal as possible. Then he rang her bell.

He heard the peephole scrape open and then the sound of a chain being removed and a lock opened. She stood there in a pink robe, her scrubbed face as clean as a child's, his Rachel, his victim, his love. She looked neither pleased nor angry, just perplexed.

"What are you doing here, Hank?" she said.

"May I come in?" Hank said. He was by her before she could answer, and he closed and locked the door. She was still looking at him, her soft lips parted, her eyes searching his face for an answer to this kind of behavior.

"What is it?" Rachel asked.

He put his enormous hands around her thin throat and led her backward to her bedroom. He had his fingers on her arteries where they led to her brain; if she tried to struggle or scream he could make her black out in an instant. She seemed to know this, or suspect worse, and she let him push her, while her eyes grew huge with fear.

Holding her neck, having her in his power at last, inflamed him almost beyond bearing. He kept one hand around her throat and with the other he unzipped his pants and let his erection spring free. He saw her glance at it, just a flicker of her eyes, and then she looked at his face again. He could feel her pulse beating wildly underneath his fingers. She was terrified. It would be so easy to crush her. He would make her do everything he had ever dreamed of, he would ravish her in every way. He was glad she knew he was the master, but for some reason her fear angered him. Was he so repulsive that she had to be terrified? Even while accepting him, waiting for his next command, she was rejecting him.

"Take off your clothes," he said, his hand still around her throat.

She let the robe drop to the floor. She was wearing a nightgown under it. He ripped that off with one hand as if it were made of paper. She was more beautiful than he had ever dreamed. When she had been his unapproachable goddess she had seemed larger, but now she seemed very small and delicate.

"You know I could kill you if I wanted to," Hank said to her. "You know that, don't you?"

She scarcely seemed to breathe.

"Slut," he said. "You deserve to be punished."

NIKKI WAS FINISHING her Christmas shopping. Most of the stores were open until nine thirty tonight because it was the week before Christmas. She left her office early so she could get to Gucci, which wasn't open late, to buy wallets for both her daughters. She wanted to get them something they would never spend the money on themselves. The rest of the list, of things they wanted, she would get at Bloomie's. Gucci was so crowded, and she had to wait so long on line, that she decided to buy herself a present too, just to make up for the annoyance. There was a dark-brown pigskin attaché case she had been longing for, just the sort of thing an executive like herself should carry, but she had put off getting it because it cost a fortune. Now, as she looked at it, try-ing to decide, the thought flashed through her mind that she should have let John Griffin buy it for her when he offered to get her a present, and she smiled because she knew that meant she was completely over him.

Season of trust and cheer, she thought, amused, watching the cop with the huge, ominous gun on his hip, patrolling the store for thieves, pickpockets, holdup men. She charged the two wallets and the attaché case and had them gift-wrapped separately.

Out in the street with her shopping bag and her handbag firmly clutched to her body against the surging crowds, Nikki walked briskly to Bloomingdale's. She glanced into the store windows on the way, cheered by the decorations and the lights. She really enjoyed shopping for her daughters. She was going to make Christmas dinner for them in her apartment, and for Lynn's boyfriend too, if he still existed. She wondered if she ought to buy him a present. No, that might make him think she was pushing him into becoming a member of the family. Goodness knows, she didn't want her daughters to get married as young as she had. She hoped they would profit from her example.

Her first stop in Bloomingdale's was at the St. Laurent department. She wasn't very well organized, she went as the spirit moved her instead of going floor by floor. But the decorations enchanted her. All the merchandise looked so desirable she had to restrain herself from buying things she didn't want or need. She bought small printed challis scarves from St. Laurent for Rachel, Margot, and Ellen, and then she had to go to the wrap desk and stand on a long line to have them gift-wrapped. It occurred to her that she could have bought gift paper and wrapped them at home herself. Well, she'd do that for Dorothy and Lynn.

She was getting hungry, but she had a lot more things to do. Down one floor on the escalator to underwear and robes. There was an electric eye on the bank that separated each escalator from the next, and some sort of matron, who couldn't fool anyone into thinking she was a customer instead of a guard (and probably didn't want to), was sitting opposite the electric eye waiting for it to signal her that a shoplifter had taken away a garment with its white plastic tag still attached to it. Once Nikki had been stopped because although the salesgirl had taken off the tag from a sweater she had bought, there was a stray one that had been dropped into the pocket. It had been very annoying.

Dorothy and Lynn wanted warm, cuddly nightgowns for college. It amused Nikki that while they were sleeping with boys and being very sophisticated, they still favored the sort of virginal, frumpy sleepwear she had worn in her college dorm in her day. In fact, they even wanted her to try to find mukluks! She bought them each two nightgowns, because she couldn't decide which she liked best, and then she wandered to the sexy at-home robes. She didn't own anything really nice to wear around the apartment, and it was time. Who knew whom she might entertain some long winter night?

She bought herself a beautiful robe for a present, too expensive—but, then, it was Christmas. Then downstairs to the gourmet shop on the lower level, where she bought imported jam and mustard and tea and fruitcake, and a big jar of brandied peaches to serve with her Christmas turkey. Charge accounts were rather reckless things to have, but in any case you wouldn't carry a lot of cash at Christmas when there were all those pickpockets lurking around crowded department stores and streets.

Now she was laden with shopping bags filled with packages. A last stop to buy gift wrap and ribbon, another interminable wait, and at last Nikki was out on the street. The smell of roasting chestnuts rose in the air and reminded her of many Christmases past. It always made her feel happy. She would have bought some, but she didn't have a free hand. Naturally there were no cabs. It was a nice night and not such a long way, so she decided to walk home.

Two Salvation Army soldiers, a man and a woman, were playing Christmas carols on the sidewalk. A man dressed as Santa Claus was clanging his bell next to a soup pot for the collection of money to feed poor people Christmas dinners. Poor drunks, Nikki thought. Everyone always felt so nice at Christmas, doing things for others, and then the rest of the year you were furious if someone tried to bum some change off you.

The crowd thinned out as she came closer to the residential streets, and the air was noticeably fresher. She looked up at the apartment windows, noticing strings of lights, Christmas cards hung on thread, pictures drawn on the glass in artificial snow. She remembered when she had decorated the whole house for Dorothy and Lynn, but she didn't feel sad for the vanished past. It had been fun, but now was fun too, and there were new things she had never done.

She turned into her block. It was so dark and empty. The people around here must all go to bed at eight o'clock, or else they went away for the holidays. It was funny how in New York you could go right from one sort of neighborhood into a completely different sort in just a moment. What seemed elegant in daylight looked ominous tonight. Damn, her keys were at the bottom of her purse, and she would have to wrestle with all these packages when she got to the steps of her building. Usually she had the keys out, it was a habit lately.

Coming down her block, between her and her house, Nikki saw a gang of kids. They were boys, black, no more than fourteen years old. In a minute she realized they were not just kids horsing around at night, they were mean kids looking for trouble. They looked at her, nudged each other, and formed a solid line. She felt perspiration trickling down her sides. She tried to cross the street, but they surrounded her, linking hands, like kids playing ring-around-a-rosy, but their eyes were absolutely empty and their faces were masks of hate. They were not amused, and they were not playing.

She realized suddenly that she was just a thing to them. She was not a person with feelings but an object that it might be fun to destroy. Something or someone had so brutalized them a long time ago that they were incapable of feeling the slightest empathy. They were moving closer to her now, still in their tight ring around her. They were deciding what to do with her. She knew only one thing: they would not let her go.

She screamed then, as loudly as she could, and they laughed at her. No one even opened a window. She kept screaming into the void of the empty, dead street until she realized that she did not exist. She who was loved and needed by so many people did not exist at all. And then the boys leaped at her like so many snarling wild cougars.

IN A CITY of many millions, crowded one atop another, you would think that people would notice each other, but they don't. The more noise you hear the less you hear. Privacy becomes anonymity, and both are prized. In a high-rise apartment house

276

you can hear when the neighbor next door or upstairs flushes the toilet, lets the water run out of the bathtub, has an argument. You can sometimes hear the scrape of the chain when a light bulb is turned on in a closet. You can hear the incinerator door clang, a key turned in a lock, a phone ring, a voice answer. And soon you block it out and hear none of it. Some people are lonely and read old letters they find in the trash left by others, but most pretend their neighbors don't exist. Suicides, domestic murders, attacks by strangers, all go on in secrecy. Each family exists in its own little cell. It is the same in the street. Violence has no reality, it is a play performed for the onlookers, who know it's only pretend unless they run onto the stage, and this they will not do. There are shots in the night, sirens, screams. They might be the cries of birds in a country hamlet. Night sounds. Awakened, the living cling to each other and procreate, celebrating the dead.

In this huge city, life is as much an accident as death.

JILL DIDN'T WANT to go near her mother's body on the kitchen floor, or even look at it. She didn't know what to do. Her mind seemed to have stopped functioning. She finished eating the chicken leg, dropped the bone into the garbage, and wiped her hands on the dish towel. Then she went to get Stacey. It seemed at this moment that her little sister was the older one and that she was the child.

"Stacey . . . I killed Mom."

Stacey looked up from her homework. "What?"

"I killed Mom. In the kitchen."

Stacey jumped off her bed and ran to the kitchen. Jill followed her, slowly, afraid to hear her sister scream. But there was no scream, and when she got to the kitchen her sister was talking on the kitchen phone. "I need an ambulance," she was saying, "immediately. No, I *tried* 911, and they're busy. It's an emergency." She gave the operator their address and hung up. "Dummy," she said to Jill, "she's just out cold. What did you do to her?"

"She's not dead?"

"Dead people don't breathe."

Jill felt something inside of her open, and she began to cry, great gulping sobs of relief and grief, of joy and frustration, at being back in the mainstream of life again and out of her nightmare. She had never cried like this before. "I didn't mean to kill her," she said. "I just wanted her to shut up."

"Part of us often wants to kill our parents," Stacey said calmly. "But only lunatics do it. I knew you didn't hit her on purpose. You threw the iron, right?"

Jill nodded, still sobbing.

"Well, she's probably got a concussion. But she'll know you didn't mean it. We'll get her to the hospital and they'll take X-rays. That's a nasty burn she's got. She'll be mad as hell when she sees that. But the main thing is she's going to be okay."

On the floor Ellen moved and groaned. Now Jill could see quite clearly that she was breathing. Stacey knelt beside her and took her pulse. "Go get a blanket," she said to Jill.

Jill ran into the bedroom and took the blanket off the bed. She brought it back to the kitchen and Stacey put it neatly over her mother as if she were tucking her into bed. "Don't move, Mom," Stacey said. "You'll be okay. The doctor's coming."

"Why does she need a blanket?" Jill asked.

"It can't hurt."

The crying had stopped now and she felt cleansed and calm. She wondered why she never cried when it felt so good afterward. She felt hungry again and she poured herself a glass of milk. Stacey was looking at her in disbelief but didn't say anything. Jill drank the milk and rinsed the glass and put it neatly upside down on the drainboard. Then the doorman rang on the housephone to say that an ambulance was downstairs and had they called for it.

"Half an hour," Stacey said, looking at her watch. "Incredible. The fastest record in New York."

They both rode with their mother to the hospital. Everyone was nice to them because they were so young-looking and Jill was so obviously grief-stricken, the marks of tears still on her face and her eyes red. Where was their father? They didn't know. Out for dinner. Jill knew there would be other questions later, but right now the nurse rushed Ellen into X-ray, and then put her to bed in a room with three other women in it. Stacey had even thought to bring along her mother's wallet with her Blue Cross card in it. It occurred to Jill that she was very lucky to have a sister like Stacey, and that if Stacey said she wanted to be a doctor when she grew up, then she meant to be one, and whatever she meant to do she would do. It was funny how the two of them were so different, coming from the same parents, the same home. But maybe they weren't so different; maybe they just coped with things differently.

After a while a doctor came to see their mother, examined her, and smiled kindly at the two girls, who were sitting beside her bed. Ellen was awake but seemed a little confused. He told her she was in the hospital and would have to stay a few days for observation until she was better. She nodded.

"What happened?" he asked gently.

"I have a headache."

"That's natural. I'll give you some medication. Do you want to tell me what happened?"

"An accident," Ellen said. She closed her eyes. "I want to sleep now."

The doctor looked at the two girls: the small, sturdy one and the taller, emaciated one, sitting side by side holding hands. His eyes told them that he had seen worse crimes in this hospital, much worse, that whatever had happened to bring their mother here was already well known to him and could not surprise him. He looked at them, and his kind, lined face told them they were not criminals, that life held all sorts of tragic and inexplicable things. Jill felt a surge of warmth toward him. He was only a little older than her father, but he looked so tired.

"What are your names?" he asked them.

"Stacey."

"Jill. What's yours?"

279

"Dr. Wilson. Why don't you girls go home and get some sleep? You can come to visit your mother tomorrow."

"Are you going to be her doctor?" Jill asked.

"Yes."

"Is she going to have a scar?"

"I don't think so."

Where had she heard that conversation before? When she was in the hospital and her mother was assuring her she would have no scar. She was saying the same thing her mother had said! Jill fought down the panic. She wasn't going to be like her mother, she wasn't! Her question had been only natural. After all, if there was a scar, it would be her fault.

"Come on," he said gently. "There's nothing for you to do now." He led them out of their mother's room and put them into the elevator and set them free.

IN THE STREET, in the dark, the gang of boys swooped down on Nikki and pulled her handbag and her packages from her numb hands, tore off her earrings, her watch, her rings. She felt them plucking at her as if they were taking bites from her skin, more shock than pain. Her heart was pounding so hard she thought she might have a heart attack and die right here before they had a chance to do whatever they were going to do to her. She felt the sidewalk hit her shoulder and leg as they threw her down, and suddenly they were gone. Gone, just like that, running off into the darkness carrying her things, tossing her gift-wrapped packages into the air and from one to another, turning the corner, gone.

She rose slowly, feeling such relief at being alive that it made her dizzy. Then she was angry. She felt violated, she wanted to kill them. Why wasn't there anybody around to protect decent, innocent people on the streets? She ran to her building and leaned on the super's bell, beginning to sob.

"Who is it?" his tinny voice came from the speaker.

"Nikki Gellhorn. I was mugged and they took my keys."

He came right out to let her in, and when he saw the state she was in he insisted on accompanying her into her apartment, until she sent him away, insisting she was all right.

"Have a drink," the super said. "A drink. It's good, you'll feel better."

"Okay, thank you. Goodbye." She locked the door and threw the heavy metal bar, knowing the boys had her address and her keys and could come back any time except for that bolt, which suddenly looked fragile. She forced herself to pour a shot of vodka, spilling most of it, and gulped it down like medicine. Then she called the locksmith. First things first. She felt as if she and the locksmith had become old friends. He said he would bring new cylinders for both locks and three sets of keys, one for her, one for the super, and one for the cleaning woman. Oh, no, he remembered, she needed four, didn't she? Four? Oh—Robert. No, Nikki told him, three sets were fine.

The vodka, or perhaps the locksmith, had calmed her somewhat. She poured herself another shot and drank it more slowly. Robert . . . Would he have been angered, horrified, or pleased if he knew of her encounter tonight? Would he have said "I told you so"? Of course he would. He would have told her that none of it would have happened if she had stayed with him in the country where she belonged. What about all the housewives who got raped and murdered in their own houses in the country while their husbands were at work? He would never think of that.

She called the police, just in case someone found her wallet and credit cards after the boys had taken her money. God, those credit cards! She'd had all of them with her. She went through her dresser drawer until she found the list of credit-card numbers she'd kept in case something happened. The department stores, of course, were closed. The credit-card companies had numbers to call, but one was busy and the other didn't answer. Nikki decided to leave them all for the morning. She wouldn't go to the office until she had everything done. She felt filthy and defiled and wanted to take a shower, but she had to wait for the locksmith. She inspected her leg. Nothing lethal. What was she going to do about the presents? They'd have to be replaced, of course, and she'd never get her money back. To have a mugger charge things on a stolen charge card was one thing, but if he took your merchandise after you'd charged it yourself, tough luck. She sighed. Why had she bought that Gucci attaché case?

Tomorrow was the lunch with Rachel, Margot, and Ellen. She'd have to replace their presents on the way to the lunch. Where could she go, with no money and no charge cards? She thought. Her driver's license, which she never used any more, was tucked into her dresser drawer with her checkbook and other important documents. She could use it for identification and go to Tiffany's. Chic, expensive places were so much more trusting than ordinary stores. Besides, she didn't plan to go into hock, just buy them each something nice in silver as a memento of their friendship. That was what Christmas should be for anyway.

She kicked off her shoes and telephoned Rachel. No answer. It wasn't very late, so maybe she was still out somewhere. Nikki dialed Ellen. She was out too? The whole family was out. Maybe they were at the stores. Margot was probably home. She dialed Margot's number. No answer. Was everybody in the world out tonight? Nikki felt very alone and deserted. She wanted to call her daughters, hoping Robert wouldn't answer, but she restrained herself. They'd only get upset, and there was nothing they could do. She knew she couldn't pretend everything was all right and she'd just called to say hello; they knew her voice and its intonations too well for that.

Who in the world could she call? She had dozens of casual friends, but it didn't seem right to call them to tell them what had happened, not because they wouldn't care, but because telling an acquaintance made it seem as if it were an anecdote instead of a personal trauma. She knew herself, and she knew she would try to pretend it was less upsetting than it had been. Was it possible, Nikki wondered, to become strong without giving up something on the way? She had come so far, but there was so much more to learn.

She turned on the television, imagining for one irrational moment that the lead story on the news would be her mugging. Then she laughed. She was alive! Her watch and rings and earrings might or might not turn up in some pawnshop, but who cared? She was alive! Her shoulder ached where she had fallen and her leg was scraped, but none of that was fatal. Her anger and hate and resentment and helplessness were not going to prove fatal either. She was *alive*. And life was the only gift she really wanted.

AT THIS MOMENT the life force in Rachel had never been stronger. Even now, as she let Hank drag her to the bed, she was thinking, terrified but trying to figure out what to do. Her thoughts rushed toward Lawrence and his love for her, the preciousness of her body, but she forced herself to put her mind on a simple course of self-preservation. If she thought of what she had become because of Lawrence—a woman who was loved beyond all others by a man she adored in turn—she knew she would break down and cry. Crying would not help her. She looked at Hank's wild, almost hypnotized eyes and wondered why she had never noticed before that he was crazy. Probably because she had never really noticed him at all. Everyone thought of him as that jerk Ellen had married. She wondered if he had always known it and if that had in part been what had driven him mad.

Who did he want her to be now, Ellen or Rachel? Not Ellen, for Hank was afraid of Ellen. Yet when he threatened to punish her, it was Ellen he hated, not Rachel, for she had never done anything to make him angry. Or had she? Had she done something without knowing it? Had his distorted mind imagined she had? She knew he intended to rape her, it was quite clear. She also considered the possibility he might kill her. He could easily kill her accidentally with those big hands of his, it would take only a small shifting of his mood. She tried to be as passive as she could and not break into hysterics, which she felt would anger him.

"Please, Hank," she said, "don't hurt me." Her soft voice

283

sounded like a gasp. "I've always been your friend. Please let go."

From the small changes in the pressure he was exerting on her throat she knew he was trying to read her mind and was reacting to what he thought he saw there, but she didn't know what he really wanted, and she suspected he didn't either. Sex, he had to want sex. It was what they all wanted, really. All those years before she met Lawrence, all those men who dated her and lied to her and wanted only to jump on her—in the end it was all they had ever wanted, to get her into their beds, to use her—and she had let them, because she was beautiful and dumb in the sixties, and that was what people did. It had ensured her survival then, she had thought, to be an acquiescent doll, a body. She had blocked it out and made it meaningless when they took her to their beds, so they could have what they insisted on and expected.

"No, Hank," Rachel said. "I don't want to. Don't do this. I don't want to."

"Shut up," he said. "You're mine. You owe me."

"Why?"

"Your fault. Everything. Your fault."

Now, suddenly, something in Rachel snapped and she was back in the past. Let him fuck her if he wanted to. Then he wouldn't hurt her any more and he would go away.

"All right," she said. Her voice was emotionless. "Do it."

HE WONDERED WHAT was going wrong. All the time he had imagined this scene it had been so perfectly choreographed, so exactly conforming to his lusts and desires that it had driven him into a sexual frenzy. But now he was here, and she was in his hands, and it was not going right at all. At first it had been perfect. Her terror, the way he had ripped off her clothes, all had been perfect. He pushed her naked body down now on the huge bed in her bedroom, and she lay there, looking at him calmly, as if he wasn't there at all. Her legs were slightly parted, as if she

284

was waiting for him. But she was not excited, she was just . . . there. Not the frightened, begging goddess of his fevered fantasies but just a limp and very beautiful woman who didn't care what he did to her. She seemed almost to be inviting him.

Inviting him? No, it was not him she invited. She had turned into a vessel, available to anyone, untouched, uninterested. She might as well be dead the way she lay there, and yet she moved one hand slightly, automatically, as if to caress him. He shrank away from her touch.

"Be Rachel," he commanded, but his voice came out like a moan of entreaty, not a firm command. "Be Rachel . . ."

She lay there, her soft lips curved in a half smile that was both invitation and introspection. She wasn't Rachel. She was just . . . anybody. He had never been so disappointed in his life. He tore off his clothes, knowing she wasn't going anywhere if he let go of her, trying to reawaken his fantasy, but it did no good. Hank hunched over her, four-legged like a beast, and saw his erection dwindle away to nothing. She didn't even seem to notice. If she had noticed, if she had laughed at him, he would have killed her on the spot. But she just lay there as if they had all the time in the world, and he knew then that there would never be a time for them.

He heard noises coming out of his throat, animal noises, and he threw himself on the bed beside her, curled up like a fetus, his back turned to her, his hands covering his face, his knees drawn up to his hated groin, and he wept.

RACHEL TURNED her head and saw Hank huddled on her bed crying. "You don't love me," he kept gasping, "you don't love me." She could hardly make it out. She raised herself on one elbow and looked at him. He was completely oblivious of her. Her hand, almost of its own volition, reached out to stroke his tormented head, and then she drew back. She got up and put on her robe again.

285

She knew she could call the doorman or the police, but she also knew with certainty that she was safe, and so she sat down on the edge of the bed, as far away from him as possible, and watched him, waiting for him to calm down. His great, white naked body was pathetic, a beached whale. She was suddenly overwhelmed with an exhaustion so draining that she nearly fell. It was over. All she wanted was for him to dress and go home so she could sleep.

But he wouldn't stop crying for a long time, and then he wouldn't stop talking. He finally pulled on his undershorts and his shirt, but he wouldn't go. He kept repeating the same things: that he had always felt unloved, inferior, that no one wanted him, no one respected him, he was a failure, he had nothing to live for. She wished he would go. Part of her felt slightly compassionate in spite of what he had done to her, because she had never seen a human being suffering such an abject and obviously painful loss of dignity. It was as if she was his mother and he a child who had come home from school to tell her he had been made the outcast: he couldn't seem to tear himself away from her presence, as if she was the only warm, comforting thing left.

He stayed there until morning. At last, when the light showed under the shades and it was eight o'clock, she persuaded him to go.

"You must go now, Hank," she said softly. "Your family will be worried to death."

He finished dressing quickly. The long night was over, and he seemed quite ordinary again. He was sane, at least for a while. Rachel walked with him to her front door and opened it. "Good night," he said in a matter-of-fact tone. She wondered if he was schizophrenic.

"Good night," she said, and he went away. She locked and bolted the door.

She went into the kitchen and put on the kettle. He had even known that the maid had taken these few days off and she would be all alone, without Lawrence. He had known everything. She realized that the creepy feeling she'd had all these months had been because he was watching her. And the white roses . . .

She shivered. She wanted most of all to call Lawrence, to tell him what had happened, but she knew it would upset and frustrate him, because he was trapped out of town with meetings all day. He would be back tomorrow. If she tried to reassure him on the phone that she was all right, that Hank hadn't hurt her, Lawrence wouldn't believe it. He would rush back, and she didn't want to put him through that. She would tell him face to face so he could see she was unhurt.

She thought of calling Ellen to warn her that Hank desperately needed a psychiatrist, but she was too tired to face it. Besides, maybe Hank was home already. She took her tea into the bedroom, pulled off the bedspread he had lain on, and threw it on the floor. She could never use it again. She would get another one later. Right now she just wanted to sleep.

Maybe she wouldn't go to the lunch. How could she possibly face Ellen today? Sleep first, and think later. Rachel was tired of always being the thoughtful one who remembered things one should do.

At ELEVEN THIRTY in the morning Margot woke up. She knew it was morning because she saw the wan light coming through the slats of her shutters. But morning of which day? She was supposed to be dead. She felt so groggy that she wasn't even depressed, just disappointed. Why hadn't the pills worked? What was she, some kind of superwoman, doomed to live forever? But her lassitude was comfortable, as if she'd been given an enormous dose of some kind of tranquilizer. It occurred to her that she was supposed to be at a lunch with Ellen and Rachel and Nikki, and she wondered if it was today or long past. She was too tired even to call. She couldn't make it today anyway. She rolled over on her side. She felt so comfortable . . . cheated, but the pain had become less. She had tried to die, and she had lived. Live to die another day. She didn't want to think about that. This feeling of being so drugged and comfortably sleepy that the pain was somewhere far away was like a blessing. She drifted off into a soft sleep, woke, and slept again. For the first time in her life she felt important, and she didn't know why.

THE CITY WAS AWAKE and going about its business. Workers were at their jobs, traffic clogged the streets, Christmas shoppers pushed their way through the stores, children freed from school for their holiday vacation rushed or loafed, the planned day and the unplanned already set in motion. At eleven thirty in the morning, just about the time Margot had awakened, Rachel woke up too, her conscience like an alarm clock. If she didn't go to the lunch at least she should call one of them. But they would all be disappointed. And now she wasn't tired at all. She had enough nervous energy to keep her going for hours. She kept wondering how she could tell Ellen. She would just have to brave it through the lunch for the sake of all of them, and then get Ellen aside afterward for a drink and tell her privately what had happened with Hank. She had to tell her. The man was dangerously disturbed.

Poor Ellen. Ellen always treated Hank so abominably, she might even have been responsible for Hank's breakdown. But Hank had picked Ellen, hadn't he? Yet Rachel suspected the textbooks she studied weren't always right. Ellen and Hank had been embryos when they got married, how could either of them imagine then how it would turn out?

Rachel took a hot shower. She felt much better. In a way she was even looking forward to the lunch. She couldn't stay home and brood, and it might be fun. She had been extravagant and gotten her three friends each a turtleneck cashmere sweater from Halston: beige for Nikki's blondness, taupe for Ellen's tawniness, and dark gray for Margot's very white skin and dark hair. They would all be delighted. She was glad she had gotten the same present for each of them. She wanted the three of them to feel equally cherished. It had seemed a good idea at the time, and now it seemed even better. Ellen would have a bad shock soon enough. What a rotten thing to have happen just around Christmas.

She hurried to dress and put on her makeup. Twelve thirty was early for a lunch and she didn't want to be late. Rachel hated to keep people waiting.

NIKKI HAD BEEN on the phone in her apartment all morning. She called her secretary to say she wouldn't be in until after lunch, got everything straightened out with the department store credit departments, called the credit-card companies, put it all in writing to confirm it, and cursed the bureaucracy that had changed the little country store where they knew everybody into a vast network of computers and numbers where anyone could be anyone. Her shoulder and leg still hurt. She stopped off at the super's apartment on her way out to deliver his new set of keys, and he said he was going to have the lock on her mailbox changed that morning and would give her the new key when she came home. It had never occurred to her that the boys who had mugged her even had the key to her mailbox. Well, then they had the key to the front door of the building too, didn't they? The super sighed. Yes, he knew that, and he was having the lock changed. He had to give all the tenants new keys, which was going to be a nuisance, because they all came home at different times and would be furious when they couldn't get in, not to mention the ones who had gone to Florida for the winter.

"Why don't we just dig a moat and put in a drawbridge?" Nikki said. "Those people had the right idea in the Middle Ages. One drawbridge, no keys."

"With alligators in the water," the super said. He laughed, pleased to see she was bearing up well after her shock of the night before.

She went to the bank to replace her spending money for lunch, and then she decided to walk to Tiffany's. The streets seemed so safe in the sunlight. People were walking their dogs, carrying groceries . . . Where the hell had they been last night when she needed them?

Tiffany's looked nice and empty until she got to the second floor. It was jammed. You would think things were cheap here! The little silver gifts were on display on a long velvet mat on one of the counters, with numbers on them, and you waited on line until it was your turn and then told the salesperson which number you wanted and were presented with a neatly tied blue box with a number on *it*. Nikki thought that all the people who received silver Christmas presents from Tiffany's at Christmas would be surprised if they saw the assembly line they came from. She tried to look over the heads of the mob that surrounded the counter to inspect the key rings, silver pencils, calendar holders, swizzle sticks, more key rings, thimbles, pillboxes, rulers . . . She looked at her watch. She would be here all day if she waited. If she didn't hurry she'd be late to the lunch. She wandered down the aisles of more expensive presents. It wasn't empty there, but at least it wasn't so crowded.

She saw just what she wanted in the showcase. Little silver mice. They were more than she had planned to spend, more than she really could afford right now. But they were so sweet. She'd write on the cards: "From the country mouse to the city mouse." Then they would all laugh and tell her she wasn't a country mouse any more, she was one of them.

Nikki finally got a salesperson and bought three silver mice, had them gift-wrapped, and charged them. She wrote the three cards and sealed them in their tiny white envelopes. All of it went into a tiny paper shopping bag. She stuffed that into her tote bag. No reason to entice any other muggers with her expensive loot. She whistled a Christmas carol while she waited for the elevator, glad she'd spent the extra money to get something really nice for her friends. The clock above the elevator said twelve twenty-five and she knew she'd be late—but, so what?

RACHEL GOT OUT of her taxi on Fifth Avenue and walked west to Rockefeller Center. The huge tree was up, overlooking the ice skaters below. Tourists were gawking at it, dragging their children; tourists were everywhere. The flags of all the different nations set around the skating rink snapped in the wind. She leaned over the wide wall for a moment, watching the skaters, listening to the music they were moving to. Little kids you'd think were too young to skate so well, old people you wouldn't think had the energy. Every year she always thought briefly that she should take up ice skating, and every year she found reasons to avoid it. This winter she had a good excuse; she had to go to classes and study. There were so many things she wanted to do, and she was going to do them too! There was no reason why she couldn't. One at a time, and she would have them all.

She left the enticing view of the skaters and walked across the street to Rockefeller Center. It was exactly twelve thirty. She looked around to see if Nikki or Ellen or Margot might be coming along, but she didn't see them. The street was full of people. Offices were letting out for lunch. Men and women, singly or in groups, hurrying to get somewhere or chatting casually about where they should go. She didn't notice the woman with the shopping bag coming toward her because she was so ordinary-looking.

When the woman was right in front of her Rachel moved away, to get to the building, still paying no attention to any detail of this wan, bland-looking stranger, neat and plain, one of a million anonymous faces on the streets of New York. She felt a pressure on her arm through her sleeve, not a pain but a pushing. She looked down. There was blood on her coat sleeve and it was coming from her arm. She looked at the woman then in disbelief, searching the face she had never seen before, looking for the first time at the shining knife the woman had taken from the shopping bag and was holding in her hand.

The madwoman looked back at her, and for one fatal moment they were both madwomen, the tall, beautiful one filled with a confusing primordial guilt she could not understand, and the smaller, plain one lost in feelings one can only begin to comprehend.

"Do you know me?" Rachel asked. "Do you *know* me?"

And then the woman stabbed her through her open coat, the knife blade going into her heart, and Rachel was dead.

EPILOGUE:
DECEMBER
1975

Epilogue: December 1975

MARGOT, ELLEN, AND NIKKI SAT together at Rachel's funeral. The coffin was closed. Lawrence's best friend, a man who had known Rachel for over ten years, made a lovely speech. Margot thought in passing that she had never been to a funeral where a woman delivered the eulogy, and she wondered why not. No one had even asked Nikki, who had been Rachel's best friend, even though Margot knew Nikki wouldn't have been up to the pain of it. Still, had Lawrence thought Nikki would have collapsed, or had he simply thought she hadn't known Rachel long enough? What was long enough in friendship? Margot knew that Rachel had been one of her own only friends in the world. How ironic that she, who had tried to die, had lived, and that Rachel, who had loved life so much, was dead. She looked at the coffin, trying not to imagine Rachel inside it, and realized for the first time that death was forever. When she had taken all those pills she had not thought of it that way, she had simply thought of ending what she could not bear. There was a difference.

295

The night of the day that Rachel was murdered, when no one could get Margot on the phone and she had not appeared at the studio for work, Nikki had come to her apartment and leaned on the bell until Margot had dragged herself out of bed to see who it was. Nikki's way of coping with grief was the opposite of Margot's; she became hyperactive. She took one look at Margot, the empty pill bottles, the filthy apartment, and she knew. She called the studio and made up a lie about Margot having pneumonia. Then she told Margot about Rachel. It was not a brutal thing to do, it was Nikki's way of jolting Margot out of her self-absorbed isolation, and it worked.

It was Nikki who had found Rachel's body, surrounded by people, police cars, an ambulance. She had phoned Lawrence's office to find him; she had discovered from calling Jill that Ellen was in the hospital. She had rescued Margot. From the time she found Margot until almost now Nikki had not left her alone, even to sleep. She had sent her cleaning woman to clean Margot's apartment, paying her herself, and had made Margot sleep on the couch in her apartment. She had prepared simple, soft foods, the kind Margot remembered as security foods from her childhood whenever she had been sick, and she had almost fed her. Nikki's two daughters had appeared. Lynn had her boyfriend in tow and all the new magazines for the convalescent, and Dorothy, who was studying to be a psychiatric social worker, had supplied Nikki with the names of several good psychiatrists. Nikki had given Margot the list.

"The rest is up to you," Nikki said. "But I think this is better than pills. Do you know how lucky you are that doctor gave you Dalmane? It's so safe, I've heard of someone who took a hundred and lived. That doctor must have suspected you were up to no good. I just wish you'd confided in me before it got that far."

At first Margot was not sure if she was Nikki's project, her therapy for her grief over Rachel, or if Nikki really cared. But then she realized that Nikki did care. "People can't help you if you hide from them," Nikki said. It was true. You had to reach

296

out. But reaching out was one thing Margot was lousy at, she knew that. It wasn't something she could change by herself. She carried the list of psychiatrists in her handbag and had it with her even now. She knew Rachel would have told her the same thing. Rachel had tried to help her, had called, had kept inviting her to come over, and Margot had finally hidden from her and lied. No one could help her if no one knew. . . .

Why had it been Rachel instead of her? But it wasn't an "instead of" proposition. That had always been one of her problems, Margot realized, that she had been so overwhelmed by mysterious guilt that she had thought everything was either-or. If she had died that night it wouldn't have saved Rachel. None of the things she had chosen to do in her life had automatically blocked out the other choices. It was just that she had believed they did.

How terrible for Lawrence, who had loved Rachel so. Margot wondered if any man would ever love her that much. Rachel was the only one of them who had truly been loved by a man. . . . Margot saw him in the first row, with Kerry beside him and some people she thought were his relatives or Rachel's. He had not wanted anyone to come to see him during the past few days except the immediate family. Lawrence, who had always been so sociable, so surrounded by friends and business acquaintances, had been suddenly overwhelmed by the knowledge that Rachel was his best friend and it was all meaningless without her. Margot knew that eventually he would go back to his social life, because it was his habit, but she knew how little it would help.

She looked at Kerry as if he was a stranger. Had it been only a little less than a year ago when she thought of him as her last chance? What an odd idea. She knew that her real last chance was a good psychiatrist. Life, since Rachel's death, had been revealed to Margot as what it was, a moment-to-moment thing, fragile, valuable. It was not an endless sentence, as she had thought. It was a gift. She had the right to throw it away if she wished, but why should she do such a stupid thing? Perhaps she had years left, perhaps only hours. She would never really be sure

297

again. But at least she should try to do the best with what she had.

ELLEN, WITH MARGOT on her left and Hank sitting stolidly on her right, was crying. She was wearing a dark veil so no one could see the bandage on her cheek and wonder, and people thought she was in deep mourning. She was crying as much for herself as for Rachel. She had almost died. If Jill had been stronger, if her aim had been better . . . Ellen had never realized Jill had a temper. Such a sweet girl, a little withdrawn and secretive, but never tears, never tantrums. Too sweet, perhaps. Jill's burst of temper had been an accident. The woman who had killed Rachel had chosen her accidentally too, and had been taken away to Bellevue to await whatever the law did to insane murderers. She had lived somewhere in Queens, and the neighbors had said she seemed like such a nice, quiet woman. Who knew what kind of insanity went on in this city? Not that Jill was by any stretch of the imagination crazy, but she had problems: she was obviously terrified of boys and of sex, and she was anorexic. For some reason, ever since the accident when she had lashed out at Ellen, Jill had been eating almost normally. But she wasn't a happy girl, Ellen realized that now, and it was more than she herself could handle. That was why she had asked Martin Wilson for the name of a good psychiatrist.

Dr. Martin Wilson . . . Ellen stopped crying. He had taken such good care of her in the hospital that she had told him, kidding, that he had the same initials as Marcus Welby. She knew right away that he was interested in her. She had seen the signs too many times not to know. And she was interested in him too. Of course he had a wife and children. He had married a girl who had helped put him through medical school twenty years ago and hadn't kept up with him since; Ellen knew the signs. He had spent an inordinate amount of time at Ellen's bedside, worrying about her. Jill even seemed to like him and hadn't noticed that his interest in her mother was more than professional. Jill had

298

liked the psychiatrist too, a nice young man whom Martin had brought to the hospital to meet her. Jill had agreed to go into group therapy with some other young kids the doctor treated. Ellen wasn't sure she liked the idea of group therapy; suppose the first boy Jill got a crush on was some maladjusted kid from the group? But Martin assured her it would be good for Jill and would cost less than individual therapy. Group therapy was the new thing for kids. Who was she, Ellen-approaching-menopause-Rennie, to make judgments on new methods of psychotherapy? She had enough problems of her own just coping with being forty and trying to realize that while it wasn't the bloom of twenty it wasn't sixty-five either.

Poor Rachel, so young, so beautiful, so happy. Such an insane, meaningless accident. Why was life so full of accidents? There was nothing sure you could believe in. Ellen glanced at Hank sitting by her side, silent, somber, staring straight ahead. Well, she thought, it's nice that I have good old Hank.

NIKKI HAD BEEN UNABLE to cry ever since she had found Rachel's body, and she couldn't cry now either. Her heart felt crushed in a vise, and sometimes when she was alone she threw up until she felt she had been turned inside out, but the tears waited. She was numb. All the frantic activity, the organizing, the holding together of those weaker than she was, had been automatic. It was her nature to be both a mother and an executive. She hardly listened to the sermon. The minister hadn't even known Rachel; he'd asked Lawrence what were the best things about her. Perhaps it was better to let a professional take care of such things as eulogies, Nikki thought. She didn't expect Lawrence to ask her. The things that she felt were most extraordinary and beautiful about Rachel were not things she wanted to share with a mob like this. And what a mob! The world had turned out, as if Rachel's funeral were the Academy Awards. She was sure some of them had appeared so they would be seen. They were from Rachel's old life. And hiding in the back row, almost timidly, was Andy, Rachel's little school friend, wearing a tie for the first time in respect for the dead. Rachel, Nikki thought, would have told him to take it off and be comfortable.

Nikki thought how much both she and Rachel had changed during the year just past. She thought of herself . . . the decisions she had made that had seemed so scary were not really scary at all because they were things she could control. But the mindless, pointless, wasteful violence that came from outside was the really frightening thing. The final decision in Rachel's life had come from a stranger.

We have no control, Nikki thought. What can I control, with all my struggles and determination? I can control the things *inside* my life. Enjoy my life, my work, my family, my friends, my loves, my pleasures, my moments, and try not to think about the other.

But how can I not?